Frederick James Furnivall, W. G. Stone

The Tale of Beryn

Vol. 2

Frederick James Furnivall, W. G. Stone

The Tale of Beryn
Vol. 2

ISBN/EAN: 9783337715106

Printed in Europe, USA, Canada, Australia, Japan

Cover: Foto ©Andreas Hilbeck / pixelio.de

More available books at **www.hansebooks.com**

SUPPLEMENTARY CANTERBURY TALES.

1.

The Tale of Beryn,

WITH

A Prologue of the merry Adventure of the Pardoner with a Tapster at Canterbury.

RE-EDITED FROM THE DUKE OF NORTHUMBERLAND'S
UNIQUE MS.

BY

F. J. FURNIVALL & W. G. STONE.

WITH ENGLISH ABSTRACT OF FRENCH ORIGINAL
AND ASIATIC VERSIONS OF THE TALE,

BY W. A. CLOUSTON;

PLANS OF CANTERBURY IN 1588, AND THE ROAD THITHER FROM
LONDON IN 1675, &c.

PUBLISHT FOR THE CHAUCER SOCIETY
BY N. TRÜBNER & CO., 57 & 59, LUDGATE HILL,
LONDON, E.C.

1887.

CONTENTS.

FOREWORDS.

IF this Tale of *Beryn* had not occurrd in a manuscript of the
Canterbury Tales, and had also not been unique and not heretofore
printed with fair accuracy, it would yet have claimd a place among
the Chaucer Society's books, by reason of its giving the only good
nearly-contemporary account, by a Canterbury man—monk, I suppose:[1] see the colophon, p. 120—of how pilgrims like Chaucer's
disported themselves in the town, and at the Shrine of the Martyr
whom from ' euery schires ende ' they sought. That Chaucer intended
to have given us such an account himself, we can hardly doubt.
The scenes at the " Cheker of the Hope," in the Cathedral and the
town, must have afforded him so many a chance for a happy line, a
humourous touch, that he *must* have thought of sketching his companions in their fresh surroundings ; but alas, this, like the Tales
awanting, was never to be ; and we have to rely on a poorer hand
for the outline and details we desire.   Still, worse than Chaucer's
though the hand of the *Beryn*-writer is, a bit, and a good bit, of the
Master's humour and lifelikeness, the later verser has in his Prologue.
Chaucer's characters are well kept up ;[2] and we can see with our own
eyes the Pilgrims strolling about the town and visiting the Cathedral,
as well as follow the after-supper adventures[3] of that loose fish, the

---

[1] See p. 137, note.

[2] Note the Miller's stealing the Canterbury brooches, by way of a change
from corn, 1. 174-5 ; the Pardoner's spite to the Summoner, 1. 184-90 ; the
Knight's courtesy and gentleness, 1. 136, 387-8, and his lecturing his son on the
defences of the town—see the walls in Smith's plan—1. 237-244 ; the Cook
drinking, 1. 410 ; the Pardoner singing, and the Summoner acting as chorus,
1. 412-15 ; the Host all through.

[3] *De la panse vient la danse :* Pro. Men are the merriest when their bellies
are fullest ; or, when the bellie is full, the breech would be figging ; (for by this
Danse is any lustfull, or sensuall, motion vnderstood).—Cotgrave.

Pardoner, with Tapster Kit, who sold him so completely.[1] "God knowes who's a good Pilgrim,"[2] says the Proverb. We may safely hold that the Pardoner was not one of the saints. As William Thorpe, a Lollard, said of Papist pilgrims in his examination taken before Archbp. Arundel at Saltwood Castle in 1407 : "such fond people waste blamefullie Gods goodes in their vaine pilgrimages, spending their goods upon vitious hostelars, which are oft uncleane women of their bodies."—J. G. Nichols. *Pilgrimages by Erasmus,* p. xxiv, ed. 1875.[3] The *Beryn* Prologue, then, is a piece of contemporary social history to be read and studied, whoever skips or skims the Tale.

For a description of the old Canterbury Inn and its present representative, of the cathedral, relics, shrine, jewels, Canterbury brooches[4] and signs, &c., I refer the reader to Dean Stanley's interesting *Historical Memorials of Canterbury* (p. 216-238, 5th ed., 1868, Jn. Murray), a book which I have already urgd all our members to buy, and which is a necessary part of their Chaucer Library. Thus much for the Prologue.

The Tale is an awfully long-winded one, based on part of a French prose romance,[5] of which Mr. Clouston has given an epitome

---

[1] *Chascun n'est pas aise qui danse:* Prov. Euerie one is not merrie that daunces ; of such a one wee say, 'his heart is not so light as his heeles.'—1611. Cotgrave.

[2] *Dieu scait qui est bon pèlerin:* Prov. God knowes who's a good Pilgrim : the hearts of Pilgrims are best knowne to God.—Cotgrave.

[3] He adds : "Also, Sir, I knowe well that when divers men and women will goe thus after their own willes and finding, out on pilgrimage, they will ordaine with them before to have with them both men and women that can well sing wanton songes ; and some other pilgrimages will have them with bagge-pipes ; so that everie towne that they came through, what with the noise of their singing, and with the sound of their piping, and with the jangling of their Canturburie-bels, and with the barking out of dogges after them, that they make more noice then if the King came there away, with all his clarions and many other minstrels. And if these men and women be a moneth out in their pilgrimage, many of them shall be an halfe yeare after, great janglers, tale-tellers, and liers."

[4] They represented the mitred head of the saint, with the inscription *Caput Thomæ.* Some may be seen in the British Museum.

[5] The added Second Part of this is summarized on p. 160—174. Note the South-Englishman's touch of the decay of Winchelsea and Rye in lines 754-6, p. 25.

and variants, the former on pages 121 to 140, the latter on pages
141 to 159. It tells how in Rome a rich old senator, Faunus,
has at last a son by his loved wife Agea; how they spoil the
boy, Berinus, during his youth; and how he turns out a cruel,
violent, gambling scamp, caring nothing for his father or his
mother, his heritage or his honour. He refuses to come to his fond
mother on her deathbed, and like a brute strikes the maiden who's
sent for him. His father Faunus, at first inconsolable for the death
of Agea, is soon married by the Emperor to a beautiful woman,
Rame; and she, after putting-up with Beryn's wildness for a time,
schemes to get rid of him, and oust him from his heritage for her
own (coming) son. She persuades Faunus to refuse Beryn further
supplies. This brings the young scapegrace to his senses; and Father
and son are reconciled at the dead Agea's tomb. Beryn then proposes
to give up his heritage for five ships full of merchandise, and try his
luck abroad. This agreed, he sets sail with his fleet of five, and
lands at deceitful Falsetown (in the land of Imagination). There he
loses a game at chess to a Burgess, Syrophane, and in consequence
has to drink all the salt water in the sea, or forfeit his ships. Then
he agrees to change his cargoes for five loads of the goods he can find
in one Hanybald's house; but on going there, he finds the house
empty. So he stands in his shoes, without either ships or cargoes.
A blind man then accuses him of stealing his eyes, and a woman of
having got a son by her, and left her to bring it up. Each has him
up before the Judge, and he is bidden to answer the charges, but has
a day's respite. He mourns, repents, and confesses that his mishaps
have come on him for his misdeeds. A Catchpoll Macaigne then
lends him a knife to bribe the Judge with, and at once accuses him
of having murdered his (the Catchpoll's) father with it. Beryn is
had up again, and is at his wit's end, when a Cripple, Geffrey,
appears. Beryn bolts, but is overtaken, and the Cripple agrees to
stand his friend if Beryn'll take him back to Rome. This is agreed,
and the Cripple tries to send Beryn to the palace of Isope, the wise
King of the land, but Beryn refuses to go, so the Cripple goes instead;
and next day, when the trials all come on, Geffrey outwits all the
lying prosecutors,—not by denying their charges, but by confessing

them and turning the tables on the rascals,—makes them pay heavy damages, and brings Beryn off a winner. The Burgess Syrophane has to separate all the fresh-water running from rivers into the salt sea before Beryn can drink its salt water, or to pay damages, which latter he does. In the empty house of the cheat Hanybald, Geffrey has let loose two white butterflies; and either five ship-loads of these have to be produced, or big damages paid, which Beryn gets. As to the blind man's lost eyes, Geffrey shows that the blind man changed his bad eyes for Beryn's good ones: if the man 'll return Beryn's good eyes, he may have his bad ones back; but if not, he must pay Beryn damages; which he does. As to the Deserted-Wife; if she's Beryn's wife, let her leave her kin, and start at once for Rome with Beryn; she refuses, and pays. For Macaigne's knife, the truth is, that Beryn found it in his own father's heart, and never knew who the murderer was, till Macaigne claimd the knife. Macaigne must therefore answer for the murder of Beryn's father, or withdraw his plaint, and pay Beryn damages. Macaigne agrees to pay. So Beryn goes back to his ships in triumph, with Cripple Geffrey, and twice as much money as he had before.

Beryn then gets five presents from King Isope; next day visits him, stays three days with him, weds his daughter, and reforms the bad Falsetown folk.

The issue of the Tales written as Supplements to Chaucer's *Canterbury Tales* was of course part of the work I laid down for the Chaucer Society; and as the Tale of *Beryn* is the best of these, I askt our friend Henry Bradshaw[1] where the MS. of the *Canterbury Tales* containing the unique copy of *Beryn* (which was first printed in Urry's posthumous edition in 1721) could be. He said " It was lent to Urry by the Hon. Mrs. Thynne,[2] a widow who afterwards

---

[1] He had a nose for missing MSS. like a bloodhound's for a fugitive.

[2] This is stated in the Preface to Urry's Chaucer written by Tim. Thomas from collections by Dart. (See the rough draft of this Preface, begun Aug. 4, ended 29, 1720, in Harl. MS. 6895, and Benn. Lintot's letter in the same MS.) "XIII. The Honourable Mrs. Thynne, Widow of the Honourable Henry Thynne Esq; Son to the late Lord Viscount Weymouth, was pleased to lend him [Urry] a MS. purchased by her, which had belonged to Mr. Long, a Prebendary of the Church of Exeter. It is a fair Book, but is imperfect at the beginning and end, and wants the *Coke's Tale*, and that of *Gamelyn;* But this Defect is sufficiently

married a Duke of Northumberland. It must be still at Alnwick. Write to the Duke there, and you'll get your MS." I wrote. The Duke said he had the MS. ; and he kindly let Mr. Martin (the Inner Temple Librarian, who also lookt after the Alnwick Library) bring the Chaucer MS. to the Inner Temple Library for me ; and there, with the MS., Mr. Brock and I collated the Beryn pages cut out of my copy of Urry's *Chaucer*. The proofs were read twice by me with the MS., and I believe the text is a faithful print of it, though unluckily, when editing it, I was affected for a time with the itch of padding out lines by needless little words in square brackets. The reader can easily leave them out in reading when he finds them unnecessary, or gratify his resentment at such impertinences by drawing a pen through them. But he will agree that the MS. is often faulty in metre, and is not a correct copy of the original poem.

For the text and side-notes of the Poem, its Forewords, and choosing its Plans,[1] I am responsible. To Mr. Stone is due the Index or Glossary, and such of the Notes as Mr. F. Vipan and Prof.

---

compensated by the addition of two new Pieces, not extant in any of the other MSS. which are there inserted between the Tale of the *Chanon's Yeman* and Chaucer's Tale of *Melibeus*, viz. The *Adventure of the Pardoner and the Tapster* at the Inn in Canterbury, and the *Merchant's Tale* in the Pilgrim's Return from thence " (sign. k. 2). Of the former of these, Thomas rightly says that "it is not properly a Tale, but an Account of the Behaviour of the Pilgrims, and particularly of the *Pardoner*, at their Journey's end, and a kind of Prologue to a set of Tales to be told in their Return " (sign. k. 2). He adds, on k. 2, back, " It may (perhaps with some shew of reason) be suspected that Chaucer was not the author of the *Adventure* and *Beryn*, but a later Writer, who may have taken the hint from what is suggested in v. 796 of the *Prologues*, that the Pilgrims were to tell Tales in their Return homewards ; but as to that the Reader must be left to his own Judgment. But supposing they were not writ by our Author, we are however obliged to Mr. Urry's diligence for finding out and publishing Two ancient Poems, not unworthy our Perusal : And they have as good a right to appear at the end of this Edition, as Lidgate's Story of *Thebes* had to be printed in former ones."

Of the *Plowman's Tale*, Thomas says on sign. k. back, it "is not in any of the MSS. which Mr. Urry describes, nor in any other that I have seen or been informed of." No MS. of it has since turnd up.

[1] Ogilby's road-plan of 1675 was the earliest full one I could find. The London to Maidstone plan is borrowd from the E. E. Text Soc.'s edition of Vicary's *Anatomie*. Smith's MS. I showd long ago to Mr. H. B. Wheatley, and he and Mr. E. W. Ashbee publisht it by subscription in 1879, with all its colourd plans, coats of arms, &c. : 'A Particular Description of England in 1588,' &c.

Skeat have not written. Mr. Vipan has also read the French *Berinus*, &c., for us, and Prof. Skeat has partly revised the Notes and Glossary; while the abstract of that portion of the Romance from which the Tale was derived, and the Persian, Indian, and Arabian variants or versions, with the notes thereon, are due to Mr. Clouston.

To these kind helpers, and to the Duke of Northumberland for lending me his unique MS., I tender hearty thanks. To the Members of the Chaucer Society I apologize for the long delay in the production of the concluding Part of this volume. But it's an ill wind that blows nobody good. The delay has led to our getting the valuable help of Mr. W. A. Clouston in his own peculiar line; and all our Members will thank him for his interesting Paper on ' The Merchant and the Rogues,' p. 121-174 below.

Canon Scott Robertson's long-promist Paper on the Pilgrim's road to Canterbury is not yet written. Let us pray that it soon will be. The second ' Supplementary Canterbury Tale,' Lydgate's ' Sege of Thebes,' has been undertaken by a Scandinavian friend, Dr. Axel Erdmann, who hopes to get it to press next year.

Our *Concordance to Chaucer* has been taken in hand by Mr. Graham, after 7 years' neglect by Prof. Corson. I hope to live to see it finisht. Now that the first volume of the Philological Society's *New English Dictionary*, edited by Dr. J. A. H. Murray,[1] has been publisht by the generosity of the Clarendon Press, one need not despair of seeing the *Chaucer Concordance* in type, tho' it is not so far ahead as Mr. F. S. Ellis's *Shelley Concordance*.

F. J. FURNIVALL.

Westfield Terrace, Bakewell, Derbyshire,
13 August, 1888.

---

[1] He is now at work on vol. ii, while volume iii is in the hands of Mr. Henry Bradley, Member of Council of the Philological Society. We started work at the Dictionary in 1858.

CORRECTION.

p. 80, l. 2619, for ageyn[se] *read* ageyn[es].

(I leave each reader to supply, according to his taste, more insertions between brackets, to make all the lines of the Poem of normal length.)

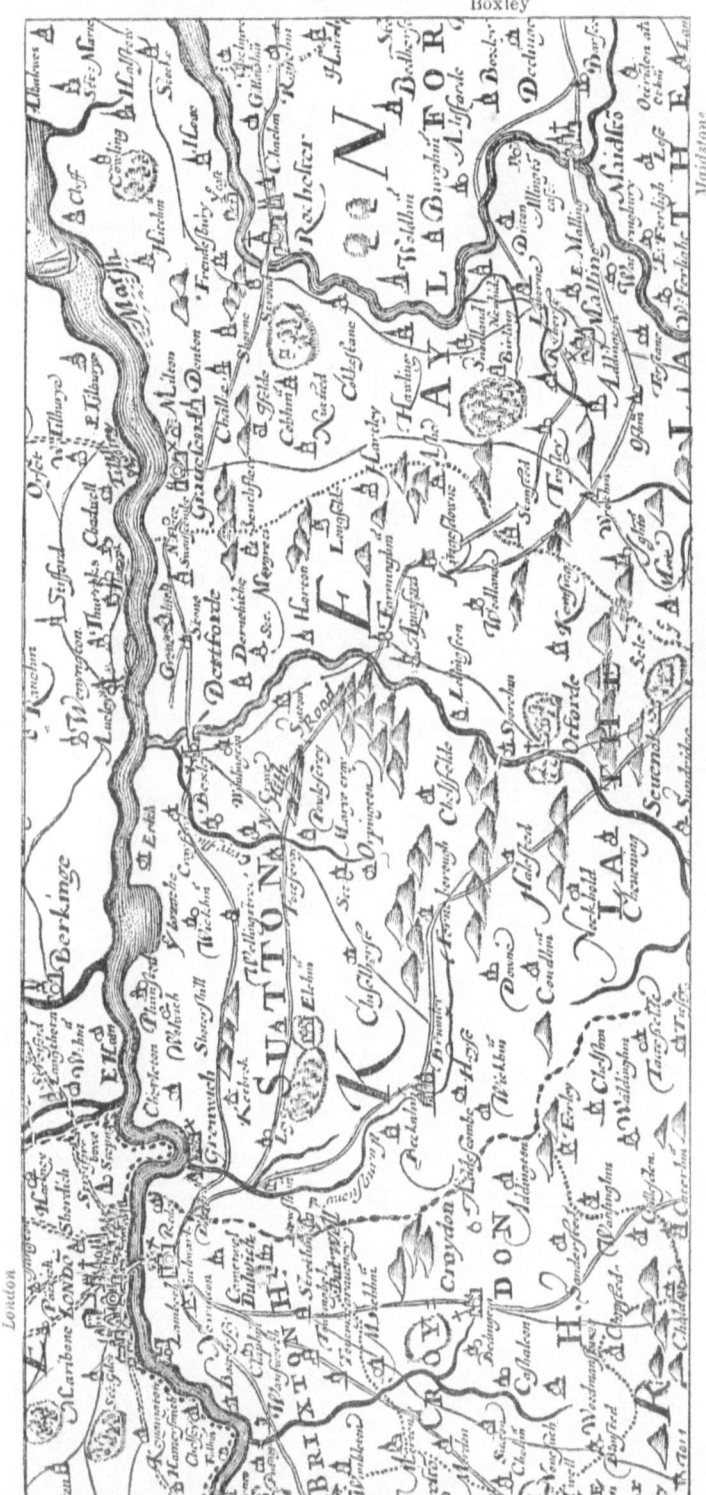

THE ROAD FROM LONDON TO MAIDSTONE AND BOXLEY.

(From Christopher Saxton's Map of Kent, Surrey, &c. (1573-9), with the Roads inserted, and other Additions, by Philip Lea, after 1690.
The names Dulwich and Butwell are inkt-in by a modern hand.)

The Merchant and the Rogues:

FRENCH ORIGINAL AND ASIATIC VERSIONS OF THE

Tale of Beryn.

By W. A. CLOUSTON,

AUTHOR OF "POPULAR TALES AND FICTIONS: THEIR
MIGRATIONS AND TRANSFORMATIONS," ETC.

THE MERCHANT AND THE ROGUES:

FRENCH ORIGINAL AND THREE ASIATIC VERSIONS OF THE *TALE OF BERYN.*

By W. A. CLOUSTON.

FOOLISH as this story may be considered by some of those who lay the flattering unction to their souls that they are, emphatically, "sensible, practical" men, there is yet a method in its foolery—which is sometimes wisdom in masquerade. Suppose—and,

> "When thought is warm, and fancy flows,
> What may not argument suppose?"

as the poet Cowper asks—let us suppose a land where wrong is right, false is true, and the rest follows quite naturally. Well, young Beryn arrives with his five richly-laden ships at such a land, where he is "entertained" by the inhabitants. Their ways, however, are calculated to make themselves rich but leave the stranger poor indeed. Clearly, as old Geoffrey was well aware, the only means of escaping such an accumulation of serious claims and accusations was to oppose lie to lie, or rather, to tell greater lies in self-defence; and by Geoffrey's so doing on behalf of his "client" the artful folk of Falsetown were caught in their own snares. To practise the sage maxim, "oppose falsehood with truth," would have been, in Beryn's case, utter and irretrievable ruin!

The Tale of Beryn is identical with the first part of the old French romance, *L'Histoire du Chevalier Berinus,* which is a singular compound of two distinct tales, interspersed with necromantic and chivalric incidents. A manuscript of this romance, of the 15th century, is preserved in the National Library, Paris ; and there is another in the Imperial Library, Vienna, neither of which has yet been edited.   It was printed early in the 16th century under the title of "L'Histoire du noble Chevalier Berinus, et du excellent et tres-chevalereux champion Aigres de l'Aimant son fils ; lequel Livre est tant solacieux, qu'il doit etre sur tout autre nomme le vrai Sentier d'Honneur, et l'Exemplaire de toute Chevalerie.   Nouvellement réduit de langage inconnu au vulgaire langage François ;" Paris : Jean Bonfons, sans date.   An abstract of it, by Nicolas-Bricaire de la Dixmerie (ob. 1791), is found in *Mélanges tirés d'une grande bibliothèque*, Paris, 1780, tome viii., pp. 225-277.   In the short preface to his *extrait*, M. de la Dixmerie says that this romance " has not been given to us as a known translation.   In what language was it first written ?   We are not told.   We are informed that the original author was called Marithiaux ; but that tells us nothing. It is supposed that it is a device of the translator to conceal his own name.   Let us see if he has made a great sacrifice to his modesty."[1] The following is a free translation of the first part of the *extrait ;* it is much to be regretted that the writer did not furnish some passages from the romance itself :

[1] There are two editions of the *Histoire de Berinus* in the Library of the British Museum, one " Imprime par la Veufue feu Jehan Trepperel." Paris (? 1525), the other, printed by Alain Lotrian, Paris (? 1537), both in 4to.   Mr. Frederick John Vipan has kindly favoured me with some extracts from the first of these, of which I avail myself in the course of this paper.
    The author says he has composed his work at the instance and request of his friend and lord, for whom he would do great service if he had enough wit and ability.   He then tells us that at the present day many men of understanding would devote themselves to the art of composition and writing, if they were provided with their living, as in old times, for then kings, princes, and great lords maintained men of talent, and held them in great honour ; but now all is changed : men are too much taken up with seeking for means of subsistence to be able to write any profitable work ; and even if they should do so, there would be little mention of their productions on account of their low estate, for the higher the rank of the writer the more widely are his works known.   " And so there was none but myself, little as I am, to accomplish the command of my lord ; and I count it no trouble to fulfil his will, and moreover the matter of which I would speak pleases me.   And think not the said matter is new, rather is it of very great antiquity, but it is not of less value on that account."—In the second chapter it is stated that this book was written by a " clerc qui s'appellait Marthiaulx ;" and in ch. 128 : " Or dit l'histoire ainsi comme *marteaulx* le raconte ;" in ch. 34 he is called *marteau*.

Abstract of French Version.

[The nos. at the side are those of the lines of the English Poem.]

THERE was an emperor of Rome, named Philip, successor of 785
Constantine, who had a council composed of seven sages,[1] two 789
of whom, Cicero and Scipio, were astronomers—that is to say, 822
astrologers, for at that time one had not sufficient knowledge to
style himself soothsayer or prophet. During the reign of Philip 828
there dwelt in Rome a very noble and wealthy citizen, named
Fawnus, who had long desired the blessing of an heir. His wife, 845
Agea, fervently prayed to Heaven for the same, and at last her
supplications were granted. She gave birth to a son, whom they 884
named Berinus. Having waited for him many years, they were
anxious that the greatest care should be taken of him, and so he was 900
never thwarted in anything, and had every wish or whim gratified.
Berinus was scarcely twelve years old when he was considered by the
children as one of the best born and worst educated in the capital.
On attaining his fifteenth year he ought to have followed the example
of other young Romans, and practised the exercises of the field of
Mars, such as wrestling, running, and throwing the javelin, as well
as leaping hedges and broad ditches, and swimming across the Tiber.
It is well known that the great warriors of Rome were excellent
swimmers : Cæsar gave a proof of this near Alexandria; but Berinus
did not wish to take Cæsar as his model. His affectionate parents
and himself considered that the exercises of the circus were of too
rough a description, seeing that those who engaged in them often

---

[1] Wright, in his edition of the Canterbury Tales, printed for the Percy
Society, vol. xxvi., p. 243, says that "from the manner in which the Seven
Sages are introduced at the beginning of the *Tale of Beryn* [see ll. 789-825],
it is evident there must have been some version of that romance [i. e. *The
History of the Seven Wise Masters of Rome*] in Europe differing from the
usual one, which does not contain this story." I don't agree with him. The
seven sages of the emperor Philip are mentioned but twice afterwards (ll. 1099
and 2659), while in the French romance, as we shall see, they figure with little
honour—old Geoffrey proves more than a match for their combined "wisdom."
It is not uncommon in mediæval stories for a king or emperor to have seven
"wise men" for his counsellors, who, unlike those of the romance referred to
by Wright, don't relate tales to their royal master.

returned with bruised limbs and gouged eyes, or had a chance of being drowned in attempting to swim across the Tiber. This would be committing to the hazards of a single day the fruit and object of the wishes of many long years.[1] Games of chance (commonly called *Tripots*) offered to Berinus exercises less fatiguing. He 923 made them his field of Mars; and he had such a predilection for dice and the game of *outre-merelle*, that he more than once lost all 928 his clothes: the rich heir of Fawnus would come home in his shirt. Agea, his mother, was comforted by the reflection that if Berinus allowed himself to be stripped in this way, it was out of pure compassion for his tailor. Good people laughed heartily at the mishap, for it was not natural to blame such a precious young shoot. But 1008 his mother died,[2] and when the news was brought to Berinus while playing at cards (and losing, as usual), he was enraged at a maid-servant for interrupting him, returned a foolish and heartless answer, and dismissed her with blows.

Now Fawnus, although wealthy, was a courtier, and sought every means of pleasing the emperor, who resolved to put his obedience to the test, and proposed that he should marry the most 1112 beautiful lady in Rome. This was the charming Raine, who had been Philip's mistress, though her fidelity to him was more than suspected. After a little consideration Fawnus consented, and the 1132 nuptials were at once celebrated. He soon became strongly attached to his new wife, who was not slow to take advantage of his doting fondness. (The author here conjectures that there must have been witchcraft in all this; but, in truth, Fawnus was old, and Raine was young, beautiful, and skilled in the art of pleasing.) As for Berinus, he changed nothing in his conduct, and would not have objected to his father's marrying ten times, if only he was not thwarted in any of his amusements. But he was not long in finding that Raine was

---

[1] There is not a word of all this passage about athletic exercises in our version, nor in the original romance.

[2] In our Tale (probably also in the French original) the dying mother of Beryn begs her husband—and it is one of the best passages in the poem—not to marry again; for they had both helped to make their son what he is by indulging his evil propensities, and a step-mother would make him still worse by unkindness. The story of Beryn's childhood and youth, as told in our version, is true to life—and "a caution to parents!"

much less indulgent to him than his mother Agea. She made no
attempt to reform him; on the contrary, her grand object was to 1145
cause his ruin and disgrace. His best actions she misrepresented to
his father, and converted simple faults into grave crimes. Fawnus,
who had so long suffered all these things from his son, found them
inexcusable when told to him by Raine. He began by not seeing
his son except after long intervals, and then only with pain, and
finished by expelling him from his house. The unhappy young man
did not venture to seek for aid amongst his own kin, whom he had
always neglected, and whose reproaches he feared. He found no
comfort from those whom he had considered as his friends, who
showed themselves merely evil acquaintances. Misfortune instructs
such as it cannot correct. Berinus reflected upon all he had done
and experienced, and felt that he had not been too severely punished.
He had lost Agea, an affectionate mother, and had not till now
realized the extent of his loss. He roamed about the city, despised
and rejected by everybody. The capital of the world would not
afford him a shelter. "I shall go and conceal myself," cried he, at 1333
length, "and die upon my mother's tomb." For two days he
remained in that mournful retreat. His relatives, feeling uneasy at
his long absence, had recourse to Fawnus, who yearned for his son. 1337
Raine, fearing lest she should be accused of having caused his death,
induced her husband to make a strict search for Berinus, and she
accompanied him. After many unsuccessful inquiries, Fawnus, in 1404
his distress, thought of visiting the grave of Agea. A young man,
with his face pressed upon the tomb, was fondly embracing it, and
bathing it with his tears. He appeared emaciated and feeble, and
oblivious of all around him. Fawnus and Raine drew nearer, and 1421
recognized Berinus. Would not the soul of any father be melted at
such a spectacle? Fawnus raised up his son and embraced him.
Both wept, and even Raine herself was much affected. They took
Berinus home and treated him kindly. Filial piety has in itself
something so touching that it can move the most heartless step-
mother. But Berinus had to struggle against something more
powerful in the heart of Rame: she loved a young Roman knight.
Fawnus suspected nothing of this intrigue, but Berinus was more

1462 difficult to deceive.[1] At length of his own accord he resolved to
    quit Rome, and besought his father to provide him with five vessels
1479 laden with rich merchandise. Raine eagerly supported this request,
    but prevailed upon her husband to demand in return that Berinus
1528 should formally surrender all his rights as successor to his father.
    The deed was drawn up and signed in presence of the emperor and
1557 his seven sages, and as soon as the five vessels were ready Berinus
    sailed away, with the design of trading in foreign countries.

1563   After Berinus had been two days[2] at sea, a great storm arose and
    forced him to seek refuge with his vessels in the chief port of the
1619 kingdom of Blandie. This was close to the capital, the citizens of
    which were thievish, cunning, and treacherous, for whom the riches
    of Berinus were a strong temptation. He was not, in any way,
    robbed, but, which comes to the same thing, they brought against
    him a great many lawsuits, and in those remote times there was
    very little chance of his ever seeing the end of them. It was the
    custom of the hosts of Blandie to be very kind towards strangers
1648 whom they suspected of being rich. That of Berinus[3] welcomed
    him with distinction and even obsequiousness. A most sumptuous
    dinner was served up, at which gaiety was joined to good cheer.
1732 The repast over, a chess-board of ivory, inlaid with silver, was
1747 brought out. Berinus reluctantly consented to play, and won three
    times in succession. The moderate sum staked at first was doubled,
    and Berinus found himself a gainer of more than he had expended
    since his arrival at Blandie. His courteous host appeared to be
    much chagrined at being defeated, and Berinus wished to cease
    playing, in order to return to the port and see the condition of his
    ships ; but he was assured that they were all in safety, and told that
1759 he ought to allow his opponent another chance. New conditions
    were imposed, the most severe of which was that the loser must do
1768 whatever his opponent should require of him, or drink up the waters
    of the sea. For some time the room had been filling with spectators,

---

[1] There is no mention of this intrigue in our version, where she artfully
plays with the old man's doting fondness and her supposititious child by him—
she'd rather have him dead than grow up like Beryn ! (1183—1222)

[2] Three days in our version.

[3] The burgess, Syrophane, in our version.

whose appearance was not the most prepossessing. A new game was begun, and the fortunes of the players were not long in changing. He whom Berinus had so easily defeated now appeared, like Antheus, to have derived fresh strength from falling. The jeers which greeted Berinus from the onlookers distracted him, and his skilful rival was not slow to take advantage of the circumstance, so Berinus was checkmated. The victor then modestly put forward his claim, 1822 which was simply to deprive Berinus of all his possessions. As he would not consent to this, they dragged him before the seneschal,[1] 1852 who, on hearing the case, showed himself as evilly disposed towards the foreigner as he was favourable to his own countrymen. Berinus 1872 requested three days in order to prepare his defence, and was accorded the favour on his providing good surety for his appearance. The provost of the city, called Sir Hannibal, was present and expressed 1878 his opinion that the five ships of Berinus were sufficient bail. He even thought that it might be advisable to unload the vessels and 1893 deposit the cargoes in his warehouse, already well furnished with every kind of merchandise, in much the same way, assuring Berinus that there was still space for his goods. The seneschal approved of this proposal, and Berinus, having no alternative, proceeded with Hannibal to the harbour. The provost went over all the vessels and 1916 carefully examined the cargoes, which he found to consist of the finest and most valuable goods. "I have something to propose to you," said he to Berinus. "Alas!" replied the disconsolate Roman, "propose and dispose; for here I see it is about the same thing." "I have told you," resumed the provost, "that my warehouse is filled with precious goods, all of the best market value. Let us agree to make an exchange : whatever may be the issue of your case, you will give me all you have here; and if you gain it, you will take for your indemnity all that will suit you in my warehouse, in order 1925 to freight and fill up your five vessels." Then he whispered in his ear, "On this condition, I undertake to arrange your case with the seneschal;" adding aloud, "in short, I shall make use of him more for your advantage than my own." Berinus agreed to everything, perforce; and there was a possibility, though a slight one, that this

[1] The steward, Evandir, in our version.

arrangement might be to his advantage. As they were beginning to unload the vessels, Berinus returned to the provost's warehouse, to examine the exchange they were compelling him to accept, but there 1948 he found nothing—all had been removed elsewhere; Hannibal, in fact, had cleared his stores to make room for the bales of Berinus. "Behold," said Hannibal, in a sarcastic tone to the Roman, who was very much astounded, "this is the place, according to our agreement: I don't wish to put any impediment in your way." Berinus could only return to the seneschal, who courteously postponed this new suit to the following day.

The Roman then retraced his steps towards the ships, cursing the 2001 swindling Blandiens. He at once became the talk of the whole town, and everybody was desirous to have a share in his ruin. A 2008 blind man, having heard the foreigner spoken about and learning that he was approaching, laid hold of Berinus as he was passing, and bawled out lustily, "Murder!—help!" Berinus was once more dragged before the seneschal. "Sir," said the blind man, "I ask justice of you." "Against whom?" "This man whom I hold." 2045 "What is his offence?" "He has my eyes, and refuses to give them back to me." Berinus was struck dumb from sheer astonishment. "What have you to say for yourself?" demanded the seneschal of him in a severe tone. "I know nothing about it," replied Berinus. 2090 "I need advice, and request that this suit be delayed like the others," to which the seneschal consented.

"Will this be sufficient?" said Berinus to himself, as he returned to the harbour. "Am I quite free, for to-day, from gamblers, provosts, seneschals, and blind men? Is there not one knave more 2096 preparing for me some other insult?" Just then, a woman, carrying an infant in her arms, accosted him with the air and tones of a Fury, calling him a faithless and treacherous man, after having pledged his troth to her and made her the mother of that child. Here was fresh cause of astonishment for Berinus: another visit to the seneschal and this new suit put off to the following day.

It was, as we have seen, to seek advice that Berinus had, at each successive accusation, requested delay. But from whom was he to 2210 seek advice? A passer-by came up to him and said, "Take my advice, stranger—give up a portion of your goods and save the rest. Offer ten talents to the seneschal: he is the man that will not refuse the money; and give him also this valuable knife, which I offer you, and he will favour you in all your cases.   I will go with you to him, and you will bless your stars for having taken me as your adviser.   In short," added he (and we will here use the author's own words, which he professes to have borrowed from Solomon), "one may willingly give up a crusty little loaf, in order to save the whole batch."   This counsel seemed good to Berinus, so he returned once more to the seneschal, only to find a new charge brought against him by his obliging counsellor.   Martin (such was the man's name)[1] 2268 modestly claimed the five ships of Berinus and their rich cargoes, which all belonged, said he, to his father, who had set out with the ships from Blandie to have them repaired at Rome, as witnesses were ready to prove.   Moreover, the knife which Berinus had in his pocket, he added, was a proof that he had murdered his (Martin's) father, to whom it had belonged.   This accusation was received like the others, and postponed to be judged along with them.

Berinus, whose freedom they granted, seeing that it was his riches and not his person they wished to possess, had now become suspicious of every human figure,[2] and as he was trying once more to

---

[1] The catchpoll, Macaigne, in our version.

[2] No mention is made here, as in our Tale—true, this is only an abstract —of poor Beryn's bitter reflections on his former wicked life, which he confesses to himself has brought all these troubles on him.   He feels that he is justly, though heavily, punished :

"For while I had tyme, wisdom I might have lernyd ;
But I drough me to foly, and wold nat be governed,
But had al myne owne will and of no man a-ferd,
For I was nevir chastised : but now myne owne yerd
Betith me to sore ; the strokis be to hard."   (l. 2321 ff.)

He curses the day he sold his heritage, for now he is like the man, who, to drive the flies off, set fire to his barn ; and, still worse, he may now lose his life, and what will become of his men, who have done no one any injury? (2306—2377)—The old English translator has followed his original pretty closely, as will be seen by comparing the passage with the following from the French romance :

"In the meantime Berinus issued from the house, sorrowing and thoughtful, and in great anxiety to have counsel.   And he departed raging, and saying such words as these : 'Alas, wretch that I am ! right well have I deserved the evil and sorrow that I have, when my heart will never persevere in well-doing, and I have madly abandoned my country and renounced my great inheritance, to get shame and trouble.   Yea, it is quite right that I have

return to the port, finally met a man who seized him by the cloak.
2379 "Is this all you want?" cried the Roman; "if so, I shall for once
2426 get off cheaply;" and unloosing his cloak, he abandoned it to the
would-be robber and escaped. "Stop!" said the man to him. "It
is not your garment I want, it is yourself." But Berinus only ran
the more quickly. The man followed and came up with him a short
distance from the port. "Listen to me," said he, "I am not surprised at your distrust, but I know very well how to remove it;"
2477 and he offered to accompany Berinus on board one of his ships.[1]
Berinus, having taken a long look at the man, smiled at his own
fear. He was of little stature, and from his appearance not one to
inspire terror;—evidently a kind of Æsop, in body and mind.
"My name is Geoffrey," said he to Berinus. "I am an earth-potter,
but formerly, in Rome, I practised a more noble calling." "In
Rome?" "Yes, I am a Roman, like you." "In that case," said
Berinus, "come with me on board of one of my ships." When
there, each related to the other the events of his life.

---

it, since I have pursued it; and, alas, I ought now to have been in Rome, with
my father and my other friends, and to be in great honour and in great lord-
ship, and to lead forth my hounds and hawks, and go a hunting with the
knights and squires of the Roman empire. And I have left it all to seek hard
adventures and meddle with that whereof I knew nothing: so that I am like
the boor who set fire to his house to rid it of the flies; for I have cast all my
honour into disrepute and afar for a little melancholy;—so do I not heed
what Solomon says, that he takes an evil vengeance on himself who lengthens
his mourning. Alas, what will my men do that I have brought with me? I
have indeed deceived and betrayed them; for they will be poor and wretched
through me, and yet they have no fault. But as for me, I have well deserved
the evil and shame that I have."

The wittol, to whom Beryn likens himself, who burned down his barn to
drive off the flies, reappears in the *Merry Tales of the Mad Men of Gotham,*
as follows:

"There dwelt a Smith at Gottam, who had a Waspes nest in the strow in the end of his
Forge. There did come one of his neighbors to haue his horse shood, and the Waspes were
so busie, that the fellow was stung with a Waspe. He, being angry, said: 'Art thou
worthy to keepe a forge or no, to haue men stung here with wasps?' 'O neighbour,' said
the Smith, 'be content; I will put them from this nest by and by.' Immediately he tooke
a Coulter, and heated it in his Forge glowing hot, and he thrust it into the straw in the end
of his Forge, and so he set his Forge a-fire [and] burnt it vp. Then said the Smith: 'I told
thee I would fire them forth of their nest.'"

The Gothamite drolleries are, none of them, home-grown: they are found—
mutatis mutandis—current from Iceland to Ceylon.

[1] In our version it is Beryn who proposes that Geoffrey should come with
him into one of his vessels.

Geoffrey was really born in Rome.[1] He had inherited a large fortune; but soon became more famous for his ready wit than his riches. More than once, although not a counsellor of the emperor, he decided state questions. He frequently answered, and always wisely, questions upon which the seven sages durst not express an opinion. An Eastern prince had submitted several questions which, according to the custom of Orientals, were so many enigmas : strong common sense was often concealed under the most familiar images. " I have," said this prince, " a rotten tooth, which causes me ceaseless pain, and gives me rest neither night nor day."[2] The second question was : " A bee creeps into my room every morning, in spite of the precaution which is taken to carefully shut doors and windows. It fastens on my hand at the moment when I have a great desire to sleep ; and if I chance to move my hand in the least, it stings it so as to make it swell." The third question was as follows : " I have in my garden a pear-tree, which surpasses all the others round about it. Its trunk is straight ; its top, leafy ; and it covers a large space of ground ; but nothing can grow beneath its shade, and its fruit is a poison to any one who ventures to taste it." The seven sages regarded these questions as too childish. It was beneath their dignity to consult them on such trifles. " We have," said they, " no balm to cure a diseased tooth ; no secret to hinder a bee from creeping into a room ; no device to improve the fruit of a tree." " There is no question of improving," cried Geoffrey to them ; " what is completely bad can never become good. Listen to the meaning of the riddle ; this would be a suitable reply to the Eastern prince : ' Get your rotten tooth pulled, or it will spoil the others ; and be sure it is pulled out by the root, so that nothing may remain, for the stump would cause new agonies : as the proverb says, " an empty house is better than a bad tenant." Kill the fly, seeing that it has honey in its mouth and poison in its tail ; it seeks to pester you in every way. Lastly, up-root the tree whose fruit and shade even are so dangerous. It may be an ornament in your orchard, but it uselessly eats up the

[1] The following account of Geoffrey while in Rome does not occur in our version.

[2] Presumably the " question "—for this is simply a statement—was : " What will cure this raging molar ?"

substance, and kills the useful plants which only require to be
allowed to spread out.'" The seven sages were rather astounded
at what they had themselves said, and what they had just heard.[1]
Geoffrey gave them other lessons, which at once roused their jealousy.
He perceived that he could not displease with impunity a council of
philosophers, and not being able to parry their malice, he thought his
most prudent course was to get beyond their reach. So he sailed
away, and a tempest drove him to the Blandiens, who laid a thousand
snares to rob him, but he had taken the precaution to have in a
portable form the best part of his treasures ; besides, he only gave
out that he was a humble potter, working for his living. As he had
nothing, apparently, to lose, they soon ceased to take any particular
notice of him.[2] Geoffrey detailed all these circumstances at great
2808 length to Berinus, adding, "I will set you free. To-morrow I will
return at cock-crow ; be not discouraged ; I undertake to get from
them more than they would have taken from you."[3]

[1] It is not easy to discover any great sagacity in Geoffrey's replies ; and
the seven sages must have been so many arrant noodles when, in the first
place, they could not prescribe remedies for toothache, a troublesome bee, and
a baneful pear-tree, and, afterwards, were astonished at the "prescriptions" of
Geoffrey. I suspect the author of this romance had but a confused recollection
of the three riddles—for such, doubtless, they were, in their original forms—
and "solved" them out of his own profound mind.—From remote times it
seems to have been a favourite practice at Asiatic courts to propound "hard
questions" as well as for eminent sages to deliver, at the desire of a king,
"good and notable sentences"—that is to say, apothegms, or striking sayings.
We learn from the Old Testament that the Queen of Sheba (or Saba, whom the
Arabian writers identify with Bilkis, queen of El-Yemen) came to prove the
wisdom of Solomon with hard questions, and that he answered them all—
"there was not anything hid from the king which he told her not." What
were the questions, or riddles, the solution of which by Solomon so much
astonished the Queen of Sheba, we are not informed by the sacred historian ;
but, if we may credit rabbinical and Muslim legends, the result of this celebrated
visit of her Sabean Majesty was her marriage with the sage Hebrew king.
[2] This account of his treatment by the knavish citizens differs very
materially from that given in our tale, where he says they robbed him of a
thousand pounds' worth of goods, and he was obliged to disguise himself as a
cripple to save his life (ll. 2497-2505).
[3] In our version Geoffrey advises Beryn to go to the palace of the good
Duke Isope, "wher thyn empechement shull be i-mevid ;" but Beryn, after
Geoffrey's account of the monsters which guard the approaches to Isope's
chamber, is so terrified that he refuses, even for the value of his five ships ;
upon which Geoffrey undertakes to go himself. Mr. Vipan informs me that in
the original Geoffrey advises Berinus to slink into the hall, slide along the
wall, slip into the king's chamber, and hide himself under Isope's couch.

Geoffrey rejoined Berinus at the appointed hour, and they went to the house of the seneschal. Geoffrey obtained leave to speak for Berinus, who did not know the customs of the country. This condescension may seem strange, but Geoffrey had on this occasion 2916 assumed the air and manners of a fool, and they did not think that such an advocate would be dangerous, but rather that he would amuse them by his conduct of the case: he was too insignificant for the opponents of Berinus, whom he answered one after another. To the chess-player he said: " You demand that my countryman should give up all he possesses, or drink up all the waters of the sea. He will give up nothing; he will drink: he has made the same vow to 3492 Saint James of Compostella.[1] He will drink all the waters of the sea, but not the rivers which flow into it. Begin, then, by turning aside the course of all these rivers, after which we will do what you require."[2] The sharper was somewhat taken aback by this proposition.

" When Berinus refuses to go," Mr. Vipan continues, " I suppose Geoffrey adopts the same course himself, though I do not find it expressly stated; he certainly goes there somehow, and gets the information he wants. Probably the English writer made a change because he thought that Isope's receiving all the rogues of the city in his chamber inconsistent with his station and high character."

The description of Duke Isope's castle and garden reads like—what it is— a leaf out of an Oriental romance. The ceiling of the great hall is of selondyne, the pavement of gold and azure, in which is one stone that scorches up whatever comes near it, and another of equal coldness. Two leopards guard a door leading into a garden—they can do no harm if blown upon very gently—the finest garden in the world, in which are birds of gold and silver that move about as if they were alive, and in the midst the fairest tree under the sky, the leaves of which are also

Of sylvir and of golde fyne, that lusty been to see.

As usual, necromancers and a white lion guard this paradise, but by simply touching a branch of the fair tree they are at once subdued. (See note on treasure-trees, *Chaucer Analogues*, p. 336.) We read of a superb palace in the Arabian romance of Antar, all of marble and carnelian. " In the centre was a fountain filled with rose-water and purest musk; in the middle of it was a column of emerald, and on its summit a hawk of burnished gold, its eyes were topazes and its beak jasper. Around it were [golden] birds, scattering from their bills on all who were present musk and ambergris. The whole edifice was scented with perfumes, and the ceiling glittered with gold and silver. It was one of the wonders of the period, and the miracle of the age."

[1] It was a very common practice in the Middle Ages to swear by, as well as make vows to, this saint (James the Greater), because of the celebrity of his relics, supposed to be preserved at Compostella.

In Tale xix. of an early English version of the *Gesta Romanorum*, edited, for the Roxburghe Club, by Sir Frederic Madden, to the question, " How many

He said they were exacting an impossibility. "That is your affair," said Geoffrey, "and it is the only way to ours. You will comply with that condition, or pay a good round sum ; and if the seneschal does not give us justice, we will appeal to good King Isope, who will refuse no one." So the sharper was compelled to pay a proportionate sum for the wrong which he had wished to inflict on Berinus.

The second accuser was called; it was the provost. "What are your charges against this stranger?" said the seneschal to him. "You know them," replied the provost : "he consented to give me the cargoes of his five vessels, and take in exchange what would be suitable for him in my warehouses." "I found nothing in them," said Berinus in a mournful tone ; "there was nothing in them to 3577 load five ships." "Let us see," said Geoffrey to the seneschal ; "we must verify the state of matters." Accordingly they go to the ware- 3582 house of the provost and find it completely empty. There was nothing, as they say, but the bare walls. Two butterflies only were 3612 seen floating about the room. "These are only insects," said Geoffrey, "which prove that the provost has deceived us. He told my client that his warehouse was full of merchandise, in good condition ; but his goods have been eaten up by insects. In proof of this we still see the butterflies which are a part of them. Is it to fill his vessels with such insects that Berinus has left Rome, and exposed himself to 3623 the dangers of the deep—of shipwrecks and of lawsuits? If so, let our accuser load with butterflies our five vessels. We shall be very well pleased, and our quarrel will be ended."[1] The provost was utterly confounded. He asked that the original bargain should be declared off. "To that we object," said Geoffrey. "You owe us for merchandise—butterflies or a fine." The provost decided to pay the fine.

---

gallons of salt water are there in the sea?" the reply is, "Let all the passages of fresh water be stopped, and then I'll tell thee." This also occurs in the old German book of the drolleries of Tyl Eulenspiegel, of which an English trans- lation was published about 1550, under the title of *A Merry Jest of a Man that was called Howleglas.*

[1] The writer of the *extrait* does not say that Geoffrey had previously pro- vided himself with the (white) butterflies, and, still better, that he claimed five ship-loads of them, as they were wanted by a Roman doctor to make an oint- ment of, which would cure all kinds of diseases.

The party then returned to the audience-chamber, where they found the blind man. Said Geoffrey: "This is a man who asserts that he has given my client his eyes. Twenty witnesses depone to the fact. We do not deny it. But twenty others depone that it was an exchange: Berinus gave him his eyes for an equivalent; let 3724 him at once return to Berinus, in good condition, those which he should give back." This proposal was ended by inflicting a fine, which the blind man paid.

The woman now came forward, carrying, as on the evening before, a child in her arms. She did not wait till Geoffrey spoke, but, taking possession of the court,[1] "Yes," cried she (and it is said she even wept), " yes, the faithless one whom you see forsook me, after marrying me, after making me the mother of this child—perhaps he wishes to say he does not know me." " Not at all," interrupted the advocate of Berinus; " we acknowledge you as our wife, and your son as our son. But I ask of the lord seneschal and this honourable 3769 assembly, ought the man to follow the woman, or the woman the man?" It was generally agreed that the woman should follow the man. " It is that which has been refused us," replied Geoffrey in a voice of thunder, striking on the railing which separated the audience. " Well! we are quite ready. I have to say that Berinus is quite 3773 ready to take away this woman, whom he knows to be his wife, and this child, whom he knows to be his son." At these words the boldness of the female accuser disappeared. She begged the seneschal not to pronounce judgment; but the pitiless Geoffrey exacted a fine, which was paid by the real husband, the real father of the child, who was soon found.

There remained Martin, the most wicked of all, since his accusation was the most atrocious. He wished rather not to risk it; he hesitated to repeat it. Geoffrey saved him the trouble. The knife, certified, formed the basis of his charge; it became his accuser. It was, 3824 according to Geoffrey, with this knife that the father of his client had

---

[1] Our English version says that "hir tunge was nat sclytt" (l. 3204). There can be little doubt, I think, that a monk wrote this romance. Those old misogynists (albeit notorious lechers, if they are not belied in song and story) seldom let slip the smallest opportunity for girding at women in their sermons and other compositions.

been murdered; it was partly to find again the owner of this knife, and consequently the murderer, that Berinus had undertaken his voyage. Martin had confessed that this knife belonged to his father, who had therefore killed the father of Berinus. Martin acknowledged that his father was dead; he had then inherited the knife with his other property; his goods ought therefore to be confiscated and handed over to Berinus, and so forth. The seneschal ordered Martin to pay a fine, like the others.

3884   So ended this memorable trial. The Blandiens went home, some utterly astounded, others quite speechless from surprise; while Geoffrey, Berinus, and his followers returned to the port to celebrate 3917 at a feast this five-fold victory which they had just gained. They were still enjoying themselves when the pages of the king were announced. Good King Esope had sent them to congratulate Berinus on his success in all his lawsuits and offer him rich presents. First of all, he was presented with a sabre of the finest quality, and richly adorned with jewels; another offered a gold cup of exquisite workmanship. All these young deputies, to the number of twelve,[1] laid before him, each in turn, some gift worthy of him who had 3939 charged them with the message. Berinus was then invited, in the name of the king, to an audience on the following day. The first question of Esope was to ask of his deputies, as soon as they returned, which of his presents seemed most to please Berinus. They answered that he had given them all into other hands excepting the sabre, 3989 which he had kept for himself. "So much the better," said Esope. "This preference shows a man of courage, and strengthens me in my project." Esope intended to give in marriage to Berinus his

---

[1] Mr. Vipan says: "In the romance we have 'v. damoiseaux,' in both editions; one of them is afterwards termed 'le varlet.'" The number of Esope's emissaries is also five in our Tale (l. 3919), but the translator (who perhaps did not know French perfectly) represents them as *maidens*. "The title of *varlet*, or valet," says W. Stewart Rose, in his notes to his free metrical rendering of *Partenopex de Blois*, pp. 33, 34, "synonymous with that of *damoiseau* in French, and *knave* in English, was given indifferently to the sons of kings and great nobles not yet knighted. In *Villehardouin* the son of the Emperor of the East is denominated 'Varlet de Constantinople;' and in an account of the house of Philip the Fair, the children of that monarch, as well as several other princes, are styled *varlets*. Hence the prince in a pack of cards is by the French still called *varlet*, and by the English *knave*."

niece Cleopatra,[1] and thus have him proclaimed as his successor.
Now Esope was himself a stranger in his kingdom, and, as he
esteemed not one of his subjects, the Blandiens, and believed that
Berinus was a wonderful man, his project was a politic one. Berinus
arrived at the court of Esope in a magnificent carriage.[2] Geoffrey
was one of his followers, and proved not less useful to him on this
occasion than he had been necessary at the court of the seneschal.
He related to the king, who knew and esteemed him, the adventures 4008
of the lately-arrived stranger, to whom he gave the honour of all that
he himself had done in Rome, and of what he had just done for him
in Blandie. Esope, moreover, knew of the noble birth of Berinus,
and all confirmed him in his plans. The union was proposed : and
a sight of Cleopatra made the proposition more precious to Berinus
than even the prospect of a crown. He did not, however, foresee
the obstacles that were to be encountered. There was a knight
named Logres, who loved Cleopatra, and, moreover, had some pre-
tensions to the crown. On learning that a foreigner was about to
wrest both from him, Logres sent a challenge to the "Roman
merchant," and the tone of his letter of defiance showed the utmost
disdain of the person and profession of his rival. Berinus was in
love, and at the same time enraged, but he was not a knight.
Geoffrey, however, had been distinguished in former years in the
noble profession, and he gave Berinus instructions in it, of which he
profited so well that, after Geoffrey had dubbed him knight, he

[1] His daughter, according to our version.

[2] In the romance, when Berinus visits Esope the wonders of his hall are
again described (ch. 25, "Des merveilles de la salle du roy isopes "), which
leads to an episode relating to the early history of Blandie : Agriano, king of
the Isle of Gamel, having a *penchant* for his own sex, expelled all the women
from Gamel ; many men joined them, and they settled in the island of
Blandie, which was also subject to Agriano. He demanded tribute, which
being refused, he invaded Blandie with an army and was defeated and taken
prisoner. Then follows a story of an incestuous king, about whose doings the
less that is said the better ; but I may mention that both the wicked kings
perished in the river, which was ever after in a state of great commotion, and
their bodies were at times seen floating on the surface of the hideous waters.
A bridge over this river conducted to Esope's palace, and Berinus and his
companions passed over it in fear and trembling when they went to visit the
king. Berinus, however, reaches the audience chamber through a different
hall from that described by Geoffrey, which affords the author an opportunity
for detailing still more wonders.

encountered Logres, and hurled him from his saddle.   Logres, 1009 covered with shame, soon after disappeared.   Berinus, as a reward of his victory, was married to Cleopatra, and shortly after, Esope dying, he succeeded to the crown of Blandie.   Geoffrey, who had up till now been so useful, resolved to return to Rome.   He set out, laden with rich presents, yet only came back to his native country in the humble garb of a potter.   He was, however, recognized, and the emperor often consulted him : he had now no cause to complain of the seven sages ; and praise from them was praise indeed.[1]

Such is the outline of the first part of the French romance from which our Tale of Beryn was derived.   But whence did the French author obtain his materials ?   That is a question not easily answered. No corresponding tale is known to exist in the literature of any other European country ; and, although a Greek version of Asiatic extraction had been in existence several centuries previous to the composition of the French romance, yet it is not at all certain that the tale of Berinus and the Blandiens was adapted from that version. The story in question is found in *Syntipas,* a Greek rendering of a Syriac text of the Book of Sindibád, which was made by one Andreopulos, during the last decade of the 11th century.   The Book of Sindibád, the original of which is lost, is believed to have been written in India, but at what period is not known.[2]   It was probably translated into Pahlaví, the ancient language of Persia, in the 6th century ; from Pahlaví it was rendered into Arabic about the middle of the 8th century ; from Arabic it was translated into Syriac, under the title of *Sindbán ;* into old Spanish (Castilian), under the title of *Libro de los Engannos et los Asayamientos de las Mugeres,* or Book of the Deceits and Tricks of Women, in 1253 ; and into Hebrew, also about the middle of the 13th century, under the title of *Mishlé Sandabar,* or the Parables of Sandabar.   The

---

[1] Abstract of remaining part of the romance, which recounts the chivalric adventures of young Aigres, and his father's subsequent career, will be found in Appendix, p. 160 ff.

[2] For an outline of the frame, or leading story, of the Book of Sindibád and its European imitations ('The Seven Wise Masters'), see *Chaucer Analogues,* p. 322

Arabic version made from the Pahlaví has disappeared, but we may consider it as fairly represented by the Greek text of Andreopulos, and the Syriac and old Spanish texts. A comparatively modern Arabic rechauffé of the work, omitting several of the original tales and substituting others, forms a member of the *Book of the Thousand and One Nights*, and is commonly known under the titles of "The Malice of Women" and "The Seven Vazírs." There is yet another version, a Persian poem, *Sindibád Náma*, or Book of Sindibád, of which a unique but imperfect MS. is preserved in the Library of the India Office, and which, though written A.D. 1379, may represent an older form of the work than the Greek and the Syriac texts. In this version our tale is thus related:

Persian Version.[1]

THERE was once a young man, a merchant, who wandered about the world like the zephyr or the north wind, and who, like the sun and moon, was on his travels every month and all the year round. Manifold are the advantages of travel, by which a man of enterprise becomes respected. He who has travelled is awake and intelligent; and when an affair of importance occurs, he is powerful; while he who has sat inactive at home can with difficulty procure a livelihood. Travel is the profit and the capital of man; its hardships are his nurse. Through it the raw and inexperienced at length become adepts; through it the great achieve renown. By travel the new moon perpetually becomes the full. What is travel, but a capital by which a fortune may be amassed.[2] By travel this young man became alert and active; and he who is active attains to wealth. He was now in Khatá, now in Khutan;[3] now in Aleppo and now in Yemen. He carried the products of Khurasan to Kh,árazm;[4] he

---

[1] From my privately-printed edition of the Book of Sindibád.

[2] "Capital is multiplied twice or thrice over, by repeatedly buying and selling, by those who have knowledge and travel in other lands."—*Pancha Tantra* (The Five Sections); a Sanskrit form of the Fables of Bidpai, or Pilpay.

[3] Both Khatá and Khutan were kingdoms, or principalities, in Chinese Tartary.

[4] Kh,árazm is a region lying along the river Oxus, and extending to the Caspian Sea.

conveyed the stuffs of Ispahán to the emperor of China. As he
sold in Bukhara the products of Abyssinia, he necessarily sold them
at one for ten.[1]

Some one having told him that at Káshgar[2] sandal-wood was of
equal value with gold, and was sold for its weight in that metal, he
resolved to proceed thither; and accordingly, having converted all
his capital into sandal-wood,[3] he set out on his journey. When he
arrived near Káshgar, a person of the country, hearing that he had a
large supply of sandal-wood (in which he himself dealt), and fearing
lest that commodity should be depreciated by its abundance, devised
the following stratagem. Going two stages out of the city, he halted
at the spot where the foreign merchant was, and having pitched his
tent and opened his bales, he lit a fire and piled sandal-wood on it
for fuel. When the merchant smelt the odour of the sandal-wood
he rushed from his tent in amazement and vexation. The man from
the city saluted him, saying: " You are welcome ; may God protect
you from evil! Say, from what country do you come, and what
merchandise bring you?" The merchant informed him. "You
have made a sad blunder," remarked the citizen. "Why have you
brought cumin-seed to Kirmán?[4] The whole timber of this country
is sandal-wood : every casement, roof, and door is composed of it.
If one were to bring common wood hither, it would be far better
than sandal-wood. Who has been so cruel as to suggest to you this
ill-advised scheme? From whose hand proceeds such a blunder as
this? Does any one bring the musk-bladder to Chinese Tartary?"[5]
"Alas!" said the young man to himself, "I have thrown away my
capital! Covetousness is an unblest passion! Alas, for my long
journey and the hardships I have endured! What have they
availed me? He who is not content with what God allots him
never prospers." The man, seeing the merchant now ready for his

---

[1] " Of all goods perfumes are the best : gold is not to be compared to the
article which is procured for one, and sold for a thousand."—*Pancha Tantra.*

[2] Káshgar, capital of a province of the same name in Chinese Turkestán.

[3] Perfumed woods—spiced woods.—*Syntipas.*

[4] A proverbial expression, equivalent to our " Coals to Newcastle," and
the Arabian " Dates to Hajar."

[5] See last note. Musk, the perfume so much esteemed by Asiatics, is
obtained from the navel of a species of deer found in Tartary and Tibet.

purpose, said to him : " The world is never free from profit and loss. Give this sandal-wood to me, and I will give you in return a measure of gold or silver, or whatever else you shall ask." [1] The merchant consented ; two witnesses were called, and the bargain was struck. The merchant considered that the sum he should receive was so much gain, and was rejoiced to be rid of so worthless an article as he had brought.

He thence proceeded to the city of Káshgar, and entering that delightful spot, that model of Paradise, took up his lodging in the house of a virtuous old woman. Of her the merchant asked a question, the reply to which brought him grief and trouble. He inquired : " What is the value of sandal-wood in this kingdom ? " and she informed him that it was worth its weight in gold. [2] " In this city," said she, " headache is common, and hence it is in demand." At this intelligence the merchant became distracted, for he saw that he had been duped. He related his adventure to the old woman, who cautioned him not to trust the inhabitants of that city, by whose cunning many had been ruined.

When morning came, he washed his eyes from sleep, and inquired the way to the market. Thither he bent his course, and wandered through bazaar, street, and field, still solitary and without a friend or companion. The alien has no portion in enjoyment ; he is a martyr wherever he dies. I will suppose him to be but second to Kay Kubád, [3] and that he has placed on his head the diadem of Farídún. [4] Even were he Joseph of Egypt, yet when he calls to mind his home and country, a palace becomes to him a prison. The young merchant was sad at heart, for his enterprise was sadly at a

---

[1] "On this account then, if you are needy, come and sell your whole business, and what you wish I shall give you upon a full plate."—*Syntipas*. "And the man said, I have great grief for thee. Since it is so, I will buy it of thee, and give thee what thou shalt wish. And now get up and give it to me."—*Libro de los Engannos*, &c.

[2] Precisely the same answer is made by the old woman in both the Greek and old Castilian versions : " It is worth its weight in gold."

[3] Kay Kubád was the founder of the second, or Kayání, dynasty of ancient Persian kings.

[4] Farídún was the sixth of the first, or Píshdádí (Achæmenian), dynasty of ancient kings of Persia. His power and grandeur are frequently referred to in Persian literature.

stand. Suddenly he observed a person playing at draughts in the
street. He stopped, and said to himself: " I will play with this
person to dispel my grief," and sat down beside the player, forgetful
of the caution which his landlady had given him. The other agreed
to play with him, on the condition that whichever of them should
lose should be bound to do whatever the winner desired.[1] The
merchant was soon beaten by his crafty opponent, who, upon this,
required him to "drink up the waters of the sea," a demand at
which the merchant was confounded and perplexed. The report
spread through Káshgar, and a crowd soon collected. Another of
the gang had but one eye, which was blue, the colour of the
merchant's eyes. " You have stolen my eye," said he to the
merchant, and he claimed it in the presence of the crowd. A third
produced a stone, and said : " Make from this piece of marble a pair
of trousers and a shirt." [2]

The story soon spread, and all Káshgar was in a bustle. The
old woman, hearing of it, hastened from her house, and saw her
lodger involved in difficulty. She was surety for him, with ten
householders, that she would deliver him, when required, to the
court of justice. When they reached home, she reproached him,
saying : " When a man listens not to advice, fresh calamities will
constantly overtake him. Did I not tell you to have absolutely
no dealings with the inhabitants of this city—no intimacy with
them ? " " It was no fault of yours," replied the young man ; "but
there is no remedy against the decrees of destiny." He was much
dispirited, but she consoled him. " Be not downcast," said she ;
" for joy succeeds to grief : there can be no cure till there be a
complaint. In this city there is a blind old man, with neither power
in his feet nor strength in his hands ; but he is of great intelligence
and acuteness. Those sharpers assemble nightly at his house, and

---

[1] " Or, surrender all his property," must, of course, be understood.—It
is a very common practice among the Arabs to play at some kind of game,
the loser of which must do what the other asks of him or pay a forfeit ; the
tasks required by the winner are often impossible and generally ludicrous.

[2] The merchant not being represented as having engaged in play with this
sharper, there is probably something omitted here by the transcriber of the
manuscript.

are directed by him how to act.[1] Do you this night dress yourself like them, and repairing to his house sit silent among them. When your adversaries shall enter and relate their adventures of the day, mark his answers and his questions. Be all ear there, like the rose; like the narcissus, be all eye and silent."

The young man did as she desired, and repairing thither at night, quietly seated himself in a corner. The first who entered was the person who had bought the sandal-wood. He related his adventure : " I have bought a quantity of sandal-wood, for which I am to give one measure of whatever the seller may choose." "O simpleton !" exclaimed the old man, " you have thrown yourself into the net. This crafty merchant has over-reached you, my son. For if he should demand of you, neither silver nor gold, but a *sá*[2] of male fleas, with silken housings and jewelled bridles, and all linked together with golden chains, say, how will you be able to extricate yourself from this difficulty ?" Quoth the sharper : " How could that blockhead ever think of such a trick ? " The old man rejoined : "However that may be, I have given you your answer."

Next entered the draught-player, and related his adventure : " I have beaten him at draughts," said he, "and have bound him to this condition (and there are witnesses to our agreement), that he shall drink up all the waters of the sea." " You have blundered," replied the old man, "and have involved yourself in difficulty. You think that you have taken him in; in imagination you have caught him in a snare from which there is no escape. But suppose he should say : 'First, pray stop all the streams and rivers which are flowing into the sea, before I drink it dry,' what answer can you possibly return ? " " How," said the knave, " could he, in his whole life, think such a thought ? "

The man with one eye then came in. " That youth," quoth he,

---

[1] " Every Muslim capital (says Sir R. F. Burton) has a Shaykh of Thieves, who holds regular levées, and will restore stolen goods, for a consideration ; and this has lasted since the days of Diodorus Siculus."—See also Burton's *Pilgrimage to Meccah and El Medinah*, vol. i. p. 91.

[2] A *sá*, according to Forbes Falconer, is a measure containing four bushels. Lane says that it is (in Egypt) very nearly equal to six English pints and two-thirds.

"has blue eyes, and I said to him : 'This is my eye that you have;
it is evident to every one that you have stolen it; restore it, and
return my other eye its fellow.'" "O ignorant of the wiles of the
age," answered the old man; "your fortune is more adverse than
that of the others. Suppose he should say : 'Pluck out your one
eye, and then I will pluck out mine, that we may put them both in
scales and judge by their weight whether you are right.' That man
will then have one of his eyes remaining, while you will be quite
blind." Quoth the fellow : "He will never think of such a trick
as that."

Lastly entered the fourth rogue—more shameless than the three
others. "I desired him," said he, "to make with his own hands
a pair of trousers and a shirt from this slab of stone." The
crafty old man replied : "You have managed worse than all; for if
your opponent should say : 'Do you first spin me from iron a thread
to sew it with,' how will you be able to answer him?" Said this
sharper : "The idea will never occur to such a noodle." [1]

The young man listened, unobserved, to all that had passed,
hastened home, and gave the woman a thousand thanks for having
put him on a plan of foiling his adversaries. He passed the night
in calmness and tranquillity. Next morning, when the parties
appeared before the kází, or judge, the man who had bought the
sandal-wood seized the merchant by the collar, saying : "Produce
your measure, that I may fill it, and give you what is your due."
But when the merchant gave him his reply, he was confounded, and
sat down mortified in the presence of the kází. In like manner he
made to each of the other rogues the reply which the blind old man
had suggested. At length, after a hundred objections, he consented
to take back his sandal-wood, and to accept several bags of gold as
compensation; and he availed himself of the first opportunity which
offered to escape from the power of those worthless people.

[1] A jest very similar to this occurs in the Talmud : An Athenian, walking
in the streets of Jerusalem one fine day, observed a tailor seated on his shop-
board, busily plying his needle, and picking up a broken mortar, he requested
him to be so good as put a *patch* upon it. "Willingly," replied the tailor,
taking up a handful of sand and offering it to the joker—"most willingly, sir,
if you will have the goodness to make me first a few *threads* of this material."

It is curious to find the incident of the merchant and the one-eyed man forming the subject of a tradition of no less a personage than the renowned Akbar. According to Knowles' *Dictionary of Kashmírí Proverbs* (p. 88), Akbar, disguised as a fakír, and accompanied by his prime minister, Bír Bal, was walking about the city one night, when he was accosted by a one-eyed man, who said to him: "You have got my eye, and I must either have it back or 1200 rupís." The emperor was mute from astonishment, but his minister readily answered for him, saying: "What you say is quite true. We have your eye, and if you will come to-morrow you shall have it again." The man consented and went his way. Bír Bal sent to the butchers for some sheep's eyes, and put each one of them in a separate box. When the one-eyed man came in the morning, the minister showed him some of the sheep's eyes, and told him that he must submit to have his other eye taken out and weighed, which was done accordingly, and so the fellow was blinded for life. Here, we see, Akbar takes the place of the sandal-wood merchant, and his minister that of the shaykh of thieves—with a difference!

In the Calcutta and Búlák printed Arabic texts of *The Nights*, the merchant, after disposing of his sandal-wood, is accosted by the one-eyed man, and obtains a day's grace, after providing surety; his shoe having been torn in the scuffle, he takes it to a cobbler, saying, "Repair it, and I will give thee what will content thee;" lastly, he plays at dice with a fourth sharper, and, losing the game, is required to drink up the sea or surrender all his property. The blind old man tells the cobbler that the merchant might say to him: "The sultan's troops have been victorious, and the number of his children and allies is increased—art thou not content?" to which he would not dare to reply in the negative; and the dice-player might be asked to hold the mouth of the sea and hand it to him, and he would drink.—In *Syntipas* and the *Libro de los Engannos*, as in the Persian version, the stopping of the rivers is the old man's suggestion, and the incident of the cobbler is not mentioned.—All that remains of the story in the unique Syriac MS., discovered by Rödiger, and printed, with a German translation, by Baethgen, is the opening sentence: "There was once a merchant, who bought a scented wood which is called aloe. When he heard"—and here it breaks off; but the story was probably similar to that in the old Castilian version.

The story is orally current in some parts of India, and it may also exist there in a written form—perhaps in the *Suka Saptatí*, or Seventy Tales of a Parrot. Under the rather vague title of "The Merchant and his Son," Mr. C. Vernieux gives a version of it in a small collection of Indian Tales and Anecdotes appended to his story of *The Hermit of Motee Jhurna, or Pearl Spring*, printed at Calcutta in 1873. Those tales he professes to have taken down from oral recitation in Urdú, Hindí, and Bengalí;—it would have been more satisfactory, however, had he specified the district where each story was told to him.

Indian Version.

A WEALTHY merchant, while lying on his bed indisposed by sickness and the infirmities of age, invited his son to his room one day, and spoke to him in these words: "My son, from this sickness I may not recover. Should I die, I fear you will squander all my hard-earned wealth by dissipation and idleness. You know that in my vocation as a merchant I have prospered and enjoyed all the blessings of this life. I fear you will not be able to conduct the business with care and discretion, yet I would recommend your following the profession of your father. In doing so I lay no restraint upon your visiting every land under the sun, but I strongly dissuade you from ever venturing into the Himálya regions." The son was desirous of knowing the reason why his father prohibited him from going with his merchandise, if he ever traded, into the Himályan mountains. "My son," observed the father, "my long experience of the world, my knowledge of all countries and their denizens, enable me to form a just and accurate estimate of the characters of men. The inhabitants of that region have been found invariably to be very artful and dishonest. They will not only rob a man of his purse, but if they can find an opportunity, or a single excuse, they will without remorse strip him naked and appropriate his clothes. Should you ever forget this my parting advice, and go into that country and fall into any disaster, remember to call on Golab Sing, the chief of the country, who is a friend of mine; mention my name to him, seek redress from his justice, and he will enable you to remain there in the peaceful prosecution of your trade."

The merchant died shortly after, as was expected, and the son, whose curiosity was excited by his father's prohibition, resolved upon visiting the lofty hills. To carry out this object, he procured a large stock of valuable goods, and such as were not only in general demand in the country but highly valued by the mountaineers. With this merchandise he loaded fifty camels, and set out on a fine morning on his perilous and uncertain journey. Having arrived in the country after two months' tedious travel through extensive forests and fields, the young merchant thought it to be appropriate to announce his arrival in the usual manner by firing a salute; but instead of wasting his powder in merely making a report, he deemed it more prudent that, while the salute was being fired, he should aim his musket at a heron which he saw seated quietly near the verge of a spacious tank, and thus accomplish two objects at once. Having shot the bird, he went to pick up his game, but in doing so he saw a washerman occupied in scouring clothes, who spoke to him thus: "What have you done? Have you not a grain of common sense? The heron was my father, who had transmigrated into the body of that bird, and he was very useful to me, watching and encouraging me in my operations, and guarding the clothes which are spread out to the sun for bleaching purpose. Now pray resuscitate my father and give him back to me, or lay down four hundred rupís, else you do not go away so easily from hence."

While this conversation was being held by the two individuals, another man who had approached the spot, and was silently listening, and who was blind of one eye, thus accosted the young merchant: " Your father, peace be to his spirit, was a just and liberal man, who traded in all kinds of things, and dealt in eyes. He took a fancy to my eyes, and purchased one of them for six hundred rupís, with a promise of paying me that sum on his next visit to this country.

Though I am suffering from the loss of one eye, I have not been paid yet for my pain and loss. I forego the interest on the sum due to me these several years, and, as you are his son, I expect that you will discharge the debt willingly, or we must proceed to court. Give me the money or restore the eye to me."

In the course of this altercation there was a third person listening. She was a woman with a child in her arms, and came forward and saluted the young merchant in a bland and soothing manner: "It is my good fortune to meet you in this country, and how happy I am to see you, of whom I have heard so favourably from your father. How well you answer his description; just those eyes and those arched brows, and those soft lineaments. I am his poor wife, and this unhappy boy is his last son by a second marriage. At the time of his going away for a short period, he told me to borrow such sums as would defray our expenses, and that on his return he would refund the money with interest. I trust you will help me to pay off the debts incurred during two years and six months, and, as you are like my own son, that you will support me and take me under your protection, that no disgrace may be cast on the honourable name of your worthy father."

The young merchant became so confounded with these novel and unexpected attacks and unceremonious demands, that he regretted he had not listened to the salutary advice of his father, the consequence of which was that he was so soon after his arrival in the country experiencing such annoyance, and was plunged into so much trouble. It occurred to him, however, in this distress of mind, that, in the event of his suffering from any adverse circumstance, his father had advised him to call on Golab Sing, the chief of the country. With this object in view, he told the people, who were pulling him on each side and almost quartering him, to go with him before the rájá, to whose decision he would submit, and be guided by his counsel. Before the merchant could arrive at Golab Sing's residence, these dexterous rogues ran and presented themselves before him to offer their respective complaints, crying out, "Help, Maháráj!" Soon after taking their deposition, the merchant also arrived, and was interrogated by the prince as to the country from whence he had

come and what his name was. On discovering that he was the son
of his friend the old merchant, the prince was moved by unfeigned
grief at the news of his father's death. The rogues, seeing the
friendly terms on which the young man stood with the prince, lost
all courage, and would have decamped from the court rather than
advance the prosecution. But it was too late to recede; they therefore screwed up their resolution to stand the investigation. The
prince, well knowing the tricks and stratagems of his subjects, took
the merchant aside and advised him what to do in this affair. He
said: "When the washerman comes and makes his claim against
you, do you make this counter-charge against him: ' When your
father became a heron, my father was a small fish in the river, who,
swimming and jumping in the shallow water, was journeying home,
up the stream, when your father, the heron, pecked at him, and
getting him in his bill, swallowed him. Produce my father first,
and then I will restore yours to you.' To the second claimant say:
' My father, it is true, traded in all sorts of things, and also speculated
in eyes; but as there are so many eyes in my possession, and I do
not know which is yours, give me the other eye, weighing which in
the scales, I could ascertain the exact weight and restore the precise
eye to you.' To the third say: ' I admit the truth of your allegation,
for I have heard my father mention to me frequently that he was
married in this country, and had a young son; he told me therefore
to bring his wooden sandal, and to give you that to wear and mount
the funeral pyre.[1] Do that, and I will believe that you are really his
wife.' "

Being thus advised and prepared by the prince, those persons,
while endeavouring by artful means to substantiate their claims,
were defeated and confounded by as cogent counter-statements from
the young merchant as those which they tendered. The merchant,
having been dismissed with marks of regard by the prince, followed
his occupation in the country without any further molestation, while
the wicked rogues were sent to prison, there to chew the bitter cud
of reflection, and to work on the roads under the weight of heavy
chains.

[1] The usual practice when a Hindú died away from his family.

Besides the story of the Sandal-wood Merchant and the Rogues, which occurs in the "Malice of Women," or the "Seven Vazírs," there is a very singular variant of our tale in another group, belonging to what may be termed the sporadic part of the great Sindibád family of romances, which is found in the Arabic text of *The Nights* printed at Breslau, namely, "King Shah Bakht and his Vazír Er-Rahwan"—for some account of which see *Chaucer Analogues*, pp. 352, 353. It is the eighth recital of Er-Rahwan, and, under the title of "The Merchant, the Crone, and the King," has been thus rendered by Sir R. F. Burton :

Arabian Variant.

THERE was once a family of affluence and distinction, in a city of Khorassan, and the townsfolk used to envy them for that which Allah had vouchsafed them. As time went on, their fortune ceased from them and they passed away, till there remained of them but one old woman. When she grew feeble and decrepit, the townsfolk succoured her not with aught, but thrust her forth of the city, saying : "This old woman shall not neighbour with us, for that we do good to her and she requiteth us with evil."[1] So she took shelter in a ruined place, and strangers used to bestow alms upon her, and in this way she tarried a length of time. Now the king of that city had aforetime contended the kingship with his uncle's son, and the people disliked the king ; but Allah Almighty decreed that he should overcome his cousin. However, jealousy of him abode in his heart, and he acquainted the Wazír, who hid it not, and sent him money. Furthermore he fell to summoning all strangers who came to the town, man after man, and questioning them of their creed and their goods, and whoso answered him not satisfactorily he took his wealth.

Now a certain wealthy man of the Moslems was way-faring, without knowing aught of this, and it befell that he arrived at that city by night, and coming to the ruin, gave the old woman money, and said to her, "No harm upon thee." Whereupon she lifted up

---

[1] They suspected her to be a witch because she was old and poor, as was unhappily the case in our own country and all over Europe in the 17th and the early year of the 18th centuries.

her voice and blessed him. So he set down his merchandise by her and abode with her the rest of the night and the next day. Now highwaymen had followed him that they might rob him of his monies, but succeeded not in aught; wherefore he went up to the old woman and kissed her head, and exceeded in bounty to her. Then she warned him of that which awaited strangers entering the town, and said to him : " I like not this for thee, and I fear mischief for thee from those questions that the Wazír hath appointed for address-ing the ignorant." And she expounded to him the case according to its conditions ; then said to him : " But have no concern. Only carry me with thee to thy lodging, and if he question thee of aught enigmatical whilst I am with thee, I will expound the answers to thee."

So he carried the crone with him to the city, and lodged her in his lodging, and entreated her honourably. Presently the Wazír heard of the merchant's coming ; so he sent to him and bade bring him to his house, and he talked with him a while of his travels and of whatso had befallen him therein, and the merchant answered his queries. Then said the Wazír : " I will put certain critical questions to thee, which an thou answer me, 'twill be well for thee." And the merchant rose and made him no answer. Quoth the Wazír : " What is the weight of the elephant ?" The merchant was perplexed and returned him no answer, giving himself up for lost ; however at last he said : " Grant me three days of delay." The minister granted him the time he sought, and he returned to his lodging and related what had passed to the old woman, who said : " When the morrow cometh, go to the Wazír and say to him : ' Make a ship and launch it on the sea, and put in it the elephant, and when it sinketh in the water, mark the place whereunto the water riseth. Then take out the elephant and cast in stones in its place, till the ship sink to the same mark ; whereupon do thou take out the stones and weigh them, and thou wilt presently know the weight of the elephant.' " Accord-ingly, when he arose in the morning, he went to the Wazír and repeated to him that which the old woman had taught him ; whereat the minister marvelled, and said to him : " What sayest thou of a man who seeth in his house four holes, and in each hole a viper offering to sally out upon him and slay him, and in his house are four sticks, and each hole may not be stopped but with the ends of two sticks ?   How, then, shall he stop all the holes and deliver himself from the vipers ?"   When the merchant heard this, there befell him such concern that it garred him forget the first, and he said to the Wazír: "Grant me delay, so that I may reflect on the reply ;" and the minister cried: "Go out, and bring me an answer, or I will seize thy monies."   The merchant fared forth and returned to the old woman, who, seeing him changed of complexion, said to him : "What did his hoariness ask thee?"   So he acquainted her with the case, and she cried : "Fear not ; I will bring thee forth of this strait."   Quoth he: "Allah requite thee with weal !"   Then quoth she : "To-morrow go to him with a stout heart and say : 'The answer of that whereof thou askest me is this : Put the heads of two sticks into one of the holes ; then take the other two sticks and lay them across the middle of the first two, and stop with their two heads the second hole, and with their ferrules the fourth hole ; and then take the ferrules of the first two sticks and stop with them the third hole.' "   So he repaired to the Wazír and repeated to him the answer ; and he marvelled at its justness, and said to him : "Go. By Allah ! I will ask thee no more questions, for thou with thy skill marrest my foundation."   Then he treated him as a friend, and the merchant acquainted him with the affair of the old woman ; whereupon quoth the Wazír: "Needs must the intelligent company with the intelligent."   Thus did this weak woman restore to that man his life and his monies on the easiest wise.[1]

Little more than a vague outline of the original story is preserved in this Arabian variant ; but the Tale of Beryn has incidents which the Sindibád and the Indian versions have each exclusively.   Thus the young Roman merchant on entering Falsetown discovers a burgess playing at chess with a neighbour (l. 1646) ; in the Persian

[1] *Supplemental Nights to the ' Book of the Thousand Nights and a Night.' With Notes, Anthropological and Explanatory.*   By [Sir] Richard F. Burton [K.C.M.G.].   Benares: MDCCCLXXXVI.   Printed for the Kama Shastra Society and for Private Subscribers only.   Vol. I., pp. 235—238.

(Sindibád) story the sandal-wood merchant, walking in the city of Káshgar, sees a man playing at draughts. In all three versions he is accused of having stolen a man's eye, or eyes. The rascal who bought the sandal-wood is required to fill a measure with male fleas, finely harnessed; in the Tale of Beryn the provost is required to load five ships with butterflies. The task of drinking the waters of the sea does not occur in the Indian story, but it has in common with Beryn the incident of the woman and the child slightly modified, while the accusation made by the catchpoll that his father had been murdered by the father of Beryn has its equivalent in the Indian story, where the washerman charges the young merchant with having shot his father in the form of a heron. In the Persian story the sandal-wood merchant is advised by his landlady to go and listen to what the blind shaykh of thieves says to each of the sharpers; in Berinus, apparently, Geoffrey secretly learns from King Escope how to defend the Roman merchant (see *ante*, p. 135, note); in the Arabian variant an old woman instructs him herself; in the Indian version the merchant consults Golab Sing, the prince of the country. It is very evident that the several versions had a common origin, but it is equally clear that the Tale of Beryn was not derived from the Persian or the Indian stories. It seems to me not unlikely that the story was brought to France from a Morisco-Spanish source.

According to rabbinical legends, the hospitality of the citizens of Sodom towards the strangers within their gates was of a very peculiar character, and the decisions of their judges bear some resemblance to the "laws" of the folk of Falsetown. When a traveller arrived, each citizen (to preserve their reputation for hospitality) was required to give him a coin with his name written on it, after which the unfortunate wayfarer was refused food, and as soon as he died of hunger each man took back his own money. It may be naturally supposed that travellers acquainted with the peculiar ways of the citizens of Sodom would either avoid entering that city or take care to provide themselves with food. But even this precaution did not avail them against the wiles of those infamous people, as may be seen from the following Hebrew story:

A man from Elam, journeying to a place beyond Sodom, reached the latter city about sunset. He had with him an ass, bearing a valuable saddle, to which was strapped a bale of merchandise. Being refused a lodging by each citizen of whom he asked the favour, the stranger made a virtue of necessity, and resolved to pass the night along with his animal and his goods as best he might in the streets. His preparations with this view were observed by a cunning and treacherous citizen, named Hidud, who came up, and, accosting him courteously, desired to know whence he had come and whither he was bound. The stranger answered that he had come from Hebron, and was journeying to such a place; that, having been refused shelter by all to whom he had applied for it, he was making ready to pass the night in the streets; and that he was provided with bread for his own use, and fodder for his beast. Upon this Hidud invited the stranger to his house, assuring him that his lodging should cost him nothing, while the wants of his beast should not be forgotten. The traveller accepted of Hidud's proffered hospitality, and when they came to the house the citizen relieved the ass of the saddle and merchandise, and carefully placed them for security in his private closet. He then led the ass into his stable and supplied him with fodder; and returning to the house, he set food before his guest, who having supped retired to rest. Early in the morning the stranger arose, intending to resume his journey, but his host first pressed him to partake of breakfast and afterwards persuaded him to remain at his house for two days. On the evening of the third day our traveller would no longer delay his departure, and Hidud therefore brought out his beast, saying kindly to his guest, "Fare thee well." "Hold!" said the traveller, "where is my beautiful saddle of many colours, and the strings attached thereto, together with my bale of rich merchandise?" "What sayest thou?" exclaimed Hidud in a tone of surprise. The stranger repeated his demand for his saddle and goods. "Ah," said Hidud affably, "I will interpret thy dream: The strings that thou hast dreamt of indicate length of days to thee; and the many-coloured saddle of thy dream signifies that thou shalt become the owner of a beauteous garden of odorous flowers and rich fruit-trees." "Nay," returned the stranger, "I certainly entrusted to thy care a saddle and merchandise, and thou hast concealed them in thy house." "Well," said Hidud, "I have told thee the meaning of thy dream. My usual fee for interpreting a dream is four pieces of silver, but as thou hast been my guest, I will only ask three pieces of thee." On hearing this very unjust demand the stranger was enraged, and he accused Hidud in the court of Sodom of stealing his property. After each had stated his case, the judge decreed that the stranger must pay Hidud's fee, since he was well known as a professional interpreter of dreams. Hidud then said to the stranger: " As thou hast proved thyself such a liar, I must not only be paid my usual fee of four pieces of silver, but also the value of the two days' food with which I provided thee in my house." "I will cheerfully pay thee for the food," rejoined the traveller, " on condition that thou restore my saddle and merchandise." Upon this the litigants began to abuse each other, and were thrust into the street, where the citizens, siding with Hidud, soundly beat the unlucky stranger and then expelled him from the city.

Another rabbinical legend is to this effect: Abraham once sent his servant Eleazer to Sodom, with his compliments to Lot and his family, and to inquire concerning their welfare. As Eleazer entered Sodom he saw a citizen beating a stranger whom he had robbed of his property. "Shame upon thee!" exclaimed Eleazer to the citizen; "is this the way you act towards strangers?" To this remonstrance the man replied by picking up a stone and striking Eleazer with it on the forehead with such force as to cause the blood to flow down his face. On seeing the blood the citizen caught hold of Eleazer and demanded to be paid his fee for having freed him of impure blood. "What!" said Eleazer, " am I to pay thee for wounding me?" " Such is our law," returned the citizen. Eleazer refused to pay, and the man brought him before the judge, to whom he made his complaint. The judge decreed: "Thou must pay this man his fee since he has let thy blood; such is our law." "There!" said Eleazer, striking the judge with a stone and causing him to bleed, "pay thou my fee to this man, I want it not," and then departed from the court.

There are many parallels to this last story, some of which may be cited in conclusion. The 50th of the 'Pleasing Stories' in Gladwin's *Persian Moonshee* relates how a dervish was charged at a police court with striking a grocer with his slipper, and the kutwal fined him eight annas, whereupon the dervish handed a rupí to the kutwal, and then, striking that official also on the head with his slipper, said : " If such be justice, take thou eight annas and give the other eight to the grocer."

In the third volume of Beloe's *Miscellanies*, which comprises a selection of amusing stories translated from a manuscript procured in Aleppo by Dr. Russel, about 1794, is one to this effect : A young man seeing a half-witted fellow, he cannot resist the temptation of giving him a blow behind his back. The crazy man drags the youth before the kází and makes his complaint. The judge fines the youth twenty small coins, and gives him leave to go and get change. Of course he remains away, and the kází falls asleep. At length the crazy fellow's patience is exhausted, and he gives the kází a blow, telling him that he can wait no longer, and as he had himself fixed the price of a blow, perhaps he would be so good as remain till the youth returned, and keep the fine for himself.

Similar stories are found in the old Italian novelists. The second of Sozzini's collection is as follows : Scacazzone, returning one day from Rome, found himself, when within a short distance of Sienna, without cash enough to purchase a dinner. But resolving not to go without one if he could avoid it, he very quietly walked into the nearest inn, and appearing quite a stranger, demanded a room in which to dine alone. He next ordered whatever he considered as most likely to prove agreeable to himself, without in the least sparing his purse, as the good host believed, and ate and drank everything of the best. When he had at length finished his wine and refreshed himself with a short nap for his journey, he rang the bell, and with a very unconcerned air asked the waiter for his bill. This being handed to him, " Waiter," he cried, " can you tell me anything relating to the laws of this place ?" " O yes, signor, I dare say," for a waiter is never at a loss. " For instance," continued Scacazzone, " what does a man forfeit by killing another ?" " His life, certainly, signor," said the waiter. " But if he only wounds another badly, not mortally, what then?" "Then," returned the waiter, "as it may happen, according to the provocation and the injury." "And lastly," continued the guest, "if you only deal a fellow a sound box on the ear, what do you pay for that?" "For that," echoed the waiter, "it is here about ten livres, no more." "Then send your master to me," cried Scacazzone—"be quick— begone!" Upon the good host's appearance, his wily guest conducted himself in such a manner, uttering such accusations against extortion, such threats, and such vile aspersions upon his host's house, that on Scacazzone bringing their heads pretty close together, the landlord, unable longer to bear his taunts, gave him a rather severe cuff. "I am truly obliged to you!" cried the happy Scacazzone, taking him by the hand; "this is all I wanted with you— truly obliged to you, my good host, and will thank you for the change. Your bill here is eight livres, and the fine for your assault is ten; however, if you will have the goodness to pay the difference to the waiter, as I find I shall reach the city very pleasantly before evening: it will be quite right."—But more closely resembling the Eastern versions is the fourth novel of Arienti, in which a learned advocate is fined for striking his opponent in open court, and "takes his change" by repeating the offence.

I suspect that not a few of the apologues and tales in the Talmud are comparatively recent interpolations; and the circumstance that that monument of human wisdom and folly was first printed at Venice in the sixteenth century, after most of the Italian novelists had published their collections, renders it at least possible that the talmudists drew some of their narrative material from Italian sources.

APPENDIX.

CONTINUATION OF THE ROMANCE OF BERINUS[1]— from p. 140.

BERINUS loved his wife, and was beloved by her, but he could never win the affection of his subjects. They regretted Logres, and sought him for twenty years in order to place him on the throne. At length they found him ruler in Corinth. Logres seized the opportunity to avenge himself and rule over Blandie, and came with a large army. Berinus mustered his troops, but they delivered him over to his enemy, together with Cleopatra his wife, Aigres their son, and the beautiful Romaine their daughter. Logres, although not approving of this act of treachery, profited by it. He remembered, however, that Berinus, after conquering him in single combat, spared his life, so he said to the Roman: "Depart, and take with you from this isle all the riches you brought to it. You have no need of pity, since you have still your Cleopatra." Logres then caused all the traitors who had given up Berinus to be put to death. He disdained to ascend the throne which they had offered him, but placed his son Ismandor[2] in his stead, who, seeing that the mild rule of Berinus had lost it, resolved to follow a quite opposite course, being of opinion that it was necessary for lions to rule wolves.

Meanwhile, Berinus was making haste for his departure. He set out as he had come, with five vessels richly laden. Cleopatra had nothing to regret; she followed her husband, who consoled her for the loss of a crown, in their departure from Blandie. They had a pleasant voyage during three days, but on the fourth day they perceived that, in spite of all their efforts, their little fleet was approaching an immense magnetic rock, which was drawing them towards itself. The old sailors declared that as soon as they touched it, no human power could detach them from the rock, and this soon came to pass. Berinus discovered a number of other ships fixed like his own to the rock, which appeared to be inhabited only by corpses. He groaned in spirit when he thought

---

[1] Dunlop, in his *History of Fiction*, has fallen into error when he says (*art.* Ser Giovanni): "This romance, of which the manuscript is *extremely* old, is the original of the Merchant's Second Tale, or Story of Beryn, sometimes published with Chaucer's *Canterbury Tales*. The first half of the story, however, concerning the treasury, has not been adopted by the English poet, or at least is not in that part of his tale which has been preserved." We have already seen the *first* part, and shall find the story of the treasury in this, the *second*, part of the romance.

[2] Yspamador in both editions in the British Museum.

that hunger would speedily reduce himself, his family, and his ships' crews to the like condition. Giving himself up to these sad forebodings, he was attracted by the appearance of a man, whose extreme thinness might have caused him to be taken for a corpse. This man was silently crawling into one of the Roman vessels to obtain some food. Young Aigres, the son of Berinus, laid hold of him, and led him to his father, in the hope that he would be able to throw some light upon an occurrence which perplexed their minds. The unhappy man informed them that he was himself a victim, adding that there was an inscription on one side of the rock, but he had not read it. Aigres, full of ardour and courage, wished to see the inscription, and after the starveling—whose name was Silvain—had partaken of some food, he led young Aigres to the place, where he read these words: "Whoever may touch this rock can only be freed after he has deposited on it all his wealth, save only what is necessary to finish his voyage; one of the company must then go to the top of this rock and cast into the sea the ring which he shall find there, when the vessel will at once be freed; but it is necessary that the lot determines the one who shall detach the ring, and he must not go in the vessel which he sets free." Berinus and his company resolved to draw lots to know which of them was to sacrifice himself for the safety of all the rest. The lot fell on Aigres, who was pleased at the result: he would have the good fortune of giving liberty to his father, mother, and sister, as well as to men who had not hesitated to follow them into exile. It requires little to determine a brave and generous soul. Aigres stole away from the embraces of Berinus, Cleopatra, and Romaine and was soon on the top of the rock. He loosened the ring, and cast it into the water; immediately the rock trembled, the wind arose, and the vessels were thrown into the open sea.[1]

Berinus now resumed his voyage, and arrived at a port in Italy. Here he paid off all his servants, and, accompanied by his wife, daughter, and Silvain, whom he had taken off the magnetic rock, repaired to Rome in a very humble equipage. Berinus had left all his wealth on the fatal rock, and he had nothing more to expect in Rome: how could his wife, whom he adored, and his beauteous daughter, who was worthy of the respect of kings, endure the misery in store for them? In this extremity Silvain said to him: "You have nothing, since the emperor has taken possession of all your fortune;[2] you have no army to demand

---

[1] The myth of a magnetic mountain often occurs in the old romances; and we have a familiar instance in the Arabian story of the Third Calender (or Royal Mendicant), and another in the miraculous legend of the Irish saint Brandanus.

[2] In chapter lxxiii. of the edition of the romance printed by the Widow Trepperel (see *ante*, note, p. 124), we are told that soon after Berinus arrived in Rome he met his old friend Geoffrey, and asked him if he could tell him anything about his father Fawnus, to which Geoffrey replied: "By my faith, sire, Raine his wife killed him with poison for a knight whom she loved, and when he was dead she so wrought with the emperor that all the race of Fawnus, both in the city and round about it, was destroyed and extinguished."—We have here an example of the manner in which Dixmerie dressed up his *Extrait*: he has transferred the lady's intrigue to

satisfaction from him for that injustice. But, without causing any trouble—without exposing yourself to any denial and persecution, which would be the consequence—it is possible to free you from a poverty to which you were not born." Berinus implored to be informed in what way this could be done. "You need run no risk," replied Silvain; "here is the secret: My father was the architect of the tower in which the emperor keeps his treasure. He took care, in the course of its erection, to contrive a secret passage, of which he intended to make use. It is marked by a stone not cemented like the others, but yet joined to them so perfectly that nobody would suspect it is moveable; it is so, however. I know this passage, and have gone into the tower more than once before leaving Rome. For you, I will go back to it, and restore, without the emperor's knowledge, some portion of the wealth he has taken from you." Berinus hesitated long before agreeing to Silvain's plan. But without means in the midst of Rome, obliged even to conceal his name, he saw Cleopatra his wife and Romaine his daughter—the former the offspring of a king, the latter born whilst he was himself a king—condemned to perish of hunger! He could not bear the horrible idea. "Bring it," said he to Silvain; "I consent to everything." He took a house close to Philip's treasury, which Silvain visited several times, and thus enabled Berinus to live in comfort. He was prudent enough to make no show of wealth; while Cleopatra and Romaine, knowing he had formerly been rich, were not surprised that he should find means of living in Rome; and they questioned him not on this matter, for his absolute silence showed that he did not wish it talked about.

Let us now return to the generous Aigres. The magnetic rock was inhabited by enchanters, who knew well how to annoy the travellers whom they drew to it; but the need of food obliged Aigres to frequently visit the vessels fixed to the rock; and he found in them more wealth than food, a circumstance which seemed to presage for him an awful fate. One day, as he was continuing his searches, he heard the neighing of a horse in the hold of one of the vessels, and going down, he saw a spirited steed, whose food was completely done, and who was now neighing for more. Silvain had taken this precaution before going away.[1] Aigres did not hesitate to take charge of him in his turn. He called him Morel de l'Aimant, both from his black colour and the place where he was found. In the same vessel hung a splendid suit of mail, and a valuable sword, on which were written the words "Pleure Sang."[2] Aigres, without thinking of ever using this armour, took

---

the early part of the romance, where there's no mention of such a thing—see *ante*, p. 127, three lines from foot.

[1] This means, apparently, that Silvain had tended the gallant steed while on the rock; yet he was himself starving when he crept on board one of Berinus' ships.

[2] The hero of romance is always provided with a wonderful horse and an irresistible blade. Antar, the Bedouin poet-hero, had his horse Abjer and his

it down, examined it, put it on, and found it a perfect fit, at which he felt a secret satisfaction, convinced that fate had not bestowed this gift upon him except to make use of it. His chief care, after guarding himself from the snares which the demons of the rock laid for him, was to look out from its top for any approaching vessel. At length he saw one which was yielding to the same power that had attracted his father's ships. Aigres pointed out to the crew the only means for detaching the vessel, and one of them went to the top of the rock, Aigres at the same time going on board, with his beautiful armour and his good steed Morel, ready to set out; the ring was cast into the sea, and the ship was set free. The young knight resolved to proceed to Rome, but fate had destined for him adventures elsewhere—his fame was to precede his arrival in Rome.

The ship in which he was embarked arrived at the kingdom of Tantalus, which was ruled over by two brothers, and he took the road to the capital. Going through a forest he was attacked by two robbers, whom he killed, and thereby set free Prince Germain, who had been captured by them. This prince was called Galopin, from his great speed in running. He was, however, so deformed that his father and mother, both handsome and well made, had for a long time refused to recognize him as their son. Aigres made him his squire. Farther on our knight met Maligant, one of the two kings of Tantalus, who was carrying away by force a young lady. Aigres fought with him and killed him. Dannemont, brother of Maligant, wishing to avenge the death of the latter, challenged Aigres, who defeated him, and spared his life on the condition that he would no longer oppress his subjects.

After these heroic achievements Aigres, accompanied by his squire Galopin, proceeded to the kingdom of Loquiferne, the king of which was called Holopherne. This prince, to whom the prowess of Aigres de l'Aimant was already known, was very much pleased to have him at his court, for he had just then great need of the strength of his arm. Holopherne was in love with the Princess Melia, daughter of a king named Absalon, who would give her only to the prince who should bring with him two knights prepared to combat with and kill two savage lions, or would attempt this great feat himself. None of the barons of Holopherne offered themselves for such a perilous adventure; but Aigres undertook it without hesitation, and was accompanied by a knight called Açars, into whose hands was committed a casket of jewels, destined for the princess as a marriage present. This knight was fit for no better employment;—it was Aigres who fought with and killed the lions, and the princess was entrusted to him to convey her in safety to King Holopherne. Aigres and the princess, accompanied by Açars, carrying the jewels, set out for their destination. Now

sword Dhami. Rustam, the Persian champion, had his horse Raksh. In the Norse sagas we read of the famous blades, Gram and Graysteel; and in other European romances, of Morglay, Excalibar, Balmung, and Durandal.

Açars was born both lily-livered and faithless, and he envied Aigres the glory which he had just achieved. As they were passing a very deep well Açars purposely allowed the box of jewels to fall into it, and affected to be very much concerned at the misfortune. Aigres at once undertook to recover the box. He joined the reins of his horse together, secured one end to the top of the well, and descended by the aid of this improvised rope. When he dived to recover the casket, the treacherous Açars drew up the reins, and then compelled the princess and her maid to follow him. But soon after Abilas, king of Pannonie, a lover of the princess, appeared and rescued her—Açars flying away without making any resistance, although Abilas had only his squire with him. The craven did not fail to return to the court of Holopherne and proclaim that the king of Pannonie, at the head of a great army, had come and snatched out of his hands the Princess Melia, while he was fighting like a lion, and that Aigres de l'Aimant had surrendered himself without striking a blow in her behalf.[1]

Let us not leave Aigres de l'Aimant, the true champion of lions, too long at the bottom of a well. He was very much astonished not to find the reins which had helped him to get down. His suspicions immediately rested on Açars, and he thought, "He who has forsaken me, can as easily have betrayed me!" But he cared little for his treachery—only how to render it of no avail. He drew his good sword Pleure Sang, with which he had luckily armed himself, and used it to cut steps in the side of the well, and thus got out, to find his horse and splendid armour where he had left them. Taking the road to Loquiferne and passing through a wood, he came upon two women, whom two unknown persons were carrying away by force; they proved to be the Princess Melia and her maid, King Abilas and his squire. The princess called out for help from Aigres de l'Aimant, who quickly responded to her cries. Challenging the king of Pannonie, he fought and conquered him, and gave him his life on condition that he should surrender the princess. Aigres then proceeded to the court of Holopherne, with Melia and the rich casket he had recovered from the bottom of the well. The cowardly and faithless Açars was unmasked and disgraced. Melia told of all that had passed, and of the glory that Aigres had gained. Açars was banished from the kingdom, and Aigres thought himself sufficiently avenged, since dishonour was worse even than death to a knight. The king bestowed the greatest favours upon the deliverer of Melia, in order to retain him at his court, but the son of Berinus adhered to his resolution of rejoining his father. He sailed away accordingly, and duly arrived in Rome, accompanied by his squire Galopin, who had remained at Loquiferne during his last adventure.

[1] It is a very common occurrence in romantic tales for the hero to be thus treated and misrepresented by his rivals in love—generally by his jealous brothers—who take credit to themselves for his gallant achievements; but in the end their cowardice and treachery are invariably made manifest, as we shall see in the case of this carpet-knight Açars.

Aigres de l'Aimant soon learned that he must conceal his birth in the native city of his father, whom he discovered with great difficulty, and only by the help of old Geoffrey.[1] Berinus gave a portion of his riches to his son, but did not reveal to him how he obtained them. He was ambitious that Aigres should eclipse the splendour of all the knights of Rome. Aigres readily fell in with his father's views, yet he shone more by his courage and skill in tournaments than by the magnificence of his armour. On such occasions he had the good wishes of the court beauties, especially of the charming Nullie, daughter of the emperor.

Now at the Feast of Pentecost the emperor Philip had a full court of his barons, and he purposed making them rich presents before their departure. For this purpose he visited the tower containing his treasures and found them considerably reduced. He accused of the theft his ten treasurers, and caused them all to be put in prison. One of them promised the emperor to discover in what manner and by whom the robbery had been effected, provided the most profound secrecy were observed. Philip determined to accompany him to the tower, where the treasurer lighted a great fire exactly in front of the door and windows, and the smoke was seen to escape through the spaces left by the uncemented stone, which they found could easily be removed and replaced, and they doubted not that it was in this way the robber entered. Concluding that he came only at night, they placed immediately below the loose stone a tub filled with a substance so glutinous that a person once in it had no chance to get out again; and keeping most secret the discovery they had made, they awaited the result. Silvain by this time was dead, and Berinus had not yet himself ventured into the tower; he felt that it was becoming more and more dangerous, but did not consider himself rich enough to dispense with such means. One night he resolved to go thither for once and once only. Accordingly he proceeded to the tower, displaced the stone, and having entered fell into the trap prepared for him. Aigres de l'Aimant, returning from the palace of Philip, was just entering his father's house when he perceived some one displace a stone from the tower wall, and creep through the opening thus made. He ran forward on purpose to seize the thief, and heard from within the tower these words, uttered amidst groans and sighs: "Alas! I am lost to honour and have disgraced my family." "Who are you, miserable being?" cried the young knight. "Approach, my son," responded the

---

[1] Here, in the original, there is a strange inconsistency: When Aigres arrives in Rome, he rides through the city till he comes before the house of a certain citizeness (bourgeoise); he sees her sitting at the door in great state, like one who was a passing rich and honourable lady. He addresses her, and ultimately takes up his lodging in her house. One day she begs him to reveal his name, as he closely resembles her deceased father. On this he asks the name of her father, and she replies that she is the daughter of Fawnus and Agea, and that their children were Berinus and herself.—Now, near the opening of the romance (as in our Tale of Beryn), Fawnus and Agea had been many years married before they were "blessed" with Berinus; and while it is not afterwards expressly stated that he was their only child, the reader is certainly led to conclude that such was the case.

same voice, for Berinus thought he knew him. "Come and save the honour of your father and of yourself." "You, my father?" The son of Berinus could say no more; he remained quite powerless and leaned against the tower wall. "My son," cried the unhappy man, "summon up your courage—lose no time, for we need it all." Then Aigres made an attempt to enter through the opening, but his father informed him of the trap into which he had himself fallen, and of the impossibility of his being extricated. Aigres exhausted his strength in fruitless efforts to draw his father out, and more than once he thought of giving himself to death. "It is my duty to die," said Berinus to him. "Listen: I exact of you the most solemn oath that you obey my last behest." "But, father!" "I exact it; hesitate no longer." Aigres, completely bewildered, repeated the oath, feeling a secret horror in so doing. Then Berinus recounted to him the whole particulars of this dire mishap; what Silvain had long done for him, and what he had now unfortunately attempted to do for the first time. Each word of the recital caused the generous young Aigres to tremble. "Now, my son," continued Berinus, "by the oath you have taken, I order you to cut off my head." "Who? I, your executioner!" cried the wretched youth—"I, the executioner of my father!" "Do you not see that a real executioner is seeking my life?" said Berinus. "I shall be the talk and horror of the whole city, and Cleopatra, Romaine, and yourself must share in my disgrace. All is saved by this act of courage; all is lost without it." "No, no!" cried Aigres, "I will never consent to the atrocious murder of my father." "You have become so in not obeying me," replied Berinus in an angry tone, "and moreover you murder your mother and sister. Remember, perhaps in a moment it may be too late—hush! do you not hear a noise? Some one is coming to the tower—the door is opening—ah, my son, will you kill us all?" Aigres, roused to madness, fancied that he also heard the sound of approaching footsteps. He was no longer himself—hesitated no longer—but drawing his sword Pleure Sang, with one blow struck off the head of his father, wrapped it in his cloak, and hastening from the fatal spot, went and buried it in a neighbouring wood.

Day had scarcely dawned when the emperor and the treasurer entered the tower. Seeing a body in the vat, they eagerly drew near, but what was their astonishment and chagrin when they found it headless. The emperor was furious. He caused the mutilated body to be borne into a room in the palace. The barons and the sages were called to examine the affair, but it seemed mysterious to one and all. The corpse was then carried to the gibbet outside the city, where it was guarded by forty mounted knights and a large number of men on foot. This great assembly, however, did not terrify Aigres de l'Aimant, who resolved to bear off his father's body from the midst of all the armed guard. In order to effect this, it was essential that he should be unknown; he therefore put on strange armour, a shield without any device, lowered the visor of his helmet, and at dawn attacked the guard with irresistible courage, put them to flight, and carried away the corpse committed to their care.

Philip caused strict search to be made to discover the author of such an outrage. The sages were again consulted, but without success. At last one of the guards whom Aigres had forced to flee before him declared to Philip that he had heard the strange knight pronounce, whilst furiously thrusting at them, the name of the Princess Nullie. As the knights of that time always called upon the lady of their love, in order to inspire them to doughty deeds, the emperor merely learned from this that the crime had been committed by one of the lovers of his daughter. And no advantage was derived by one of the sages, when he suggested the following device, which pleased Philip, though it seemed rather strange. He said: "Since the robber of the headless body is in love with the Princess Nullie, I advise that all the barons and lords of high degree be assembled to supper; afterwards order them to lie down in the great hall, each on a bed of his own, and place in the centre that of Princess Nullie. Now he who is not in love will fall asleep, but he who is in love will keep awake, and will not fail to visit the princess, who must take care to mark his forehead with her thumb, previously steeped in a black liquid, which all efforts of the gallant cannot obliterate. Forget not," added the sage counsellor, "that the room must be perfectly dark."

The emperor adopted this advice from anger; Nullie yielded to the plan from filial obedience. The barons were astounded that the princess was to sleep in the same room with themselves, and no one approach her under pain of death. All, save Aigres, fell asleep. He drew near the bed of the princess and mutely kissed her hand. Nullie, not knowing that it was Aigres, pressed her thumb upon his brow. The young knight took this imposition of her hand for a favour; he flattered himself that he had been recognized, and showed by the most loving words all his gratitude to the princess. She knew him by his voice and fell in despair. "Alas!" said she, "give me no thanks: I have killed you unawares! I have given you over to death! I will never survive it!" How flattering to the amorous knight was Nullie's grief. He thought his life no penalty for this proof of her affection, and he dared to ask for yet another. She could not refuse a lover who was doomed to die, and he obtained Love's gift.[1] Afterwards, profiting by the sleep of the barons, Aigres drew near in succession to each bed, and put on every brow a mark like his own.[2] He then returned to his own bed and fell asleep.

---

[1] "Le don d'amoureuse merci" are the words of the writer of the *Extrait*, who slyly remarks: "We do not know whether the wary sage, if he had foreseen this incident, would have thought it his duty to forewarn the emperor."

[2] This device occurs in many tales besides most of the numerous versions of the Robbery of the King's Treasury, and we find something similar in "La Mort de Tong-chao," one of the *Nouvelles Chinoises* translated by M. Stanislas Julien, 1860.

Great was the astonishment of the emperor when he saw, on entering the hall in the morning, all his barons and knights marked alike on the forehead. He asked his daughter in an angry tone whether they were all guilty, but she stubbornly kept silent and was shut up in her chamber. Cursing the sage who had given him such an absurd advice, he had recourse to the other sages, but they seemed as perplexed as himself. At this juncture, Geoffrey arrived at court from Constantinople, where some special affair had required his presence. He knew nothing of the robbery of the treasury and its results. The emperor told him all,[1] as well as of the trial made by the Princess Nullie. Geoffrey caused all who wore the black mark to assemble, examined them, and said to the emperor that he would point out the guilty one if he would grant him a boon. This Philip solemnly promised, and Geoffrey, pleased to mortify the sages once more, looked at them with a sarcastic smile as he said to the emperor: "The knight who has the smallest mark is the guilty one;—all the marks of his companions have been made by the thumb of a man." It was then found that Aigres alone bore the impress of the thumb of Princess Nullie. The latter was in despair; Aigres expected nothing but death. Geoffrey, however, reminded Philip of his oath, and asked the life of the guilty one. His fault did not appear so great to the barons as to the emperor, and they joined with Geoffrey to obtain his pardon. Philip granted it on condition that Aigres de l'Aimant should leave Rome. He only did so after secretly obtaining the troth of the princess;—the emperor little thought that in exiling the young knight he was banishing his own son-in-law! And when Philip died, Nullie, recalling her own husband, raised him to the throne. His banishment had been nothing but a succession of glories and triumphs; his return to Rome prepared him for new laurels. He re-established his mother on the throne of Blandie; went and conquered Constantinople for Prince Orlas, who was the friend of the good Geoffrey, and who married his sister Romaine.[2] After so many adventures there remained for the son of Berinus only to live in happiness and peace; this double advantage he enjoyed, and it was a source of great felicity to his subjects.[3]

---

[1] That is to say, all *he* knew.

[2] After conquering Constantinople for Geoffrey's friend, Aigres sails, with more than 20,000 men, for the Holy Land. They remain at Acre 26 weeks, during which period they make divers raids on the Saracens, and by their prowess so beset them that they dare not go out of their fortress. When the gallant Aigres has done his duty against the paynims, he goes to the Holy Sepulchre, where he offers up prayers and orisons, and makes rich presents—all for the purpose of doing penance for having caused his father's death (ch. cliv.).

[3] In the last chapter but one of the original, Geoffrey dies in the odour of sanctity, is buried near Berinus, and the emperor Aigres erects a magnificent church over their remains.

Mr. Vipan, in concluding the interesting extracts and notes with which he has favoured me, makes the following observations: "There is one great difference between the French and English versions. The latter, though very amusing, is

Thus ends the Romance of Berinus, in the second part of which, we have seen, his gallant son is the most conspicuous figure.—In the account of the robbery of the treasury there are several important differences between Dixmerie's *extrait* and the romance in the British Museum: (1) According to the *extrait*, after the death of Silvain, Berinus went but once to the treasury and lost his life; while in the romance (ch. lxxiii.) he goes often and takes as much treasure as he requires, and leads that kind of life for a long time. (2) In the *extrait* Berinus goes to the tower without the knowledge of his son, and it is only by chance that Aigres comes across him. In the romance, when Berinus hears that the robbery of the treasury is discovered, he determines to go once more, and take his son with him, in order to remove a greater quantity of the treasure than usual, as he fears that precautions will be taken before long to prevent his entrance into the tower. Aigres steadily refuses to go, and tries to dissuade his father from his purpose. However, that night, finding he is gone, he follows and discovers him in the tub of glue. (3) In the *extrait*, Aigres attempts to enter through the opening; while in the romance he does enter, his father having first given him directions so that he may avoid falling into the tub. (4) In the *extrait*, Berinus exacts from his son a solemn oath that he will obey his behest. In the romance Berinus says: "Sweetest son, now cease your sorrow, for you can gain nothing thereby. But bethink you of your own safety, and of putting me out of this grief; for if you will do as I counsel, soon will you have relieved me of my trouble. For God's sake, fair son, hasten you, for the night is quickly gone." "Dear father, God-a-mercy, tell me," said Aigres, "and I will do it

---

hardly edifying. Beryn is at first utterly worthless; mends a little, but shows no kind of merit; at last, however, he is dismissed to high station and happiness. In the French version, on the contrary, I think the author *intended* to be highly edifying: Berinus, badly brought up, after a short period of decent behaviour, falls again into error, turns robber, and comes to a wretched end. Aigres, on the other hand, who on many occasions shows a spirit of most generous self-abnegation, after many trials is dismissed to happiness. His two faults, the cutting off the head of Berinus and the affair with Nullie, the author probably thought excused, or partly so, considering the most extraordinary circumstances under which they were committed; besides, he suffers from long persecution on account of them. I think in every case vice is severely punished in the French romance."

It seems to me that the author's design in causing Berinus to fall into such a depth of unworthiness was to exhibit the evils that result from ignorance, which Shakspeare terms "the curse of God." The English versifier of the first part of the romance does not appear to have had any particular moral in view, although the Merchant in the prologue (p. 24, l. 725) says to his fellow-pilgrims that he will tell a tale " in ensaumpill" to them. Beryn, even in his early boyhood, is lewd and dissipated, mischievous and cruel, in consequence of the over-indulgence of his doting parents; and in manhood, when he falls into the toils of the knaves of Falsetown, he shows no force of character—in fact, he is throughout (in the English tale) an arrant poltroon; yet, by no merit or action of his own, he not only comes out of his law troubles a considerable gainer, but is amply compensated for the loss of his heritage by becoming the son-in-law of the good duke Isope. If there be any "moral" in this tale, it must be that the unworthy and profligate are the favourites of Fortune! We see, however, in the sequel, according to the complete story, that Beryn's prosperity was only temporary, and that at last he perished miserably.

most willingly." Berinus then tells him to take enough treasure to keep himself from want all his life. Aigres says he will first set him at liberty. Berinus declares that he will never leave the place until his son has complied with his request. Aigres accordingly takes a large quantity of treasure home and returns. (The author is careful to inform us that Aigres did not do this from covetousness of wealth, but solely to obey his father's command.) On his return to the tower Berinus orders him to cut off his head. Aigres expostulates through a whole chapter (cxix.). At last his father proves to him that much will be gained by his doing it, and nothing will be lost; while if he (Berinus) does not die at once he will perish under frightful tortures. On this Aigres falls on his knees before his father, and begs him to pardon him for causing his death. The father answers that he pardons him, and gives him his blessing. Then Aigres rises and goes to kiss his father, "weeping very copiously." Then Berinus confesses all his sins to God, and prays for God's mercy, recommending to God his soul, his wife, and his daughter. After this he says to Aigres: "Now quickly, my son, despatch thee—promptly end my sorrow; let me languish no longer." On this Aigres draws his sword and cuts off his head.[1] (5) In the *extrait*, Aigres recovers his father's body by boldly attacking the guards single-handed and causing them to fly for their lives; while in the romance he paints his horse on one side yellow, on the other blue, he covers his armour with a white robe, one side of which he stains with a vermilion dye, leaving the other of its proper colour, and round his horse's neck he hangs a number of bells—the guards take him for a goblin and make off at full speed. (6) In the *extrait* the device, to discover the person who stole the body, of causing the knights to sleep in the same chamber with the Princess Nullie, is suggested by one of the seven sages; but in the romance the emperor consults an enchanter, who raises a demon, and it is the demon who devises the stratagem. The demon tells him to order the knights not to approach the bed of Nullie under penalty of "the rope": the one who stole the body is of "such wondrous boldness" that he will disobey the order, and being marked on the forehead will be detected next morning.

M. de la Dixmerie, at the end of his *extrait*, remarks that "this unique, foolish, and ridiculous story of the treasury of the emperor Philip," with almost all the details, is found in the novels of Ser Giovanni Fiorentina, *Il Pecorone*, Day ix., nov. 1, whence it was taken. He omits to state that the original is given in Herodotus (Euterpe, 121), where it is the treasury of Rhampsinitus, king of Egypt, that is robbed by the two sons of the architect who erected the buildings, and purposely left a stone uncemented. The same story had been current in Europe long before the time of the Italian novelist, being found in the earliest written version

---

[1] M. de la Dixmerie has worked up this incident into a quite "thrilling" scene, albeit in the original it is told very effectively.

of the Seven Wise Masters, a Latin prose work, entitled *Dolopathos;* *sive, de Rege et septem sapientibus,* composed in the latter years of the 12th century, and in the French metrical version, *Li Romans des Sept Sages,* about 1284.[1] The author of the romance of Berinus might have adapted his story of the Treasury from *Il Pecorone,* since the latter dates as far back as 1348;[2] yet both versions may have been independently derived from a common source. Be this as it may, the foregoing story differs considerably from Ser Giovanni's version, of which Dunlop, in his *History of Fiction,* has given an abstract as follows, which I have compared with the translation of the Italian story given in Painter's *Palace of Pleasure* (first printed in 1566), vol. i. nov. 48, and found fairly accurate:

"The doge of Venice employed an architect, called Bindo, to erect a building which should contain all the treasures of the republic, and should be inaccessible to depredators. This ingenious artist reserved a moveable stone in a part of the wall, in order that he might himself enter when he found it convenient. He and his son [Ricciardo] having soon after fallen into great poverty, they one night obtain access by this secret opening and abstract a golden vase. The loss was some time after remarked by the doge while exhibiting the treasury to a stranger. In order to discover [the perpetrator of] the fraud, he closed the doors, ordered some straw to be burned in the interior of the building, and found out the concealed entrance by the egress of the smoke. Conjecturing that the robber must pass this way, and that he would probably return, he placed at the bottom of this part of the wall a cauldron filled with pitch, which was constantly kept boiling. Bindo and his son were soon forced by poverty to have recourse to their former means of supply. The father fell up to the neck in the cauldron, and finding that death was inevitable, he called to his son to cut off his head and throw it where it could not be found, in order to prevent further discovery.[3] Having executed this command, the young man returned home and

---

[1] Under the title of "The Robbery of the King's Treasury," in my work on the migrations and transformations of Popular Tales, vol. ii. p. 115 ff., after citing the narrative as related by Herodotus, I have brought together translations or abstracts of mediæval Latin, Italian, Sicilian, modern Greek, Albanian, French, Breton, Gaelic, Dutch, Tirolese, Danish, Russian, Algerian (Kabaïl), Mongolian, Tibetan, Bengali, Indo-Persian, Indian (Sanskrit), and Singalese versions, and, in Appendix, pp. 486-8, a curious modern Egyptian variant, of this world-wide story, to which the fascinating Arabian tale of Ali Baba and the Forty Thieves is near akin.

[2] There are two MSS. of the romance of Berinus (not one, as stated at foot of p. 124) in the National Library, Paris, both of which, according to M. Delisle, the Librarian, closely agree with the printed editions. One is a folio volume, written on parchment, and dates about the middle of the 15th century; the other is a quarto written on paper, imperfect at the beginning, of about the end of the 15th century. The date of the Vienna MS. is 1482: "Fait et acomply le dit Romant le vj Jour de Septembre Lan *Mil quatre cens quatre vings et deux.*" This is doubtless not the date when the romance itself was finished, but that of the transcription of the Vienna copy.

[3] A man who was "up to the neck" in a cauldron of boiling pitch would hardly be able to give his son such an order: the pain would either deprive him of consciousness or his anguished cries bring in some of the royal guards.

informed his neighbours that his father had gone on a long journey; but he was obliged to communicate the truth to his mother, whose affliction now became the chief cause of embarrassment. For the doge, perceiving that the robber must have had associates, ordered the body to be hung upon a gibbet, in the expectation that it would be claimed. This spectacle being observed from her house by the widow, her cries brought up the guard, and her son was obliged, on hearing them approach, to wound himself in the hand to afford a reasonable pretext for her exclamations. She next insisted that her son should carry off the body from the gibbet. He accordingly purchased twelve habits of black monks, in which he dressed twelve porters whom he had hired for the purpose. Having then disguised himself in a vizard and mounted a horse covered with black cloth, he bore off the body in spite of the guards and spies by whom it was surrounded, and who reported to the doge that it had been carried away by demons. The story then relates other means to which the doge resorted, all of which are defeated by the ingenuity of the young robber. At length the curiosity of the doge is so much excited that he offers the hand of his daughter to any one who will discover the transaction. On this the young man reveals the whole, and receives the promised bride in return."

Among the "other means to which the doge resorted" Dunlop passes over the fruitless device of the beds in the great hall: By the advice of a senator, "the most riotous and lecherous young men, such as the doge had in the greatest suspicion, to the number of twenty-five, were summoned to appear before him;" they were made to sleep in separate beds in one of the great chambers, and in their midst was the doge's own daughter. The doge says aloud that should any of them approach her bed she is to mark him on the forehead. This frightens all but Ricciardo. He visits the young lady, who marks him; but, in his turn, he marks the other sleepers, some with two, some with six, some with ten marks, and himself with four, besides the one placed on him by the doge's daughter.—There seems to me little reason to conclude that the story of Berinus and Philip's treasury was adapted from Giovanni's novel, besides the circumstance of the beds ranged around the young lady's bed. We have nothing in Giovanni about the culprit being discovered by the smaller mark on his forehead, and nothing in Berinus about each sleeper having a number of marks. Moreover, in Giovanni the treasury is only once entered, and a golden vase stolen, while in Berinus, as in Herodotus and all other versions, frequent visits are paid to the treasury before the catastrophe.

GLASGOW, *June 1887.*

ADDITIONAL NOTES.

pp. 125, 126. The remarks about the athletic exercises of the young Romans, and Fawnus' and Agea's aversion from Berinus practising them, do not occur in the romance, and are therefore to be regarded as M. de la Dixmerie's own: he frequently indulges in excursions of this kind in the course of his *extrait*, which I have for the most part left out.

p. 126. Raine, the second wife of Fawnus, is called Rame in the Tale of Beryn, possibly by a clerical error.

p. 133. There is no mention of the three questions put to the seven sages in this part of the romance, but there is much later on (chs. xxxix. and xl.), when Geoffrey introduces Berinus to Esope. In order to recommend Berinus to Esope's favour, Geoffrey gives his quondam "client" the credit of having discovered that the aching tooth, the fly, and the pear-tree were figures of speech, and signified treacherous flatterers of different kinds. Geoffrey goes on to say that the Romans became so jealous of Berinus on account of his sagacity, that they laid plots against his life, and this was the cause of Berinus leaving the country and taking to the occupation of a merchant. It comes out ultimately that the king who sent the messengers to ask the three questions was Esope himself, who wished to test the wisdom of the seven sages. Geoffrey was one of the messengers, and on their return the Blandiens, being envious of the honour done them, murder all but Geoffrey, who escapes by disfiguring and disguising himself.—The Eastern origin of the "parables" of the aching tooth, &c. is, I think, apparent from the following passage which occurs in *Kalila and Dimna*, the Arabian version of the Fables of Bidpaï: "A tooth which is decayed," said Kalíla to the Lion, "will never cease to ache as long as it remains in the mouth; nor is there any other remedy for the disagreeable sensation arising from having eaten unwholesome food than that which will remove it from the stomach, which is the seat of the disorder. The application of these maxims to the case of a dangerous enemy points at once to the necessity of taking away his life." In the Sanskrit version, *Hitopadesa*, the wily jackal Damanaka cites the sentiment thus: "A pulling up by the root of poisoned food, of a loose tooth, and of a wicked minister, gives ease."

p. 135. In the Planudean Life of Esop the fabulist it is related that Xanthus (Esop's master), getting drunk at a symposium, wagered his house and all it contained that he would drink up the sea. Esop gets him out of this scrape by advising him to demand that all the rivers should be stopped, for he did not bargain to drink them too.

p. 135; note on Duke Esop's castle. Gibbon, quoting Abú-'l-Feda, states that in the palace of the Khalíf Moktader, "among the other spectacles of rare and stupendous luxury was a tree of gold and silver, spreading into eighteen large branches, on which, and on lesser boughs, sat a variety of birds, made of the same precious metals, as well as the leaves of the tree: while the machinery affected spontaneous motions, the several birds warbled their natural harmony. Through this scene of magnificence the Greek ambassador was led by the vazír to the foot of the Khalíf's throne."

p. 136, l. 16. "Two butterflies only were seen floating about the room."—In the romance, as in the Tale of Beryn, Geoffrey had provided himself with two butterflies, but there does not appear to be any reference, as in *Beryn* (p. 109, l. 328 ff.), to the doctor in Rome.

p. 153, l. 22 ff. "What is the weight of the elephant?"—Forbes, in his *Oriental Memoirs*, vol. ii. p. 455, cites, on the authority of Colonel Wilks, the following anecdote of Shahjí, father of Sevají, the founder of the Mahratta empire, "from which," he remarks, "some conjecture may be formed of the general state of the arts and sciences in India, in the commencement of the seventeenth century": The minister Jaga-deva Row had made a vow to distribute in charity the weight of his elephant in silver; and all the learned men of the court had studied in vain the means of constructing a machine of sufficient power to weigh the animal. Shají's expedient was certainly simple and ingenious to an eminent degree. He led the animal along a stage prepared for the purpose to a flat-bottomed boat, and marking the water-line removed the elephant and caused stones to be placed in the boat sufficient to load it to the same line. The stones, being brought separately to the scales, ascertained the true weight of the elephant, to the astonishment of the court of the wonderful talents of Shahjí.—This is precisely the device suggested by the old woman in our Arabian analogue of the story of the Sandal-wood Merchant.

p. 165. In the romance, ch. cxv. *ad fin.*, when the robbery of the treasury is discovered the author breaks out into a long lamentation over the pending fate of Berinus: "Here is an illustration of the peasant's saying, that 'no one knows when his chance and his hour cometh.' Alas, how unhappy was the birth of Berinus, and how he was born under a stern constellation! For in all his life he had not a single day of peace and quietness; and, moreover, he was never freed from his ill-fortune; rather did his mischance approach him relentlessly, for Fortune used all her efforts to bring him under."

Here, in accordance with the belief in astrology which prevailed throughout Europe during the middle ages and even much later, as it does still in Asiatic countries, the author ascribes the misfortunes of Berinus, not to his improper up-bringing and defective education, but to the circumstance of his having been born under an unlucky planet— a comforting doctrine to sinners of all degrees.

W. A. C.

NOTES TO THE TALE OF BERYN.

[The notes with the letters F. J. F. appended are by Dr. Furnivall, those with W. W. S. by Professor Skeat, those with S. by W. G. Stone, and those with no letter appended by F. J. Vipan.]

p. 1, l. 8. *Hurlewaynes meyne.* This meyne is sketcht in the second book of François de Rues' *Roman de Fauvel,* A.D. 1314:

.. Puis faisoient une crierie,
Onques tele ne fut oïe :
Li uns montret son cul au vent,
Li autre rompet un auvent ;[1]
L'un cassoit fenestres et huis,
L'autre getoit le sel ou puis.
L'un getoit le bren au visage,
Trop estoient lés et suavaiges ;
Es tetes orent barboeres,
Avoec eus portoient deus bières,
Ou il avoit gent trop avable (?),
Pour chanter la chanson au diable.
Il i avoit un grant jaiant,
Qui aloit trop forment braiant ;

Vestu ert de bon broissequin ;
Je croi que c'estoit Hellequin,[2]
Et tuit li autre, sa mesnie,
Qui le suivent toute enragie.
Montés est sus un roncin haut,
Si tres gras que, par saint Quinaut,
L'en li peut les costes compter. . .
Avec eus avoit Hellequines
Qui avoient cointises fines,
Et ce deduisoient en ce
Lay chanter qui si ce commence :
" En ce dous temps d'esté,
Tout droit ou mois de may," &c.

P. Paris. *MSS. François de la Bibliothèque du Roi,* i. 324-5. (Paris, 1836.)—F. J. F.

---

[1] A penthouse of cloth, &c., before a shop window, &c.—Cotgrave.
[2] *Hurlewayn* is also in l. 90, Passus 1, of 'Richard the Redeles' ·

" Oþer hobbis ȝe hadden · of *hurlewaynis* kinne,
Reffusyuge the reule · of realles kynde."
Piers Plowman, Text C, p. 477, ed. Skeat.

ib, p. 507, is Mr. Thomas Wright's note on the word : " *Hurlewaynes meyné* is the *Maisnie Hellequin* of old French popular superstition ; in Latin, *familia Harlequini.* The name is spelt in different ways : Hellequin, Herlequin, Henequin, &c. The legend was, that Charles the Fifth of France, and his men, who fell all in a great battle, were condemned for their crimes to wander over the world on horseback, constantly employed in fighting battles. Some derived the name from that of the Emperor, Charles quint, Charlequin, Herlequin, Hellequin. Of course this derivation is wrong, and the legend a fabrication of later date, to explain it. See Grimm's *Mythologie,* p. 527 ; Le Roux de Lincy's *Livre des Legendes,* p. 148-150, 240-245 ; and Michel's *Benôit,* vol. ii, p. 336, where in a note is given a most extraordinary story about them. See also Paulin Paris " (as above).

See also Tyrwhitt's *Chaucer*, Gl. s. v. *meinie;* he refers us to *Ordericus Vitalis*, who gives a strange story of the *familia Herlechini*, also to Gervase of Tilbury, who speaks of the *familia Arturi*. As to the etymology of the word *Hurlewayne*, see Skeat's Dict., s. v. *Harlequin*.

p. 1, l. 16. *Hope* is a *hoop:* see Larwood's *Signboards*, p. 488.— W. W. S.

p. 2, l. 18. *Such vitailles as he fonde in town.*   Here *in town* = at hand : cf. *Sir Thopas* (ed. Skeat), l. 1983 and Note : also *Guy of War-wicke*, l. 5841 :

> "God let me neuyr dye in londe."

On which Professor Zupitza says : " *in londe*, used here as often with no great force " ; he then compares with it the expression *in toune*.   Other instances are :

> "Hyt befell in the month of June,
> Whan the fenell hangeth *yn town*,
> Grene in semly sales."
>
>> *Lybeaus Disconus* (Ritson), l. 1225.

> "And ich him schal with myn hond teche
> Hou Goddes grame com *to toune*
> Ryght amidelward his croun."
>
>> *The Seuyn Sages* (Weber).

> "Had she brought some forty pounds *to town*,
> I could be content to make her my wife."
>
>> R. Green's *George-a-Greene* (ed. Dyce), p. 260, col. 2,—

where Dyce's Note on the word "town" is : Qy. dower. The expression might still be heard in the present century in East Anglia : in my early youth an old servant by way of informing me that some friends of ours had an addition to their family, said : "A new Miss —— has just come to town."   Cp. also the usage of " in place " and " in the stede."

p. 2, l. 20. *The Pardoner beheld and aside swervid.*   ? perhaps *diskennyng* agrees with *statis*, and we may translate : "The Pardoner saw how the people of good station were served, and how, ignoring him quietly, they slipped away from him."

p. 2, l. 40. *Benedicite*, pronounce *ben'cite*, or *ben'cit;* see Skeat's Gl. to *Prioresses Tale*, &c.

p. 2, l. 42. *she gan to fnese.*   ? *snese*, as *fnese* elsewhere means to blow, as Prof. Skeat has pointed out.

p. 2, l. 43. *Aha! all hole.*   In Germany when any one sneezes, the custom is for the bystanders to cry out *pros't* (*prosit*), in Austria *Gesundheit.*   In France, Belgium, and Italy, they say in their respective languages, "God bless you": also in some parts of England, for instance in Suffolk.

It is said that this custom arose at the time of the plague, a sneeze being supposed to indicate a change for the better in the condition of the sufferer.

p. 3, l. 56. *þat ye* [been] *unaservid.*   The words, I suppose, as they stand with *been* inserted, will mean, "but you havn't been served with your morning-meal"; from l. 60, however, it appears that the

Tapster was not aware that the Pardoner was fasting.   ? Perhaps the words *that ye unaservid* may mean : "you didn't deserve *that*, viz. to suffer such extreme sorrow."

p. 3, l. 66.   *now broke wel thy name.*

> " þanne hym spak the god king :
> Wel bruk þu þi nevening ;
> Horn, þu go wel schulle (shrill)
> By dales and bi hulle ;
> Horn, þu lude soo sune
> Bi dales and bi dune."
>
> *King Horn*, l. 206.   (Specimens by Morris.)

"Dan John, quod he, now well brouke ye your name."

> Lidgate's Prologue to the *Tale of Thebes.*

p. 3, l. 70.   *trown & feyn this song.*   ? For *trown* read *crown* or *croon* = murmur ; the scribes frequently interchange *t* and *c* : see note on l. 822.   ? Also for *feyn* read *seyn ;* in *Chaucer* we find " *seyn* a song " : later in this tale, l. 2462, we have : " I will not *feyn* one word, as makers doon to ryme " ; but there the word *feyn* relates to composition of verse, not to singing.

p. 4, l. 99.

> "*Now certen, quod the tapster, yee have a red ful even,*
> *As wold to God yee couth as wel undo my sweven.*"

ared ful even = interpreted rightly, in this passage the Tapster's behaviour, but *arede* is frequently used for to interpret a dream, and we find it with the word *even* attached in *The Boke of the Dutchesse*, l. 284 :

> "Ne nat scarcely Macrobeus
> [Coude] . . .
> I trow, *arede* my dremes *even.*"

Rede is so used in modern poetry ; as in Campbell's

> "Glenara, Glenara, now *read* me my dream."

Also "read me my riddle" we find several times in Bishop Percy's Folio.

Undo my sweven.   Cp. *Romaunt of the Rose*, l. 7 :

> "An authour that hight Macrobees
> That halteth not dremes false ne lees,
> But *undoth* us the avision
> That whilom mette king Cipioun."

p. 5, l. 109.   *a lover glad. glad* does not suit the context, unless we take it in the sense of "anxious."   See *Lancelot of the Laik*, l. 2798, "gladly desyrit," and l. 2946.

p. 5, l. 122.   "* * * *howe the Tapster made the Pardoner pull*
> *Garlik all the longe nyghte.*"

? pull = pill or peel ; cp.

> "Wyll, Wyll, Wyll, Wyll, Wyll,
> He ruleth always still.
> Good reason & good skyll,

> They may *garlic pyll*,
> Cary sackes to the myll,
> Or pescoddes they may shyll
> Or elles go rost a stone."
> Skelton's *Why come ye not to Courte*, ? 103-109.

Todd in his Dict., s. v. *pilled-garlick*, says : " one whose hair is fallen off by a disease : 'A pleasant discourse between the authour & pild-garlick ; wherein is declared the nature of the disease,' " 4to, 1619.

Sir John Denham, in his *Directions to a Painter*, p. 21, published in 1667, terms a certain officer " poor Peelgarlick," the reason for this appellation being that part of his posteriors had been shorn away by a cannon-ball. We find the term as late as 1770 in *Foote's Lame Lover*, *ad fin.* where Sir Luke says of himself :

" So then it seems *poor Pilgarlik* is discarded at once."

It is easy to understand why a man whose hair has fallen off, or part of whose body has been flayed, should be compared in derision to peeled garlick, but not so easy to see why " to peel garlic " should be regarded as a degrading occupation, as it apparently is in the passage before us. Mr. Wedgwood compares the Fr. saying : " Il en pelera la prune "—he will smart for it, he will have the worst of it. The question is also discussed in *Notes and Queries*, 1st S., i. and ii., and in Latham's Dict. It may be, however, that the expression was originally " to make a man *peeled-garlik* or *pilgarlik*," which is intelligible, and was then corrupted into " to make a man pill *garlic*."

p. 5, l. 125. *þouȝe she aquyt his while.* Cp. *Man of Lawes Tale*, 584, where Skeat's Note is : " *quyte her while*, repay her time ; *i. e.* her pains, trouble ; as when we say : ' it is worth while ' ; *wile* is not intended."

p. 6, ll. 137-8.
> " *Put forth the Prelatis, þe Person & his fere.*
> *A monk that toke the spryngill with a manly chere.*"

Substitute a comma for the full-stop after *fere*. Perhaps also for *A monk* we should read *The monk ;* in any case this monk is the monk of the *Canterbury Tales ;* the words " manly chere " agree with the description given of him by the Host in the Prologue to the *Monk's Tale*.

p. 6, l. 141. " *The ffrere feynyd fetously the spryngill for to hold,*
> *To spryng upon the remnant.*"

? For *feynyd* may we here read *feyndyd*, from the A.S. *fandian*, to attempt, try. In *Chaucer* the word appears as *fonde*, and in *Gologros and Gawayn* as *faynd*.

p. 6, l. 151. *for the story mourned.* The word " mourn " seems sometimes to mean " to be deep in thought," unconnected with sorrow. Cp.

> " And in gret thout he was
> Wher it was his wyfe, er hyt nas.

> Alse he sat in *mornynge*,
> Anon he thout upon the rynge."
>
> *Seven Sages*, l. 3013 (ed. T. Wright).

> " he murned ful swiðe
> to habben þat mæiden to wiue."
>
> *Layamon's Brut.* (Specimens by Morris and Skeat), l. 585.

p. 6, l. 160. *kynd of brode* = native breeding.

p. 7, l. 172. *out of contrey*, out of his own country. Cp. l. 2294 : "sith he of contre past." Halliwell, *s. v. country*, says : "county. Var. Dial."; this usage is frequent.

> "And commandede barouns thre
> Her to lede *out of cuntré*
> To the wyldest forest that myght be
> Of Crystendome." *Octovian Imperator* (Weber iii. 285).

> "And outte of cuntré wille I wende." *Sir Amadas* (Weber iii. 35).

> "Seth he went *out of cuntré*." *Sir Cleges* (Weber i.), 485.

p. 7, l. 178. *Save the Sompnour seid somewhat.* ? For *seid* read *sey* = saw.

p. 7, l. 188. *þouȝe wee shoul set at sale Al the shrewdnes that I can.* For *wee* read *I*, *wee* being caught from preceding *wee*. This error is frequent with our scribe.

p. 7, l. 192. *to the dynerward.* A late instance of this construction occurs in Sidney's *Arcadia*, lib. ii., p. 98, ed. 1638. "And so went she from them to the *Lodge-ward*."—S.

p. 7, l. 195. *till girdill gon arise.* Cp. *Man of Lawes Tale*, l. 789 (ed. Skeat) :

> "He drank and wel his *girdel underpyghte*."

p. 9, l. 247. *He was of al factur, aftir fourm of kynde.* He was made for everything by natural formation or constitution.

p. 9, l. 250-1. Probably some lines between these two are lost. As the prologue stands, the Sompnour had said nothing to the Frere since their arrival in Canterbury, though, l. 186, he says he will do so on their way home.

p. 10, l. 284. *rowe* = rest (cp. G. *ruhen*).—W. W. S. Cp.

> "She wolde never rest nor *rowe*,
> Till she came our king unto."—Percy's *Folio MS.* ii. 548/606.

Also *roo*, s. rest, in *Guy & Colebrande.*—Jamieson.

p. 10, l. 290. *ffor many a herbe grewe.* Insert *there* after *grewe ;* it is required both by sense and metre.

p. 10, l. 293. *And other beddis by & by*, one beside the other. For *by & by*, see note by Professor Skeat in N. & Q., 11th S., ix. 37.

p. 11, l. 306. *he drank without the cupp.* Cp. 460 : "He shall drynk for kittis love without cup or pot," *i. e.* in abundance.

p. 11, l. 310. *And fond hir ligging liry-long.* Cp. with this :

> "Somme leyde her legges *a liri* (leri)." *Piers Plowman*, vi. 123.

I venture to suggest that *liry-long* means "at length like a dormouse (*loir*)," and *a liri* after the manner of a dormouse.

Littré (*s. v. loir*) tells us that the Berry pronunciation of *loir* is *lire ;*

also that there are two diminutives of *loir*, viz. *liron* and *lérot*, which
signify *une espéce de petit loir gris*.   Again (s. v. *lérot*) he tells us
that the pronunciation of *loir* in Normandy is *ler*.   From this and the
Berry form we may have taken our *leri* and *liri*.

It appears that the dormouse, when eating, hangs suspended by its
hind-feet from a bough, and is consequently stretched out at full length;
again, when asleep in winter, it rolls itself up in a ball.   The former
attitude probably is that of the Tapster in *Beryn*, the latter that of the
Losels in *Piers Plowman*.

p. 11, l. 326.   *Wher coud I, [I]yewe prey, when ye com efftsone?*
For *when* read *wen* = wene, think; "Whether could I, I pray you,
think you would come again?"   Perhaps *when* may stand; cp. *yhit* for
yet, and *yhere* for *yere* in the *Pricke of Conscience*.

p. 12, l. 361.   *And al ascaunce she loved him well.*   The word
ascaunce has been discussed, N. & Q., 6th S. xi. and xii.; see also Skeat's
Gl. to *Man of Lawes Tale*, &c., and Murray's Dict. *s. v.*

p. 12, l. 362.   *As þouȝe she had learned cury favel of some old frere.*
See Hunter's Dict., s. v. *curry*, "*To curry favour*, a corruption of Mid.
Eng. *to curry favell;* Fr. *étringler le fauveau* = lit. to rub down the
chesnut horse: *favell* was a common name for a horse, and the same
word, but from an entirely different source (Lat. *fabula*), was used for
flattery."

p. 12, l. 362.   *As þouȝe she had lernyd cury fauel.*   "But if such
moderation of words tend to flattery, or soothing or excusing,   Paradiastole,
                                                                   or the
it is by the figure *Paradiastole*, which therefore nothing   Curry fauell.
improperly we call the *Curry-fauell*, as when we make the best of a bad
thing, or turne a signification to the more plausible sence: as, to call
an vnthrift, a liberall Gentleman: the foolish-hardy, valiant or couragious:
the niggard, thriftie: a great riot or outrage, an youthfull pranke, and
such like termes: moderating and abating the force of the matter by
craft, and for a pleasing purpose," &c.—Puttenham's *Arte of English
Poesie*, ed. Arber, p. 195.—S.

p. 13, l. 372.   *As he þat hopid sikerlich to have had al his will.*
Here the perfect "to have had" is used for the present.   This is not
unusual; cp. l. 3150, "made him redy to *have swore*."   Also cp. 2075,
"To make his pleynt on Beryn & *suyd* upon his goode," where *suyd* is
for "have suyd," as Prof. Skeat has pointed out.

p. 13, l. 374.   *howe-so-euir it gone.*   Cp. l. 791, "or I ferther goon."
Also l. 3008, "no man on hem pleyn."

"For sothe as I the *sayne*."   *Sir Isumbras*, l. 536 (Thornton Rom.).

"The sothe thou me *sayne*."
          The Avowynge of Arthur, 33/8 (Robson's Rom.).

p. 13, l. 380.   *þat had no spice of rage.*   *Rage* = playfulness.   Cp.

"Ac ever in ernest and *arage*
    Ever speketh French langage."   *Sir Beves of Hamtoun*, l. 2790
                                                  (Maitland Club).

p. 13, l. 388. *And then the officers & I.* Cp.

> "The Squier came fro chambre tho,
> Downe he wente into the hall,
> The *officers* soon can he call,
> Both usher, panter, & butler,
> And other that in office were ;
> There he them warned sone anone
> To take up the bordes everych one."
>
> *The Squier of Lowe Degre*, l. 388 (Ritson's Rom.).

p. 13, l. 398. *ffor he met with his love, in crokeing of þe moon.*
"Also the same yere [1421] betuen Cristemasse and Candelmasse, the
town of Milen' [Melun] was yolden to the kyng [Henry V.], and alle
cheveteyns with the sowdyours were ledd to Parys *in the croke of the
mone* they myght seyn, for of them there skaped thens but fewe on
lyve."—*A Chronicle of London*, ed. Sir H. Nicolas, 1827, p. 109.

"Also this same yere [1436] the xiij day of August, the kyng of
Scottes and hys wyf lyenge at the sege of the castell of Rokysburgh
[Roxburgh], with a gret power of Scottes and a gret ordinaunce, brak
up the sege and wente his way shamfully, and lefte his ordinaunce and
his stuff behynden hym as a coward, and mo than vij score of his
galgentires [? gallowglasses] sclayn and taken at the same sege : and
so myghte he wel sey, that *in the crook of the mone* com he thedirward,
and in the wylde wanyande [waning] wente homward :

> ' With reste and pees,
> A man schal best encrees.' "—*Idem*, p. 122.

From the last passage quoted here it seems that it was thought
unlucky to begin anything when the moon was either in her first
or last quarter: in the "crook of the mone"; that is, when she is
crescent-shaped.—S.

p. 14, l. 422. *al they route.* For *they* read *the* or *that.*

p. 14, l. 424. *& weytid hym a trest.* *trest* = *trist*, of which
Jamieson says : "trist" is used in O. E. as denoting a "post or station
in hunting."

> "Ye shall be set at such a *triste*,
> That hart and hind shall come to your fist."
>
> *Squire of Low Degree.*

weytid him a treste therefore = "looked out for a post for himself."

p. 15, l. 459. *& he com by my lot.* Halliwell gives *lote :* a loft, a
floor. *South.* The host was going to bed.

p. 16, l. 471. *dischauce yewe nat.* According to Littré *chausses*
in old time comprised all the coverings for the lower part of the body,
answering to our word *hose.* *Dischauce yewe nat* therefore means,
don't take off your lower garments. The word *chauce* is very rare in
English, but we find it again in the name *Chaucer.* See *Le Héricher's
Glossaire des noms propres*, p. 39, s. v. *calc.*

p. 16, l. 474. *nere hond quarter night*, nearly nine p.m., the night
lasting from six p.m. to six a.m. See also Camden's *Remains* (ed. 1870),
p. 133 : he says, chauser = hosier.

p. 16, l. 478.

> *And went to have fond the dor up by the hasp & eke þe twist*
> *Held him out a whyls.*

Does *up* here = open? The German *auf*, and the Dutch *op*, have the two meanings *up* and *open*: may not the corresponding word in a kindred language have the same two meanings? In the Imperial Dict., s. v. *open*, we find: "it would seem to be a past part. of a verb formed from *up*, or at least is based on *up*." If so, in the line

> "The colde deth wyth mouthe gapyng upryght."
> *Knight's Tale*, l. 1150,—

"gapyng upryght" will mean "gaping right open." Again, when a knight in an encounter with his adversary is thrown from his horse, we are told over and over again that he "lay upright": *i. e.* lay quite open or unprotected, his arms by his sides, and his spear fallen from his hand. Sometimes, instead of the words "lay upright," we are told that he "wyde open lay."

> "*Wyde open* on here back,
> Dede in the lyng."—*Sir Degrevant*, l. 3352 (*Thornton Romances*).

> "And strykes the duk throw the scheld
> *Wyde open* in the feld."—*Id.* l. 1293.

> "sweltand knyghtez
> Lyes *wyde opyne* welterande on waloparde stedez."
> *Morte Arthure*, l. 2147.

Perhaps the meaning is preserved in the modern phrase "to set *up* shop," where *up* seems to mean *open*. Cp. "For this is the first day I *set ope shop*."—Rowley and Webster's *Cure for a Cuckold*, p. 294, col. 1. Webster's Works (ed. Dyce).

Perhaps "to cut *up* a fowl" may be explained in the same way. Also

> "the hevynly portis crystallyne
> *Upwarpis* braid."—Gawin Douglas. *Prolong of the XIIth Buk of Encados*, l. 19,

where *upwarpis braid* seems to mean "cast wide open." Again in Gl. to Morris and Skeat's *Specimens* we have *upon*, open, and three instances are given from *Allit. Poems*.

bye the hasp, &c. *bye* seems here to = *but*. Either it is an error of the scribe, or a dialectical corruption—probably the latter. See Prof. Zupitza's Note on *Guy of Warwick*, l. 7853.

> "Nay," seyde Gye, "but Mary sone,"

where the MS. has *be*. He also cites three lines in *Generydes*, where the editor prints *but* for *be* of the MS. To these instances I may add

> "Ne bidde ich no bet, *bie* ich ['beo] a losed a domesdai o bende."
> *A Moral Ode*, l. 136. Trinity MS. (Specimens by Morris),—

where I have inserted *beo* from the Jesus MS. to make the line intelligible. For *bie* the Jesus MS. has *bute*.

p. 18, l. 534. *the feliship þat shuld nevir thryue.* Cp. l. 1035,
" To such maner company as shuld *nevir thryue.*"

p. 18, l. 536. *Jak, þow must be fele.* ? For *fele* read *fell;* then
the meaning will be: "Jak, thou must be crafty: thou must have
thy wits about thee." Cp. ll. 310-11: "with half slepy eye, Pourid
fellich vnder hir hode." Also l. 1833; "þat sotil was & *fell.*" Occleve
(*De Regimine Principum,* st. 607) has :

> " What doth this *felle* man & prudent ? "

Again, " fykil was and felle,"—*Tale of Gamelyn,* and *feille,* skill, in
Lancelot of the Laik, l. 2854.

p. 18, l. 538. *this is a noble chere That þow hym hast i-found.* Here
chere = chare, and the meaning will be "this is a splendid turn of
luck." If we pronounce it as *chore,* as the Americans do, the rime with
dore will be perfect.

p. 18, l. 550. *I have too gistis a-ryn.* Cp. 569, " beth these pannys
a-ryn ? "

In Murray's Dict., s. v. *aroint,* we find: " rynd-ta is merely a local
(Cheshire) pronunciation of ' round thee, move round, move about ! ' "
Perhaps therefore *aryn* may = around, about, which meaning will suit
the two passages given above. See, however, the Glossary.

Some maintain that the Shakesperian *aroint* is a doublet of " around,"
and this view seems to be supported by the following lines, which are
found in a Moral Play, *Mind, Will, and Understanding* (Collier's *Hist.
of the English Drama,* ii. 208, new ed.) ; where Lucifer says :

> " Reson I haue made both dethe and dumme ;
> Grace is out and *put aroin.*"

Mr. Halliwell-Phillips in his *Life of Shakespeare,* i. 142 (7th ed.),
gives us another form of this word ; he tells us that " *arent* the, wich,"
is found in one of the records of the town of Stratford-upon-Avon, which
was written about Shakspere's time.

p. 19, l. 563. I think it certain that the Paramour begins here :
he came frequently to visit the Tapster (see ll. 54-55), so that he would
know that the water-cans were in the place ; besides this the line 568
in this speech is nearly the same as line 542, which is spoken by the
Paramour.

p. 20, ll. 612-13. *astert* rimes with *mark;* also ll. 676-7 *rype* with
pyke; ll. 781-2 *londis* with *wrongis.*

p. 20, l. 625. *St. Juliane,* the patron Saint of travellers, who
provided them with a good night's lodging. Cp.

> " He says : ' Dame, for Saint July !
> This night let me have herbary
> And als some vittalls till the morn.' "
>
> > *Roswall and Lilian,* l. 253, in *Laing's Early
> > Metrical Romances.*

> " ' This night,' quoth John, ' you shall not spill,
> Such harbour I shall bring you tille,
> I hett it you to day ;

See that ye take it thankfully
In Gods name and St. Joly,
I aske no other paye.'"
John de Reeve, 166 (*Bp. Percy's Folio*, ii. 564).

"they thanked God & St. Jollye,
to tell the Queene of their harbor
the lords had full grete pryde."—*Ibid.* 581-572.

See also *Rauf Coilyear*, p. 5, l. 63, and note.

p. 21, l. 640. *warrok.* Mr. Skeat offers three conjectural explanations of this word. 1. The A.S. *wearg*, a wretch. 2. Possibly connected with *ware*, wary. 3. Cf. the Sc. "warrock, a stunted, ill-grown person, or puny child," which Jamieson connects with the A.S. *wear*, a wart; *wearrig*, callous with labour, knotty, rough.

p. 21, l. 640. I venture upon a fourth conjecture. Prof. Skeat in Gl. to the *Wars of Alexander*, s. v. *warloked*, says : "pp. fettered, 769*. The same as *warroked*; see Gl. to *P. Plowman*." May not *warrok* here mean "the fettered (one)"? The dog had a clog about his neck.

p. 22, l. 667. *for auȝht that þey coude pour.* for þey read *he*, þey being caught from preceding *they*.

p. 22, l. 674. *helde him to hys harmys.* ? does *to* here govern preceding *him:* then the meaning will be "kept his injuries to himself."

p. 23, l. 687. *Lo! how the trees * * * somer clothing [wear]!*

? read : Lo! how the trees grenyth, þat nakid wer, & nothing
Bare þis month afore, but now her somer clothing!

p. 23, l. 701. *unlace his male.* Cp. *undid the bag* of treachery, l. 1182.

p. 23, l. 715. *my last knot.* Cp. Thou sholdest *knitte vp* well a greet matere. *Prologue to Parson's Tale*, l. 28 (ed. Skeat).

To *knitte up* al this feste & make an ende.—*Id.* 47.

p. 24, l. 728. *good will shall be my chaunce. chaunce* here means "good fortune." Littré, s. v. "2° Absolument et abusivement, heureux hasard, bonne chance." Then the meaning of the sentence will be, "my wish to please will cause me to succeed."

p. 24, l. 728. *With this I be excusid.* with this = on condition that. Cp. l. 3972, "*With this* I have saue condit;" and see Mätzner, Sprachproben, 109/192, and note.

p. 25, l. 750. *these olde wise poetes.* Cp. l. 196, *these* olde wise, where *these* = the well known. This usage is frequent in M.E. In Latin we have *ille* used in this way, as in *Antipater ille Sidonius.* Forcellinus, s. v. *ille*, says : "*ille* nominibus, vel etiam adjectivis, tam in bonam quam in malam partem additur majoris evidentiæ ac emphasis gratia." So in Italian *quello* is used, and in German *jener.* Grimm, s. v. *jener* says : "auch sonst bei hervorhebung von etwas bekannten, wo *jener* fast nicht mehr sagt wie der blosse artikel." I give some instances from Faust :

1st part. "Fluch *jener* höchsten Liebeshuld.
in *jener* ersten Nacht" (first night after Creation).

2nd part.   "wie *jene* Katze.
       Stimmen *jener* Himmelstage."

Why the followers of Beryn are always termed "these Romeyns," I am unable to explain.

p. 26, l. 776. *doseparis* = douceperes, *douʒe pairs*, 12 peers of France. Spenser's use of the word is most amusing. He says :

    "Big-looking like a doughty *doucêpere*" (*Faerie Queene*, III. x. 31).

i. e. looking as bold as *a twelve peer.*—W. W. S.

p. 26, l. 779. *bon-cheff* = good achievement, opposed to *mys-cheff* = bad achievement.—W. W. S.

p. 26, l. 789. *dessantly.* continuously, incessantly.

          "Þe *seven sagis* were
      In *Rome dwelling dessantly.*"

Cp. with this, "ffor thre dayis *dessantly* þe darknes among hem was," l. 1562. Also :

        "iii hunderit baptist men and wivis,
        Þat *desseli* bathe late and are
        Ware tendant to þe apostlis lare."
                Cursor Mundi, 1587/19033.

    "Als if he *desseli* did ille."—*Id.* l. 26881 (Cotton MS.).

The corresponding word in the Fairfax MS. is *iþenli.* For *iþen* Stratmann gives *assiduus, diligens.*

        "Þat at þe last þai ordeined tuelve
        Þe þoghtfulest among þem selve,
        And did þem in a montain dern
        [Biseli] to wait þe stern."
     Cursor Mundi, 70/31.   (Specimens by Morris and Skeat.)

The Cotton MS. reads *desselik* for *biseli*, and at p. 490 we have a note by Mr. Goodchild of Penrith. "*Dess* is common in Swaledale in the sense of 'to pack tight or fit closely together.' Possibly the word *desselic* (p. 70, l. 34), which is the reading of two MSS. (Cotton and Göttingen), may mean crowded together or gathered closely together. Cf. Icel. *hey-des*, a haystack. W. *das*, a stack ; *dasu*, to stack."

The word *desselich* in the five passages given above seems to refer to "time," and Halliwell's equivalent for it "constantly," s. v. *dessable*, suits the context in each case. In his Dict. Halliwell gives also *dessment*, stagnation ; *dess* therefore will mean "close, without intervals," whether applied to hay, time, or water.

As to the form of the word, I suppose *desse* in *desselich* represents the past part. of the word *dess*, viz. *dessen*, and that *dessant* in *dessantli* is the Northern form of the same. On this point the use of the present for the past part. in Lowland Scottish, see Sir David Lyndesay's *Monarche*, l. 5517, and note (*E. E. Specimens* by Skeat).

p. 26, l. 789. *Seven Sages.* See Mr. Wright's ed. and his dissertation in Hazlitt's ed. of *Warton*, i. 305-334. In the poem ed. by Wright, the sages are :

1. Baucillas.
2. Ancillees   = Asulus?
3. Lentulus.
4. Maladas.
5. Cato.
6. Jesse.
7. Marcius.   —W. W. S.

p. 26, l. 797. *sownyd out of reson.* ? For *reson* read *seson.*

p. 27, l. 810. *as wele me myȝht haue clepid.* ? For *clepid* read *crepid; crepe* = crepitate (see Cockeram's Dict., 1626), break wind.

p. 27, l. 812. *changit onys chere ;* before *chere* insert *his.*

p. 27, l. 817. *Angir or disese.* Halliwell s. v. *anger* gives : " sorrow (A.S.)," and cites instances, in one of which we have *angere and disese. Angre* in this sense is frequent in Hampole's *Pricke of Conscience.*

p. 27, l. 822. *Stypio and Sithero.* It's the old mistake of *t* for *c* : many scribes write *Si* for *Sc.* " Stypio " means *Scipio,* and " Sithero " means *Sichero* (Cicero).—W. W. S.

In the French Romance they are termed cipio and cithero, which confirms preceding note.

p. 27, l. 822-3. They were named Stypio Astrolage, and Sithero Astrolage. Astrolage = astrologer.—W. W. S.

p. 27, l. 824. *Astronomy*—in O.E.—means often what we now call astrology.—W. W. S.

p. 27, l. 824. *of Astronomy al the fences.* ? Here *fences* = defences, and means prohibitions of setting out on a journey on a certain day and the like ; see Skeat's note to the *Man of Lawes Tale,* l. 312.

p. 28, l. 837. *His sportis & his estris.* ? For *sportis* read *portis ;* " his doors and his apartments."

p. 28, ll. 855-6. *delites, pris.* A strange rime. Is this another instance of a *t* being written for a *c,* and may we read *delices* (= pleasures)? See Halliwell, s. v. and " delices," *Cursor Mundi,* l. 23284.

p. 28, l. 867. *inlich gentil.* Cp. l. 1098 : *inwardlich sory.* Halliwell, s. v. *inly* says : " inwardly, deeply, thoroughly." The words *inlich* and *inwardlich,* used in this sense, were great favourites with the M.E. writers. The writer of *Generydes* uses them frequently.

p. 31, l. 959. *Save that tournith al to cautele,* except that *that* (viz. glosing) turns entirely to deceit.

p. 32, l. 974. *But of my remembraunce.*

" *Yeur deth wol nevir, I woot it wele, but evir be in mynde* "—

i. e. your death will never, I know well, be out of my remembrance, but be ever in my mind.

p. 32, l. 987. *& I lafft yew behynde.* A blunder of our author's ; he means " & yew lafft me behynde."

p. 33, l. 1012. *lewde visenage.* ? *visenage* = vixen, with suffix *age ;* cp. *Rosan* for *Roxana* in the *Wars of Alexander* (E. E. Text Society).

p. 33, l. 1019. *Ner thou my father's messenger wer.* Cp. *Ner* = ne wer : for this Hampole uses *warn* = war ne.

" Elles suld þe hert, thurgh sorow & care,
  Ouertyte fayle, *warn* som hope *ware ;* . . .
  And men says, '*warn* hope *ware*, it suld brest.' "
                    Hampole's *Pricke of Conscience*, ll. 7259-7266.
    "*war ne* syn *war.*"—*Id.* 2342.

These lines are cited in note on l. 220, *Sunday Homilies in Verse* (A).
(*Specimens* by Morris and Skeat.)

p. 33, l. 1032.   *The death of Agea sprang about the town.*   Cp.
l. 3213, " It was *I-spronge* þurh the toun."   This word is very frequently used in this sense by the M.E. writers : we find a still earlier
use of it in the A.S. Gospel of St. Mark i. 28. Thorpe's *Analecta*, p. 130.

p. 35, l. 1087.   *the serkill celestyne* is the *primum mobile.*   After
enumerating, in their ascending order, the Moon, Mercury, Venus, the
Sun, Mars, Jupiter, Saturn, and the Fixed Stars, Dante goes on to say :

ᴑ ᴑ ᴑ ' lo nono [sito] è quello che non è sensibile se non per questo
movimento che è detto di sopra, lo quale chiamano molti Cristallino,
cioè diafano, ovvero tutto trasparente.   Veramente, fuori di tutti questi,
li Cattolici pongono lo Cielo Empireo, che è a dire Cielo di fiamma,
ovvero luminoso ; e pongono, esso essere immobile, per avere in sè,
secondo ciascuna parte, ciò che la sua materia vuole.   E questo è
cagione al primo mobile per avere velocissimo movimento ; che per lo
ferventissimo appetito che ha ciascuna parte di quello nono Cielo, che è
immediato a quello, d'essere congiunta con ciascuna parte di quello
Cielo divinissimo, Cielo quieto, in quello si rivolve con tanto desiderio,
che la sua velocità è quasi incomprensibile : e quieto e pacifico è lo
luogo di quella somma Deità che sè sola compiutamente vede.   Questo
luogo è di Spiriti beati, secondo che la santa Chiesa vuole, che non può
dire menzogna : e Aristotile pare ciò sentire, chi bene lo 'ntende, nel
primo *di Cielo e Mondo.*'—*Convito*, Tratt. II., cap. iv.—S.

p. 35, l. 1098.   [And] With the vii sagis.   ? For [*And*] *With* read
With [*that*] = thereupon.   Cp. l. 1181, " Rame *with* þat gan siȝhe."

p. 36, l. 1112.   *þat she myȝt be shryne to all other wymmen*, an
object for other women to visit and gaze on.   Cp. with this :

              " She is playnly expresse
                Egeria, the goddesse
                And lyke to her image,
                Emportured with corage,
                A lovers pilgrimage."
                    Skelton's *Phyllyp Sparowe*, l. 1157-1161,—

where I take a lover's pilgrimage to mean an object for a lover to make
a pilgrimage to ; I bring forward this explanation, however, with
diffidence.

p. 37, l. 1167.   *spak ful feir with hym.*   Perhaps the reading of the
MS. *spal* may be retained, as preterite of *spell*, ' speak ' ; possibly it
means " she spoke bewitchingly" (cp. the sbst. *spell*), " talked him over."

p. 38, l. 1196.   *so hiȝe & mode.*   In *Le Bone Florence* (Ritson), l. 90,
we have " swete and sware."   Perhaps for *&* in both cases we should
read *on*, or *of.*   Cp. " so *lowe* I was *of* mode," l. 2129.

p. 39, l. 1217. *I had levir he were I-sod.* Ogilvie's Dict. gives a verb *sod*, to cover with sod, to turf. At the present day "he's under the sod" may now and then be heard.

p. 39, l. 1229. *The devill hym spech.* ? For *speche* read *spede.* The words "the devill hym spede" occur four or five times elsewhere in this tale. Probably the *che* in *speche* was caught from *reche*, which follows.

p. 39, l. 1244. *aweynyd. aweyn*, disaccustom, cp. G. *entwöhnen*, seems to be the correct form of the word, the later *wean* having lost a significant prefix; the same is the case with *manse*, excommunicate, for *amanse.* See Stratmann, s. v. *mânsian.*

p. 40, l. 1250. *merellis.* A game somewhat like fox and geese,— called also nine men's morris, and five-penny morris,—played upon a board by two persons, each having nine pawns or counters. It was often played in the open air, the lines of the merelle board being then cut out in the turf. Shakspere mentions the game in this form, *Mid. N. D.*, II. i. 98. Further particulars, and a woodcut of a 14th cent. merelle table, will be found in Strutt's *Sports and Pastimes*, ed. Hone, 1845, bk. IV. chap. ii. pp. 317-18. Sherwood calls it: "(The boyish game) five-pennie morris. *Le jeu de merelles.*"—Cotgrave, ed. 1632. Eng.-Fr. *s. v.* Morris. 'Mereau * * * selon Monet, jeton pour compter.' —Roquefort, *s. v.* 'Mereau,' and see also 'Merellier.'—S.

p. 40, l. 1267. *rekelagis* = rigolagis = diversions. Littré gives a verb *rigoler*[*se*], of which he says : "*v. réflex.* Terme vieilli. Se divertir, faire une petite débauche ; *v. n.* Terme populaire. Rigoler, même sens." The word is found also in the *Cursor Mundi*, 1652/47, Laud MS.

> "Ensample hereby to hem I say,
> That rage in her ryot allewey,
> In Riot and iu *rygolage.*"

Here Bedford MS. has *Ricolage.* See also *Cursor Mundi*, 10/49, where Cotton MS. has *rygolage*, Fairfax and Trinity *ricolage*, and Göttingen (which is a Northern MS.) *rekelaye.*

p. 41, l. 1283. *Vel fikill flaptail. Vel* = wel, very, *fikill*, deceitful ; cp. Heo ne couthe of no *fikelyng*, and answerede not so (said of Cordelia). *Laȝamon* (in Mätzner), 156/32, and note.

p. 41, l. 1288. *And lepe out of the chambir, as who seyd "cut",* "as if one said to him '*cut.*'" *Cut* was a term of reproach, probably meaning gelding. See Nares, *s. v.*

p. 41, l. 1295. *willokis.* ? undergarments. Perhaps it is connected with *wilie-coat*, the origin of which word is unknown ; see Jamieson.

p. 41, l. 1300. *ffor seth min aray! for thy vilany.* ? after *for* insert *God*, which perhaps the scribe omitted from reverential feelings ; cp. l. 1275. At the same time I should remark that Geoffrey begins a speech, l. 3253, with the word *ffor.* For *thy* read *thys*, *thys vilany* meaning "the vilainous appearance I make."

p. 41, l. 1308. *ffor tho he first gan to glow a sory mans hede.* Here *glow* = clow = claw. *g* and *c* are frequently confounded by the scribes; which may easily be explained in the case of those who wrote from dictation. In this tale, l. 8, we probably have *capes* for *gapes*.

Cp. also
> "ȝe be so fayre, lyme & lythe,
> And therto comly *glad* tharw",
> That cemmely hyt ys to see."
> *Syre Gawane and the Carle of Carelyle*, l. 190 (ed. Madden),

where for *glad* read *clad*. Again we are told that *Gengis Khan* becomes *Cambynscan* in the *Squieres Tale*; *glaize*, the white of an egg, is from the Latin *clarus*, and we find *knawen* for *gnawen* in the MS. of the *Mirrour of Magistrates*, p. 296 of Skeat's *Specimens*; perhaps also in this way arose the early use of *can* for *gan*. As to *clow* for *claw*, Halliwell tells us that this is a Cumbrian usage. It is evident that our author wrote his tale in the dialect of some Northern county, with a sprinkling of Southern forms, which he picked up when a monk at Canterbury.

As to the meaning of the expression, Jamieson tells us that *to claw an auld man's pow* is a vulgar phrase, signifying to live to old age, and that it is often negatively addressed to a man who lives hard, *Ye'll never claw*, &c. If therefore "to claw an old man's head" means to become an old man, "to claw a sorry man's head" will mean "to become a sorry man," and the line before us will mean that Beryn then became really sorry for the first time in his life.

p. 41, 1309. *kepe thy cut*, be faithful to thyself. The editors of *Nares*, s. v. *keep cut*, cite:

> "A pretty playfellow, chirp it would,
> And hop & fly to fist;
> *Keep cut*, as twere a usurers gold,
> And bill me when I list."
> Cotgrave's *Wits Interpreter*, 1671, p. 176.

Keep cut therefore seems to = keep touch, stand the test, like gold; but how it got this meaning I cannot say.

p. 42, l. 1342. *That he had part of sorowe, me thinkith þat myȝt avowe.* Cp. l. 2467, part of sapience; and l. 3122, parcell of his sapience. The meaning of the line is: "that he fell into a swoon, I think, shows that he was sorry."

p. 42, l. 1350. *alto tare his cre*, . . . *With many a bittir tere* = tore his hair, at the same time shedding many a bitter tear.

p. 43, l. 1365. The poet here makes Fortune masculine; so also Nature, l. 689; and the City of Rome, l. 736; Beryn's mantell, l. 2428; Foly, l. 2319, and a knyfe, l. 2345.

p. 44, l. 1393. *wel a fyne.* Cp. Professor Zupitza's note in *Guy of Warwick;* he decides that *well and fyne* is the correct form.

p. 44, l. 1410. *And herde Beryn made his mone.* Cp. "Has doon fraught."—*Man of Lawes Tale*, l. 171 (ed. Skeat), and note thereon; also

> "Whose fathers he caus'd murder'd in those wars."
> Greene's *George-a-Greene* (ed. Dyce), p. 269, col. 1.

" The lorde halpe with myrthe & play
Tollyd his oune wyf away."

                              Seven Sages, l. 3051 (ed. T. Wright).

p. 45, ll. 1425—1442. Faunus usually addresses his son as *thou:*
so in this speech he begins with *thou*, but being softened by his recol-
lections of Agea, at l. 1437 he changes to ȝewe. The son always
addresses the father as ȝewe. Faunus addresses Rame, l. 1536, as *thou*,
though he usually calls her *you:* on that occasion he is upset with joy-
fulness. This change from *you* to *thou* is found as late as the year
1757. In Foote's *Englishman returned from Paris* (*Modern British
Drama*, vol. v. p. 263), Crabb first addresses Mac-ruthin as *you;* then
getting out of temper, *thou's* him; then subsiding a little, he returns
to *you*, and finally breaks out again into *thou*. Again, at p. 270,
Lucinda, conversing with Burke, commences by addressing him as *you*,
but soon breaks out into *thou*, upon which he retaliates with the same
disrespectful pronoun. On the whole the use of *thou* may be said to
indicate strong feeling, good or bad, or superior station.

p. 45, l. 1439. *I shall ȝit, or eue [come], that Bergeyn vndirtake.*
Cp. l. 1486, " onys *or it be eve* that I shall do my devoir." This expression " or it be eve " we find very frequently in the M.E. writers,
who borrowed it from the French; in the *Histoire de Berinus*, chap.
liii. *ad fin*, we have : " sil eut este dans leur puissance, logres fut de
royaume de blandie saisi, *avant quil eut este la vespree.*" Cp. also " ere
it was nyght."— *Squieres Tale*, l. 460, ed. Skeat.

p. 46, l. 1460. *a redy for to snache.* Cp. l. 659. Perhaps the *a*-
represents the older ȝc. Dr. Morris in his note on the word ȝeredie,
An Bispel, l. 152 (*Specimens*), says : " in *Piers Plowman* we find *iredi*
and *aredi; aredinese* occurs in Bacon's *Advancement of Learning*, and in
our English Bible, 2 Cor. x. vi."

It may be observed in favour of the meaning *all*, attributed to it in
the Gl., that at ll. 23, 484, we have *al redy*.

p. 46, l. 1473. *And as sone as—And hiȝrd—And told and made.*
There is no apodosis in this sentence. We find a similar one in
Chaucer's *Prologe of the Wyf of Bath*, ll. 818—822, when—and—and.

p. 46, l. 1477. *She hullid hym & mollid hym.* For *hullid*, covered
with her arms, embraced, cp.

" how hertily þe herdes wyf *hules* þat child,
& hov fair it fed, & fetisliche it bathede."

                              William of Palerne, l. 97 (E. E. Text Soc.).

As to *moll*, slobber over, see Gl.; perhaps this word appears in the
term *mollicoddle*, and that may be explained as " one who has been
molled and coddled."

p. 46, l. 1478. kite = belly; *see* Jamieson.

p. 48, l. 1536. my *hertis* swete. ? for *hertis* read *herte*. So again,
l. 2801, for " a mannys *hertis*" read *herte*.

p. 49, 1560. *had wedir at will.* Frequent in the M.E. writers, who
have taken it from the French; cp. *Histoire de Berinus*, sign. II 1, col.

2, "ils eurent vent *a gre et voulente:*" ibid. sign. NN 4, col. 1, "ils eurent vent *a voulente.*"

p. 49, l. 1580. *strothir.* l. 1884, *strodir* = *steor-roþir* = steering rudder. This was corrupted into *strothir.* See Wright's *Vocab.* i. 48, col. 1. "Remus, steor-roþir," lit. a steering paddle.

p. 49, l. 1582. *That myȝte abaten of the Shipp the þiknes of a skale.* ? for *Shipp* read *myst, Shipp* being caught from *Shippis* in preceding line.

p. 50, l. 1604. *Lace on a bonet or twain.* An additional part laced to the foot of the jibs, or other fore- and aft- sails, in small vessels in moderate weather, to gather more wind. They are commonly one-third of the depth of the sails they belong to. Thus we say : "Lace on the *bonnet,*" or "Shake off the *bonnet.*"—Admiral Smyth's *Sailor's Word-book,* 1867, p. 118.—F. J. F.

In the French romance the description of the storm and succeeding mist is despatched very briefly, and no nautical terms are used ; our author gives us fifty lines or so on this subject, and uses nautical terms, from which I infer that in early life he was a seafaring man : he also uses the word *cond,* l. 3995, which we are told is a seaman's term.

p. 51, l. 1652. *Now wold to God I had wherof, or coude make yewe cher.* Cp. l. 1729, "*had wherof* plente ;" *to have wherof* is a translation of the French *avoir de quoi :* of which Littré says : "*familièrement être dans l'aisance.*" At the present day we say : "I havn't the *wherewithal,*" and "one doesn't know his *whereabouts.*" Cp. also "every man, who *had whereof,* shulde peynen him."—Mandeville, Prologue to the *Voiage,* l. 60.

p. 52, l. 1682. *þat failid neuer of lakk.* *lakk* = fault ; cp. *lac,* Gl. to *Havelok* (ed. Skeat). Dutch *lak,* fault. Dr. Furnivall suggests "game," from A.S. *lakan.*

p. 53, ll. 1709-10. *And had enquerid of the Child and told his master's name.* The subject (viz. *the Child*) is omitted before *told.* This is frequent in this poem and elsewhere. Cp. l. 1746, and see Prof. Zupitza's note to *Guy of Warwick,* l. 10.

p. 54. *half a myle,* the time it takes to walk half a mile. This is a common usage, probably adopted from the French ; cp. *une grande loëe* (lieue Stunde) in *Gl.* to Bartsch's *Chrestomathie.*

p. 55, l. 1762. To "shake a ring" seems to be O.E. for "ring the bell."—W. W. S.

p. 55, l. 1790. *þurh-out the world.* Read *worlde wyde* to rime with *ryde ; worlde wyde* is a common expression.

p. 57, l. 1837. *gesolreut the haut.* i. e. G-*sol,* re, ut the high, or G-sol, re, upper C. G-sol means the note G, called *Sol* by singers. *Re* is the note D, and *ut* is the note C ; ut the haut is C in the octave, or upper C. *Ut* is never used now : *Do* is used for it.—W. W. S.

"Gesolreut *the haut*" means "at an exceedingly high pitch of voice. There are two Gesolreuts in the old scale, the one an octave above Gamma, and the second two octaves above Gamma. It is to the last gesolreut *the haut* applies. The name is a long one for a single note, but it means only one, viz. G."—Oct. 23 [1871], W. Chappell.

p. 57, l. 1838. *in kenebowe.* See Skeat's Dict. s. v. *akimbo.*

p. 57, ll. 1847-48. *tyme* rimed with *by me* occurs in Chaucer (see *Ryme-Index*), and gives a final *e.*—W. W. S. See also *to me* rimed with *lome*, ll. 1700-1.

p. 57, l. 1851. *endenting every pase*, in zigzag manner, like the edge of an indenture. Cp.

> " they took
> Their staves in hand, and at the good man strook,
> But by *indenturing* still the good man scaped."
> > Heywood's *Hierarchy of Angels*, 1635, p. 134.

p. 59, l. 1916. *what charge þe Shippis bere.* *charge* = cargo, which latter word is Spanish ; the two words are doublets. See Skeat's Dict.

p. 59, l. 1918. *in his uoice.* For *his* read *hiȝ* = high.

p. 59, l. 1922. *let tuk le meyn*, let touch the hand. A bargain was settled by joining hands. See Prof. Skeat on the word "tucker." *Transactions of Phil. Soc. for* 1885-6, p. 328.

p. 60, l. 1948. *& fond a-mys.* Perhaps the hyphen may be deleted, as the verb requires an accusative after it.

p. 60, l. 2061. *howe euir so yee taue.* ? for *yee* read *he, yee* being caught from preceding *yee :* then the words will mean, "however he may pull against you." Jamieson gives *tawe*, to pull, and *tawan*, reluctance, and Halliwell *tave*, kick. Cp. also "to *tow* a boat," and for the rime ll. 1257/8, *withdrawe, have.*

p. 61, l. 1978. *ȝis trulich, the tite ; the tite* = it betideth thee *i. e.* thou must do it. Cp.

> "Opbreyde *me tyt* of many on
> Of þyne riche kynne."
> > *St. Alexius* (E. E. Text Society), Trinity MS., l. 155.

p. 61, l. 1987. *Now fele in hir wittis & eke undirstonde.* The M.E. writers frequently use *fele* in this sense, especially the author of *Generydes.* Cp. also

> "Ne ilef þou nouht to *fele*
> uppe the see þat floweth."
> > *Proverbs of Alfred*, l. 196 (*Spec.* by Morris)—

where *fele* = think, meditate.

p. 62, l. 2010. Read *cried* "*out & harowe.*"

p. 63, l. 2039. *they com into þe plase.* *Plase* here means Court-house. Cp. l. 3451, " therfor, Sir Steward, ye occupy our place ; " here *our* is a form of *your*, and *our place* (= your plase) does not mean your seat on the bench as it would at the present day, but *your court-house. Plase* sometimes signifies a mansion, chief house of the neighbourhood ; so l. 1636, we have : " waytid on his ryȝht-hond a Manciples place." Also see Skeat's note on *Sir Thopas*, l. 1910 : " At Pepering, in *the place.*" Cp. *New Place* at Stratford-on-Avon ; the name, however, is frequent in England and Wales.

p. 64, l. 2075. *& suyd* = and to have sued.—W. W. S.

p. 64, ll. 2083-4. To make *condempnyd* and *examened* rime, we must delete the second *e* in *examened* and pronounce *examned.* At ll.

2380-1, *for-skramyd* rimes with *examenyd*, where we must pronounce *examyd*.

p. 64, l. 2092. *þat on me ben surmysid.* We have the corresponding English term, l. 2103, "Of þing that I shall *put on* ȝew."

p. 65, l. 2123. *for offt time.* *for* is here intensive and = very; cp. l. 268, *for curteisly.*

p. 65, l. 2128. *his:* the old idiom. We now say—"For sucking of him," or "As for his sucking."—W. W. S.

p. 67, l. 2194. *þan he did his shippis or his good.* dele the words *he did:* the metre of this Tale is very irregular, but will not tolerate a line of this length.   ˌ

p. 67, l. 2196. *a-mure.* At l. 2806 we have *a-myrid* apparently in a directly contrary sense. Perhaps in the passage before us we may read *i-myre*, put in the mire, as in l. 3388; cp. l. 304, "i-loggit al nyȝt *in a myere;*" our author is always repeating himself. It may possibly however be from A.S. *amyrran*, to mar, destroy.

p. 68, l. 2213. *ensensid* = insensed = informed. To 'insense' is to drive sense into people: common in Norfolk. [And in Devonshire also, I've been told.—S.]

"It's a wonder somebody doesn't *insense* him about it," he continued, "but I hope they'll not, for I want him to come down to our part just once more, that I may sattle wi' him for what he said to Miss Mary."—*Ralf Skirlaugh*, by Edw. Peacock, 1st edit. 1871, vol. iii. p. 99.—W. W. S.

p. 68, l. 2227. *doith eke man appeir.* For *eke* read *eche;* appeir = impair, from Fr. *pire*, worse.

p. 68, l. 2228. *& falle in dispeir.* The context seems to require "fallith," the subject *he* being omitted.

p. 69, l. 2266. *þey had no cause to yelp.* For *þey* read *he*, viz. Beryn.

p. 70, l. 2275. *vii dromodarijs.* *Dromodarijs* is here put for *dromonds*, swift vessels. Cp.

> " Wyth eighty shyppes of large towre,
> Wyth *dromedaryes* of great honour."
>
> *The Squyer of Lowe Degre*, l. 817.

In *Guy of Warwick*, l. 5805, we find the converse error, *dromonde* for *dromedary*, which Prof. Zupitza thinks probably arose from the author's ignorance of natural history. In the *Morte Arthure* (ed. Brock), l. 2286, we have—

> "They drewe out of *dromondaries* dyuerse lordes"—

where *dromondaries* evidently = dromonds. In the *Taill of Rauf Coillyear* (ed. Herrtage), l. 807, a "knicht on ane *camell*," who is a Saracen, comes to encounter Sir Rauf, and after the encounter we are told that "baith thair hors deid lay," l. 817; besides which the animal on which the Saracen rode is termed a "blonk" and a "steid"; therefore here the word "camell" is evidently used for a horse. It is not surprising that this confusion has arisen : the words *dromond* and *dromedary* have both the same meaning, viz. runner, the only difference between the two words being that the latter has an adjectival suffix, so that they are both equally applicable to a ship and a horse. The author of *Rauf Coilyear* seems to have fallen into his error in this way; first, he thought that the word "dromedary" might be used for "horse"; then having learnt that a dromedary was a sort of camel, he used the word "camel" also for a horse. Possibly, when we read of a Christian knight riding on a dromedary, as in the *Morte Arthure*, l. 2941, "dromedary" only means a swift horse. The surname *Drummond* is probably from this word, *dromond*, ship.

p. 70, l. 2289. *neuir have mery.* *mery* seems to be put here for *merriment.* The absence of the substantival suffix is frequent in M.E. writers; cp. l. 3493, *desperate* of mind. Again, l. 1431, we have: "our dicte shall be *mery* & solase:" here either *mery* = merriment, or *solace* = solacious, as the two words must either be both substantives or both adjectives.

p. 70, l. 2293. *Ther may no man hale murdir, þat it woll out at last.* The negative is omitted in the secondary sentence; this arises from a confusion of two constructions; see Prof. Zupitza's note on *Guy of Warwick*, l. 1301-3. To instances there cited, may be added,

> "There was none that he mette,
> And his spere on hym wold sette,
> That after within a lyttel stounde
> Hors & man bothe went to ground."
>
> *Ipomydon*, l. 541 (Weber).

Also *Richard Coer de Lion*, l. 3500 (Weber); *Sir Beves of Hamtoun*, l. 1412 (ed. Kölbing); and *Tale of Gamelyn*, ll. 511-12.

p. 71, l. 2319. *ffoly, I hauntid it evir*, &c. A redundant object.—S.

p. 72, l. 2348. *to speke of had-I-wist.* Prof. Earle (*Philology of E. Tongue*, p. 514) cites:

> "And kepe þe wel from *hadde-y-wiste.*"
>
> *Babees Book*, p. 15 (ed. Furnivall).

> "When dede is doun, hyt is to lat;
> be ware of *had-y-wyst.*"

p. 72, l. 2349. *the man, that he stert.* Here *that he* = who; this is frequent in Chaucer and other M.E. writers.

p. 72, ll. 2356-7. *raftris, aftir.* Cp. this rime with that of *wers, ther*, ll. 3444-5.

p. 73, l. 2388. *began to preche.* For *preche* read *prece*, press on. Both sense and rime require the change.

p. 73, l. 2397. For *liȝte* read *lite.* Dr. Furnivall however suggests that *liȝt* may stand, as *lightly.*

p. 73, l. 2408. *outid all yeur chaffare.* Jamieson, s. v. *outing*, a vent for commodities, cites: "sale & *outing* of his wares"; see *id.* s. v. *out*, and *Canon Yeoman's Tale*, l. 834 (ed. Skeat). This phrase is used in a metaphorical sense in *Marchant's End Link*, l. 3438. See also *Wyf of Bathe's Prologe*, l. 521 (ed. Morris).

p. 74, l. 2436. ? For *contremen* read *contreman*.

p. 75, l. 2450. *Sir Clekam*, from *cleiks*, *s. pl.* a cramp in the legs, to which horses are subject; so denominated, because it *cleiks*, and as it were holds up their hinder legs.—Jamieson's Dict. But see Gl.

p. 77, l. 2515. *clyȝte*, closed; cp.

"Than comen her frendes hem to,
And seide: 'alas! whi seie ye so,
In your armour so fast *ycliȝt?*'"—*Cursor Mundi*, 1648/717.

The word is from A.S. *beclusian;* cp. "*beclused* inne castle."—*Laȝamon* in Mätzner, 31/14138.

p. 78, l. 2563. *at all þat I shuld stonde cler.* *i. e.* that I should stand clear of all charges. These inversions are frequent in this tale. Cp. ll. 3133-4, "so forforth atte laste Thurh vertu of myne office, þat," which = "so forforth, þat atte laste, thurh vertu of myne office."

p. 78, l. 2569. *That ye woll hold me couenante, & I will ȝew also* = if you will keep word with me I will keep word with you; cp. ll. 3547-8. This construction is frequent. It appears in many of our proverbs, as "Marry in haste, and repent at leisure," "Stuff a cold, and starve a fever," and others. It is found in mediæval and modern French.

p. 78, l. 2583. *I-seclid & fixid them a nye.* Again *c* for *t;* for *I-seclid* read *isetlid*, as Urry does, and cp. l. 1742, "*ysetlid* ne fixid in the wose."

p. 79, l. 2590. ? before þey insert þouȝe.

p. 79, l. 2606. *þe lawe wold graunte anoon.* ? For *anoon* read *noon*, *i. e.* no opportunity of proving your case.

p. 80. l. 2624. *ffor of wele & ellis it is thy day final* = this day will decide finally as to whether you have good fortune or other fortune. Cp. l. 1122, "So what *for drede & ellis* they were bothe ensuryd," *i. e.* for fear and other feeling, viz. fear of the Emperor and personal liking. *Ellis & else* are sometimes used as adjectives or pronouns; cp. *King John*, Act II. scene i, where the King says: "I bring you witnesses," and the Bastard interposes with: "Bastards *and else.*"

p. 80, l. 2637. *Deupardeux* = *de part dieu;* see Prologue to *Man of Lawes Tale*, l. 39, and Prof. Skeat's note thereon. The corresponding English oath seems to have been: "a Goddes half," where half = part.

p. 81, l. 2661. *Grew* = Greek. Cp.

"And fast disputed with the *griues.*"—*Cursor Mundi*, 1597/19739.

For the dropping of the final *k*, cp. *warlau* = warlok, and *sli* = slik = suilk, which are both common in the *Cursor Mundi*.

p. 81, l. 2673. *In denmark he was goten and I-bore also.* In the French romance also Esop is represented as having been born in Denmark; why so, it is difficult to say; but perhaps the following extract from the *Foreign Quarterly Review*, No. XXXV. p. 193, will throw some light upon the subject. "We are inclined also to think that during the 12th and 13th centuries, and perhaps later, it was very common, when people would tell a legend, supposed to have happened in another land, to place its locality in Denmark : we have thus in *Giraldus* a story of a household spirit who served a bishop in Denmark (perhaps the oldest form of the story of *Hudekin*) ; we have several stories among our saints' legends whose scene is in Denmark ; and the oldest form in which we have yet met with the story of Shakespeare's *Shylock* is in an Anglo-Latin Manuscript, where it is said to have occurred in Denmark. Had the name of Denmark been thus accidentally introduced the story might have been adventitious to that country, and yet might at a later period have localized itself there."

p. 82, l. 2697.   *wonde* = fear, see Stratmann, s. v. *wandien.*

p. 82, l. 2701.   *And eve afore* = on the evening before ; perhaps for *and* we should read *an* (= on).

p. 83, l. 2723.   *The keveryng of-bove, is of selondyn.*   In the French romance we have in this passage *cassidoine* (= modern *calcédoine*) : and for *salidone*, l. 3302, we have *sardoine* (= sardonyx).   Probably both *salidone* and *selondyn* are corruptions of *sardoine.*

p. 83, l. 2726.   *he my3t be disware of his owne lyve* = he might unawares lose his life.   Cp. l. 3393, " of þe lyve They wishid that they were," *i. e.* they wished that they were dead.   In the phrase " to be of þe lyve ; " *of* = " off, out of ; " cp. also the common phrase, " to do of dawe."

p. 83, l. 2728.   *what thing come forby.*   *for* in *forby* = forth.   Cp. "*forthby* as they go," Chaucer's *Legend of Phillis.* ad fin.   *Forby* = by or past.

p. 84, l. 2758.   *And mowe, as they were quyk, knawe the sotill engyne.* The only meaning I can extract from this perplexing passage is " and they may, as if they were alive, acknowledge the subtle skill (of Tholomeus) ; " but ?—

p. 84, l. 2772.   *tregetours,* jugglers ; see Tyrwhitt's note on the *Canterbury Tales,* l. 11453.   He derives the word from *treget,* frequently used by Chaucer for *deceit,* and *treget* from *trebuchet,* the French name for a military engine, which is called by Chaucer *trepeget.*   *Trebuchet* in French signified also a machine for catching birds.

p. 84, l. 2774.   *þe arte of apparene.*   For *apparene* read *apparence,* the art of producing apparitions, which word we find four times in the *Frankeleyne's Tale* (ed. Morris, ll. 412, 426, 529, and 858); also in Lydgate's *Dance of Macabre,* cited in Tyrwhitt's note, which is referred to in note next preceding this ; *aperance* we find in the *Testament of Crescide,* l. 142 (ed. Laing).

p. 84, l. 2775.   *That they make semen wormys,* i. e. that they cause serpents to appear seemingly.

p. 84, l. 2791.   *as a dentour wriythe,* goes zigzag like an indenture. " If a deed be made by more parties than one, there ought to be regularly as many copies of it as there are parties, and each ' was formerly ' cut or indented (' either ' in acute angles *instar dentium,* like the teeth of a saw, 'or more usually' in a waving line) on the top or side, to tally or correspond with the other; which deed, so made, was called an indenture."—Blackstone's *Commentaries*, ed. Kerr, 1862, vol. ii. p. 290. Further particulars may be found in Spelman's *Glossarium Archaiologicum*, and Cowell's *Law Dictionary*, s. vv. 'Indentura,' and 'Indenture.'—S.

p. 87, l. 2874. *imade al my wanlase*, driven all my deer to a stand. Jamieson, s. v. *wanlas* says: "*at the wanlas*, accidentally, without design." We find a word much resembling this in A.S. only inverted; *leaswene*, false opinion, from *waenan, wenan*, to think, and *leas*, without. This was evidently used in E. as a term of the chase. *Wanlass* (a term in hunting), as *Driving the Wanlass*, i. e. the driving of deer to a stand; which in some Latin records is termed *Fugatio Wanlassi ad stabulum*, and in *Doomsday Book, Stabilitio Venationis.* Phillips. " Illi custumarii solebant *fugare Wanlassum ad stabulum*, i. e. to drive the deer to a stand, that the lord may have a shoot; *Blount ap. Cowell.*"

The word therefore seems to have meant, 1st, thoughtless or thoughtlessness; 2nd, a deer running thoughtlessly or at random; and 3rdly, the act of driving the deer so running to a stand, in which sense it is used in the passage before us. We also find *wanlessour* for *huntsman:*

> "The wandlessoures went throw the forest,
> And to the lady brought many a best,
> Hert & hynde, &c."—*Ipomydon*, l. 387 (Weber).

We also find the word *wanles* in the *Cursor Mundi*, l. 23996:

> "Bot quhen i sagh thaa juus snell
> Rise again my son sa fell,
> Ful *wanles* wex I then,"

where *wanles* = destitute of thought, at a loss what to do. Cp. also " will of *vayn.*"—*Barbour's Bruce*, l. 225 (Morris and Skeat's *Specimens*).

p. 87, l. 2886. *ovir the bord.* " * * * the Frenchemen had the victorye, and toke two great shyppes of Englande with great ryches, and caryed them with them into the Frenche stremys, and cast the men *ouer the borde.*"—Rastell's *Pastime of People*, 1525, ed. T. F. Dibdin, 1811, p. 215.—S.

p. 87, l. 2899. *the saylis stonden al a-cros.* p. 90, l. 2995. *make cros-saill.* A friend obliged me with the following note on these phrases.—S.

" Neither of the phrases you mention is used now, nor in truth any words very like them that I know of. I can only guess that '*make cros-saill*' may refer to the course to be sailed, in which case it would well express tacking = a zigzag course at half a right angle from either side of the wind. 'The saylis stonden al a-cros' is explained by the fact that it is said of a boat about to sail,—provided we may presume that the wind is right aft, or quite fair,—as then whether the rig be that (e. g.) of a yacht called 'fore and aft,' or that (e. g.) of most merchant-men, 'square,' the boom of the mainsail in the former case is let going out as nearly at right angles as possible with the keel of the vessel, and in the latter the yards are hauled quite square across—so that in both rigs *the sails stand all across—before the wind.*"—J. W. L.

p. 90, l. 2984. *good sir John.* This was properly a term of ridicule for a priest; see Skeat's notes to *Shipman's* Prol., l. 1172, and to *Nonnes Prestes* Prol., l. 1000; it is here applied to a layman.

p. 90, l. 2996. *feche more last;* cp.

"God yeve this monk a thousand *last* quad yeer."
Shipman's End-link, l. 1628, and Skeat's note.

p. 90, l. 2997. *ȝemen* = yeomen, men of small estate; see Skeat's Dict.

p. 90, l. 3006. *fell* = fill. *See* rime and l. 3117.—W. W. S.

p. 91, l. 3017. *made him angry.* ? pretended to be sorrowful: cp. note on line 817; an angry man in the modern sense of the word does not "siȝh wondir sore."

p. 91, l. 3020. *Geffrey chasid him aȝeyn.* ? for *chasid* read *chastid*, chastened, reproved; see *chaste,* ll. 1058 and 3440. The Steward, though very indulgent to Geffrey, would hardly have permitted him to chase Beryn about the Court.

p. 92, l. 3056. *a company I-met; a* = on or in.

p. 92, l. 3063. *in the mene whils.* ? after *whils* insert *that.*

p. 93, l. 3115. *I telle trewly.* After *telle* insert *yewe.*

p. 95, l. 3163. *That God him grant wynnyng, riȝte as he hath aservid!* An imprecation: the words "I pray" may be understood before "that". Cp. l. 3277, "þat sorow com on thy hede!" also ll. 601, 1012. It is frequent in M.E. writers.

p. 96, l. 3185. *by thee I meen,* I speak concerning thee. Cp. l. 10, "by hem I *meen,*" and l. 1791, *be Beryn I may wele sey.*

p 97, ll. 3213-14. *Rimes.* noweȝ—mowith. *See* also ll. 3231-32. —W. W. S.

p. 97, l. 3302. *salidone,* l. 2723, we have *selondyn,* on which see note. Also cp. "Ribes and *salidoines.*" *Owain Miles,* p. 97 (ed. Laing).

p. 100, l. 3315. *Gylhoget,* in the French romance *guigne-hochet,* which is from *guignol,* une sorte de polichinelle, and *hochet,* plaything. Wade's boat was termed *Guignelot;* see Tyrwhitt's *Chaucer,* l. 9298.

p. 101, l. 3366. *to pot who cometh last* = who cometh last to pot.

p. 104, l. 3456. *And euery man til othir lenyd with his hede. And seyd,* &c. Cf. the Homeric "ὧδε δέ τις εἴπεσκε ἰδὼν ἐς πλησίον ἄλλον." —*Il.* II. 271.—S.

p. 104, l. 3476. *þouȝe I it sey, can nat half so muche.* Before *can* insert *that.*—F. J. F.

p. 104, l. 3477. For *ne* read *nowe, ne* being caught from preceding line.

p. 105, l. 3489. MS. *to se the the sepulkir.* ? again *t* written for *c;* for *se the* read *seche,* the word always used for a pilgrimage.

p. 106, l. 3527. *ynmagytiff.* Cp. *ignomy,* which is found in Shakspere four times; also *attame,* from Low Latin *taminare.* Gl. to *Prioresses*

Tale, &c. (ed. Skeat). "*Determyt* furth therewith in myn entent." *King's Quair*, l. 13. We find *ignomious* in Peele's *Sir Clyamon and Sir Clymades* Prologue, p. 490 (ed. Dyce); also *Ignomy*, p. 508, 1st col. ; and in the tale before us, l. 2382, *examyt*; on which see note.

p. 106, l. 3549. *Let him go to in haste.* Cp. l. 3229, "*Go to*, & kis them both." Also

> "*gaþ till*, and bareþþ heþenn ut
> whatt-like þise þinges."—*Ormulum*, l. 15570.

These words are put into the mouth of Christ, when driving those who sold doves out of the temple.

> "þu *gest* al *to* mid swikelede."—*Owl and Nightingale*, l. 838.

Go to is found also in *Hamlet* V. i., and in the *Book of Genesis*, chap. xi. 3, 4, and 7. The meaning of "go to," in these eight passages, seems to be "to set briskly about some business;" when we have "go to" in the imperative, the modern English equivalent will be "now then," the French "or ça." Flügel in his *English-German Dict.*, s. v. *go*, translates "go to" by *wohlan, daran, frisch darauf an.* In *go to*, *Macbeth*, V. i. 46, *to* seems to = the German *zer-*.

p. 107, l. 3554. *þouȝt ye sotil pry;* for *pry* read *be*, which rimes with *iniquite*, and cp. l. 3592, "as sotill as þey be."

p. 107, l. 3562. *& ye work in eny poynt.* Possibly *work* may here mean "trouble us," see Jamieson; but in that case we should rather expect "work us," which, however, does not suit the metre.

p. 107, l. 3586. For *they* read *he*, viz. Beryn.

p. 108, l. 3588-9. *they sawe no maner selve ffor soris of hir hert.* Either *selve* = salve, or for *selve* read *salve*.

p. 108, l. 3596. For *him* read *hem*, i. e. "these romeyns."

p. 111, l. 3724. *vnyd.* Cp.

> "þis love & þis wilninge, þat ioyneth & oneþ zuo þe herte to God."
> Dan Michel's *Ayenbite of Inwit*, l. 43 (Zupitza's *Uebungs-buch*).

p. 113, l. 3764. *the pleyntyfs.* For *the* read *thre*.

p. 114, l. 3803. *vii yeer & passid.* ? For *& passid* read *i-passid*.

p. 117, l. 3914. [*quod*] *Beryn, and al the remenaunte; the remnaunte* seems here to mean "the other Romans"; cp. l. 3884. It occurs frequently in that sense.

p. 118, l. 3946. Cp. with this *Octouyan Imperator*, Weber, iii. 187/ 729, 192/847, where Florentyn, brought up as a butcher's boy, betrays his high birth by similar tastes.

p. 118, ll. 3948-9. *þat with al hir witt To serve hem.* A change of construction which is found frequently: cp. *All. Morte Arthure*, 1281/2.

p. 119, l. 3995. *To cond him saff.* *To cond*, in seamen's language to conduct a ship: see *N. and Q.* 6th S., xi. 355. To *Balke, Conde*.

---

p. 179, note to p. 11, l. 310. As to the word *aliri*, Prof. Skeat in *N. & Q.* 6th S. i. 318, 386, suggests that it is connected with A.S. *spear-lira*, where *lira* means the fleshy part of the leg.

ADDITIONAL NOTES.

p. 3, l. 56. *unaservid.* *aservid*, ll. 2371 and 2377 = deserved, and in *Troylus and Creseide* (Bell's ed.), p. 145, st. 1, we find *untrist* for " mistrust ": again at p. 244 st. 3, *unswelle;* it must however be admitted that *unaserve* is nowhere found in the sense I attribute to it.

p. 5, l. 109. In the *Legende of Goode Women* Egiste looks on his daughter " with *glad chere* "; then tells her to murder her husband; here again *glad* requires explanation.

p. 6, l. 152. It should be : " And a-red [it] also right, as [be] rammys hornyd," *i. e.* and explained it as right, as are horned rams. " As right as a ram's horn " is an open joke, rams' horns being proverbially crooked. A pun on *right*, which = (1) correct, and (2) straight.—W. W. S.

p. 10, l. 271. *brothir in possession.* Cp. *Sompnoures Tale*, l. 13 (Aldine ed.), where the Frere says :

> " Neither it needeth not for to be yive
> To *possessioneres*, that now lyve
> (Thanked be God) in wele and abundaunce."

Of the word *possessioneres*, Tyrwhitt in Gl. says : " an invidious name for such religious communities as were endowed with lands," &c.

p. 10, l. 282. *stalk* = to go on tiptoe, or noiselessly : see Skeat's *Dict.*, s. v., and cp. l. 299.

p. 10, l. 292. *ifrethid* = friþed in Gl. to *Piers Plowman.*—W. W. S. Also in *Allit. Morte Arthure*, l. 3247, we have *frithede*, hemmed in with trees.

p. 12, l. 362. Here the dislike of the author to Freres breaks out, as again at l. 1643.

p. 14, l. 423. *cushy :* French (*se*) *coucher.*—W. W. S.

p. 16, l. 478. Other instances of *up* = open are :

> "Goo *upon* the chaumber dore, she seide."
> *Generydes* (E. E. Text Soc.), l. 5721—

where a syllable is wanting to the line : therefore perhaps we may read, " goo, *do upon*," i. e. open. Again, "cast *up* the gatis wide," *Troylus & Creseide*, ii. 615, and " dupp'd the chamber-door " in Ophelia's song, where *dup* = do up or open. We have it again in *Beryn*, ll. 1639 and 2736, and as Prof. Skeat points out, *char up*, l. 355 = [on] char up = on the jar open = open on the jar. In the note at p. 182 on this line, dele words from " *be* of the MS." to the end.

p. 16, l. 493. *cardiakill*, Fr. *cardiaque*, Low Lat. *cardiaca* (Prompt. Parv.).—W. W. S.

p. 16, l. 498. *wood rese*, mad fit : *rese* = A.S. *rǽs.*—W. W. S.

p. 17, l. 511. *evil preff.* Here *preff* = success. See *Encyclopædic Dict.*, s. v. *prove.*

p. 18, l. 562. For *leue* read *lene*, and cp. the phrase "to lend a blow."—W. W. S.

p. 21, l. 640. Dele note marked W. W. S. and substitute : *warrok* = warlock, *i. e.* ill-tempered ; see *warlo* in Jamieson.—W. W. S.

p. 21, l. 651. *growning* = growling. See Stratmann, s. v. *groinen.* Fr. *grogner*, Lat. *grunnire.*

p. 22, l. 674. *vpward gan she pike.* Here *pike* = peep ; see Skeat's *Dict.*, s. v. *peep :* where a line from *Troylus and Cryseide*, iii. 60, is cited ; "gan in at the curtein *pike.*" I may remark that the sun is here *she*, in Chaucer always *he.*

p. 22, l. 764. *held hym to* = put up with.—W. W. S.

p. 23, l. 687. *twynyth.* Halliwell, s. v. *twine*, says : "to whine or cry—*Yorksh.*"

p. 23, l. 690. Dele note on *he* (Glossary, p. 213).—S.

p. 27, l. 824. *fences*, safeguards ; see *Defence* in Cotgrave, alluding to the protection of men's fortunes by the planets.—W. W. S.

p. 28, l. 855. *delices* is found frequently in Chaucer, especially in the *Persones Tale ;* in verse however it is elsewhere a trisyllable ; but in the passage before us we must pronounce it as a disyllable for the sake of the rime.

p. 31, l. 967. *elyng.* See Murray's *Dict.*, s. v. *alange.* He cites *Wif of Bathes Tale*, l. 433, where one MS. gives *elenge*, another *alenge.* The meaning is "protracted, tedious, wearisome." Cp. also *Schipman's Tale*, l. 222, and *The Cuckow and the Nightingale*, iv. 340, st. 2 (ed. Bell).

p. 35, l. 1084. *halffyndele*, half-part. A.S. weak acc. *healfan & dæl.*—W. W. S. In *Troylus and Cryseide*, p. 140 (ed. Bell), we have *halvyn-dele.*

p. 37, l. 1167. Dele this note.

p. 38, l. 1196. For *bloderid* perhaps read *bloberid.*—W. W. S.

p. 39, l. 1217. *isod* = in the sod = under the turf = buried. W. W. S.

p. 40, l. 1268. *heritagis.* Perhaps we may retain the reading of the MS. *hostagis.* Cp.

"To my *hostage* ye go by nyght."
Ipomydon (Weber's Romance), l. 773.

"She said he was welcome to that *ostage.*"—*Generydes*, l. 64— where *ostage* = hostelry.

If therefore Faunus's property consisted of houses, *hostagis* might stand, but on the whole it must be admitted that *heritagis* is more suitable.

p. 41, l. 1288. *as who seyd cut.* Here *as who* = as if one. Cf. l. 3407—

"The Romeyns stode still, as who had shor hir hed."

p. 46, l. 1478. Add : *kyte ;* in Northern English the form is *kite.*

p. 48, l. 1536. *my hertis swete.* Perhaps *hertis* may be retained : cp. "My harts swete" = sweet one of my heart.—*Sir Lambwell* (Percy Folio MS.), vol. i. 149/139. The usual form is "Myn herte swete."

p. 52, l. 1682. Dele words after *lak*, fault in the note on p. 191. Prof. Skeat says : *of lakk* = for lack, " for lack of matter," as Shakspere says.

p. 52, l. 1692. For *nethirless* read " nerthiless " or " nertheless " : so again at l. 2477.

p. 62, l. 2010. For *oute & harowe* read " oute " and " harowe," i. e. *out* and *harowe* are separate exclamations.—W. W. S.

p. 63, l. 2039. We have a very modern instance of *place* used in this sense : " my Lady Dedlock has been down at what she calls her *place* in Lincolnshire."—*Bleak House*, chap. ii. *ad init. Place* in M.E. also means = " lists " : see *Knightes Tale*, l. 1541, " winne her in the place," and again l. 1836.

p. 65, l. 2110. *of fyne force.* We have the same expression in *Troylus and Cryseide* (ed. Bell), p. 251, st. 2. Littré says *fin* sometimes merely gives force to the word to which it is attached ; see also Genin's note to *Pierre Patelin*, v. 29, and cp. the modern expressions " fine fun " and " a fine frolic."

p. 67, l. 2196. *amvre ;* also *amyre*, l. 2806, possibly " ripen " in both places. Fr. *ameurir.* Cotgrave.—W. W. S.

p. 74, l. 2241. Dele words after *jolif* in Glossarial Index, s. v. *iuly.*—S.

p. 77, l. 2515. *clyȝte.* In note, dele words after lines cited from *Cursor Mundi*, and substitute : from *clechen*, clutch : which word see in Gl. to Mätzner's Sprachproben.

p. 80, l. 2626. *ymmemorat of lyes.* These words are very perplexing ; perhaps *ymmemorat* agrees with *Beryn*, and the words will mean : Beryn, unmindful of the deceptions previously practised on him, and now inclined to trust another stranger. See Forcellinus, s. v. *memoror*, memorsum.

p. 81, l. 2661. *Grew.* In note dele words that follow the line cited from the *Cursor Mundi*.

p. 82, l. 2697. *wonde ;* dele this note.

p. 91, l. 3020. Dele last sentence of the note.

p. 94, l. 3136. *for to go at large.* After *for* insert *hym*.

p. 103, l. 3434. *have the wordis* = be spokesman, the regular phrase ; see Tyrwhitt's Note to *Canterbury Tales*, l. 17378.—W. W. S.

p. 106, l. 3529. *ynmagytyff*? = suspicious. Prof. Earle in his *Philology*, p. 56, laments the disparagement of many respectable words in the 12th and 13th centuries: among others, he says, that *imaginatif* acquired the meaning of " suspicious." Cp. also *Frankeleynes Tale*, p. 500, l. 2 (ed. Bell).

> " Nothing list him to be *imaginatif*,
>   If any wight had spoke, while he was oute,
>   To hire of love."

I give some other errors of the scribe which are of no great importance : p. 16, l. 486, read *hym* for *hem.* p. 33, l. 1015, for *outȝ* read *nouȝt.* p. 37, l. 1170, dele *it.* p. 65, l. 2098, for *ȝit* read *it.* p. 75, l. 2466, dele the former *as.* p. 79, l. 2603, dele *gyve.* p. 96, l. 3182, dele *as.*

GLOSSARY AND INDEX.

By W. G. STONE.

a, *adv.* all, 46/1460.

a, *pron.* he, 113/3771.

abigg, *vb.* pay for, 20/593. A.S. *abycgan.*

abill, *adj.* apt, fit, 9/245, 97/3237. 'Able, or abulle, or abylle. *Habilis, idoneous.*'—Prompt. Parv.

accordit, *pret. pl.* agreed, 50/1615; *pp.* 8/212, 86/2834, 95/3148, 107/3578, 116/3871.

a-combrit, *pp.* hampered, overcome, 85/2800; accombrid, 109/3644; comberid, 73/2386.

acordement, *sb.* agreement, 48/1521, 78/2571.

a-dred, *pp.* afraid, 62/2006; a-drad, 68/2231, 86/2839. *See* drede.

a feir, *adv.* on fire, 71/2310.

Affirmative, an, in Civil Law, rule relating to, 64/2070.

affray, *sb.* terror, 102/3384. O.F. *affre.* L.Lat. *affraiamentum.* Roquefort, *s. v.* affre.

a force, *adv.* perforce, 65/2118.

a-foundit, *pp.* foundered, 21/631. See note in *Prompt. Parv.* s. v. 'Fownderyñ.'

aftir-mete, *sb.* afternoon, 8/227, 13/391. Noon was the dinner-hour in the middle ages. See *The Babees Book,* E. E. T. S., 5/128.

a fyne, or & fyne. *See* wel.

AGEA, first wife of Faunus, bears him a son, Beryn, p. 29; her dying injunctions to Faunus, p. 32; her funeral rites described, p. 34.

a-geynes, *adv.* again, 76/2511.

ageynward, *adv.* again, in return, 100/3314.

ago, *pp.* gone. *See* goon.

al = all that, 33/1025.

al & som, altogether, 5/115.

al at, ? all that, 119/3984.

al bothe, *adj.* both, 98/3252.

a-leyid, *pp.* laid, 118/3936.

Alisaundir, Alexandria, 49/1556.

a londe, *adv.* ashore, 73/2405.

alowe, *vb.* praise, 4/94; lowe, allow, 51/1653. O.F. *aloér.*

al so, *adv.* even as, also, 6/152, 17/504; also, 29/874, 72/2370, 76/2483, 97/3220. A.S. *eal-swá.*

altercation, *sb.* 76/2500.

al, ? = albe, although, 69/2261.

amayid, *pp.* dismayed, 56/1807; a-mayide, 102/3379.

a-mend, *vb.* correct, 81/2658; mendit, *pp.* amended, 34/1045.

a-mongis, *adv.* at intervals, from time to time: evir more a-mong, 110/3686; othir whils amongis, 30/933; oþir while a-mong, 38/1197; ther a-mong, 105/3435.

a morow, next morning, in the morning, 22/656, 62/1998; a morowe, 22/667, 117/3909.

a-mvre, *vb.* ? = amure, wall up, bury, 67/2196; *pp.* a-myrid = amurid, defended as by a wall, 85/2806. Halliwell has 'mure', *vb.* to wall. See note, p. 193.

a-myrid. *See* a-mvre.

amys ase, *sb.* double aces, 89/2955.

ambiguite, *sb.* ambiguity, 78/2577.

and, *conj.* if, 18/546, *et passim.* Often written thus: &.

anenst, *prep.* concerning, 15/442; a-nenst, 113/3764.

angir, *sb.* sorrow, 27/817.

angir, *vb.* be angry, 116/3883.

an hond, *adv.* nearly, 95/3173.

anothir, *adv.* otherwise, 106/3538.

a nowe, *adv.* now, 77/2526.

ANTONYUS JUDEUS, one of the Seven Sages, 27/809.

a nye, ? *vb.* annoy, harm, 78/2583. 'Anoier, *anueir, anuer, anuier:* Ennuyer, nuire, &c.'—Roquefort.

apassid, *pp.* past, 85/2827.

apayde, *pp.* satisfied, pleased, 39/1238; a-payde, 46/1467; payde, 13/399.

a-pele, *sb.* appeal, 107/3562.

a-pele, *vb.* accuse, charge, 96/3206; *pres.* 1 *s.* a-pele, 99/3294.

a-poyntid, *pret. s.* pointed out, 9/240.

appareno, *sb.* appearance, delusion, 84/2774. See note, p. 196.

appeir, *vb.* harm, 68/2227.

appid oppon, *pret. s.* hapt on, lighted on, 21/632.

aquyt, *pret. s.* repayed, 5/125.

aray, *sb.* company, assemblage, 9/233, 90/2978; conduct, 40/1255; clothing, equipment, 41/1300, 44/1391, 51/1655, 65/2119, 92/3045, 3064.

aray, *vb.* afflict, 20/603; *pp.* arayed, 72/2375.

aray, *vb.* dress, 116/3882.

arblast, *sb.* cross-bow, 9/241.

areche, *vb.* utter, 112/3734. A.S. *areccan.*

a-rede, *vb.* conjecture, guess, 17/527. *See* Stratmann, *s. v.* arædon.

arere, *adv.* in the rear, backward, 61/1972. *Cf.* 'Sometime aside, and sometyme *arrere.*'—*Piers Plowman,* Text B. (E. E. T. S.), v. 354.

arerid, *pp.* raised, set up, 113/3764. A.S. *arœran.*

armys, *sb. pl.* harms, injuries, 96/3208.

Armys, lawe of, Heraldry, 81/2667.

a-ryn, *adv.* ? in a course, in order, 18/550, 19/569. A.S. *ryne,* a course. ? Cp. Yankee, 'around.'—F. J. F. See footnote, p. 18, and n te, p. 183.

as = as far as, 103/3414.

as, 75/2466; that.

a-say, *vb.* essay, try, 18/532; asay, 44/1396; assay, 54/1740, 67/2187; *imp. s.* asaye, 42/1318.

ascapen, *vb.* escape, 67/2188; *pp.* a-scapid, 118/3953.

a-scaunce, *conj.* as if, pretending that, 12/361; ascaunce, 51/1627, 59/1918; as skaunce, 55/1797.

a-sclakid, *pp.* abated, 39/1226.

a-servid, *pret. s.* ? deserved, 72/2371; *pp.* 73/2377, 95/3163.

a seyd, 113/3771, he saw? *See* seen.

a square, *adv.* on the square, aloof, 20/596, 21/643. *See* a-sware.

assoyll, *imp. s.* absolve, 53/1716.

assurid, *pp.* answered, satisfied, 113/3763.

a-stert, *vb.* escape, 20/611, 63/2058.

a-stonyd, *pp.* astonished, bewildered, 77/2544; -stonyed, 104/3455; stonyd, 64/2088.

Astrolages, *sb.* astrologers, 27/822.

a-stryvid, *pp.* divided, perplexed, 95/3164.

a-sware, *adv.* on one s'de, 19/586.

at, *prep.* to, 77/2536, 117/3913.

at, ? that, 119/3984.

a-tast, *vb.* taste, 15/458; a-tast, prove, test, 54/1745. O.F. *taster.*

a-tend, *vb.* set fire to, 83/2728. A.S. *atendan.*

ateyn, *vb.* reach, 103/3414; ateynt, *pp.* attainted, 102/3406; atteynt, 107/3586, 112/3752.

a-toon, be, *vb.* be at one, in accord, 71/2338.

atta, at a, 89/2945.

atte, at the, 1/14, *et passim.*

attonys, *adv.* at once, 79/2614, 74/3125.

a-vaile, *vb.* avail, help, 66/2151; *pres. s.* vaillith, 65/2098; vaylith, 116/3883, 118/3958.

auaunte, *adv.* forward, 61/1972.

auercH, April, 23/691. F. *Avril.*

auntir, auntris. *See* aventure.

aventure, *sb.* fortune, chance, 38/1185, 67/2195; aventur, 46/1470, 88/2913, 105/3517; auntir, 109/3639; *pl.* auntris, 103/3436. 'Awntyr or happe (aunter, P.). *Fortuna, fortuitus.*' — *Prompt. Parv.*

a-vise, *sb.* counsel, 80/2640.

avisely, *adv.* advisedly, 118/3946.

avowe, *sb.* vow, oath, 105/3506, 3514, 106/3543; a-vowe, 92/3049, 101/3353, 108/3599; *pl.* a-vowis, 105/3488, 3509.

aweynyd, *pp.* weaned, 39/1244.

a-weyward, *adv.* away, on one side, 77/2516.

axe, *vb.* require, exact, 8/219; *pres. s.* axith, 7/196, 14/403, 81/2654; *pres.* 1 *s.* axe, ask, 92/3071, 93/3090; 2 *s.* axist, 107/3580; *pret. s.* axid, 12/346, *et passim.*

axing, *sb.* request, 94/3126. A.S. *acsung.*

a-ȝe, *adv.* again, 43/1373, 62/2026, 111/3714, 111/3720; a-ye, 44/1384, 99/3276, 112/3729.

badder, *adj.* worse, 96/3187.

bafft, *adv.* abaft, 49/1576.

bale, *sb.* woe, sorrow, 58/1862, 118/3956. A.S. *bealu.*

ball, *sb.* head, 115/3860.

ballid, *pret. s.* smote, 33/1026. 'bollen, *O. Dutch* bollen?'—Stratmann. 'palle' = beat occurs in *Piers Plowman*, Text B. (E. E. T. S.), xvi. 30.

balstaff, *sb.* balk-staff, quarter-staff, 6/153. Mr. Vipan thinks that 'bal' may be a corruption of *pale* or *pail.* Cf. Cotgrave: 'Courge:... a Stang, *Pale-staffe,* or Colestaffe, carried on the shoulder, and notched (for the hanging of a Pale, &c.) at both ends.'

barme, *sb.* bosom, 75/2457. A.S. *bearm.*

barr, 93/3087, bar of a Court of Justice.

bate down, *vb* beat down, 76/2482.

'baw bawe!' a dog's bark, 98/3243.

be, *vb.* be, 102/3389; *pres.* 2 *pl.* been, are, 53/1722; beth, 53/1719, 115/3839; 3 *pl.* beth, 19/569, *et passim;* bethe, 100/3313; *imp. pl.* beth, be, 32/976, 50/1593, 87/2891, 88/2915; beith, 4/77; *subj. pres. s.* by, 108/3595; 2 *pl.* be, 4/96; *pp.* i-been, 35/1087; i-be, 43/1357; be, 4/81, 113/3902.

be, *prep.* by, 3/50, *et passim. See* by.

bede, *imp. pl.* offer, 69/2258. A.S. *beodan.*

be-dotid, *pp.* infatuated, 36/1137.

be-fele, *vb.* ? feel about, 18/536. See note, p. 183.

be-hest, *sb.* promise, 101/3353; behest, 76/2488, 91/3029; beheest, condition, 47/1510.

be-hongit, *pp.* hung round, 27/832; hongit a-bout, hung about, 21/636; hongit, adorned with trappings, 51/1632.

behote, *vb.* promise, 69/2252; by-hote, 75/2472; *pres.* 1 *s.* be-hote, 11/332; *pret. s.* be-hiȝte, 36/1126; *pret.* 2 *pl.* be-hete, 63/2059, 78/2562; behete, 117/3912; *pp.* behote, 77/2529. *See* hiȝte.

bekk, *sb.* obeisance, 46/1478.

be-menyd, *pret. s.* bemoaned, 33/1033.

be-nym, *vb.* take away, 64/2073; 79/2588; by-nym, 61/1981; *pp.* be-nome, 40/1279.

benyng, *adj.* benign, 120/4011.

bere, in, on the bier, dead, 85/2826.

bergeyne, *vb.* 105/3507; deal in, sell.

BERYN, or BERINUS, son of Faunus and Agea, his birth and bad upbringing, pp. 29-30; disreputable life, pp. 30, 34; unconcern at his mother's death, pp. 33-4; quarrels with his father, pp. 40-1; repents of his misdeeds, pp. 41-3; reconciled to his father, p. 45; releases his heirship for five ships-ful of merchandise, pp. 46-8; sails and meets with a storm, p. 49; lands at Falsetown, and is betrayed by Syrophane, a burgess, pp. 51-7; cheated by Hanybald, Provost of Falsetown, pp. 58-61; wrongfully accused by a blind man, pp. 62-4; and by a woman, pp. 65-6; duped by Macaign, a catchpoll, pp. 68-70; bewails his past life, pp. 71-2; meets Geffrey, a cripple, who offers to help him, pp. 73-8; he and his men distrust Geffrey, and prepare to sail, pp. 85-6; is angry with Geffrey, p. 91; appears for trial, p. 92 ; his trial detailed, pp. 93-116 ; is acquitted, and obtains damages from the plaintiffs, p. 116 ; his gratitude to Geffrey, p. 117 ; accepts the gifts and invitation of Duke Isope, but asks for a safe conduct, pp. 118-19 ; visits Isope, p. 119 ; marries his daughter, p. 120.

be-sey, *pp.* provided, adorned, 51/ 1632.

beshrewid, *pret. s.* cursed, 98/3252.

be-shyne, *vb.* shine on, 36/1113.

besines, *sb.* busyness, utmost endeavour, diligence, 78/2560 ; besynes, 74/2437.

bet, *adj.* better, 6/162, *et passim ;* better, 18/555 ; bettir, 20/596 ; bet like, *adj.* better like, more like, 88/2920.

be-þouȝt hir al about, carefully considered, 43/375. *See* bythynck.

be-tid, *pret. s.* happened, 27/813.

beuerage, *sb.* refreshment taken between dinner and supper, 12/359. *See* Halliwell, *s. vv.* ' Beverage ' and ' Bever.'

beyard, Bayard, a name for a horse, 96/3184. ' Bayart : M. Arde : f. as Bay, (*whence we also tearme a bay horse, a bayard*).'—Cotgrave.

blab, *sb.* 91/3022, chatter.

blabir, *sb.* chatter, prate, 99/3276.

blase, *vb.* blazon, describe arms properly, 6/150.

blenchid, *pret. s.* turned away, swerved, 98/3250 ; blynchid, 22/ 669 ; *imp. s.* blenche, 82/2713 ; *subj. pres.* 2 *pl.* blenchen, 110/ 3659.

bler, *vb.* blear, dim, 15/445. ' To blear ones eye, begyle him, enguigner.'—Palsgrave.

Blind man, a, of Falsetown seizes Beryn, and brings him before Evandir, pp. 62-4 ; his accusation of Beryn, pp. 95-6 ; agrees to share Beryn's goods, p. 101 ; his accusation answered by Geffrey, pp. 110-12 ; finds sureties for damages, p. 112.

blodcrid, *pret. s.* blubbered, 38/1196.

blowe vp, *vb.* sound loudly, 88/ 2906.

blowing, *sb.* 83/2742.

blyn, *vb.* cease, delay, 17/507, 58/ 1893. A.S. *blinnan.*

blynchid, *pret. s.* turned away. *See* blenchid.

blysyng, *verbal sb.* blazing, 18/ 561.

blyve, *adv.* quickly, 18/533, *et passim ;* blyve, *dissyl.* 33/1008.

bode, *pret. s.* stayed. *See* bood.

boncheff, *sb.* good fortune, 26/779, 117/3900.

bonet, *sb.* a small sail, 50/1604. See note, p. 189.

bood, *pret. s.* stayed, 47/1494, 87/ 2898 ; bode, 100/3320.

boon, *sb.* a die made of bone, 89/ 2957.

bord, *sb.* jest, 41/1304, 91/3022.

bord, *vb.* jest, 89/2941. O.F. *bourder.*

bord, *sb.* the side of a ship, 87/2886. Ovir þe bord, overboard.

borow, *sb.* surety, bail, 58/1876 ; *pl.* borowis, 112/3753, 113/3778, 115/3841.

borowe, *vb.* bail, 16/490.

bote, *sb.* remedy, help, 3/60, 118/ 3956. A.S. *bót.*

bote, *pret. s.* bit, 21/641, 60/1957, 101/3351.

bothen, *adj.* both, 3/67, *et passim ;* bothe to, both two, both, 17/506, *et passim.*

botirflijs, butterflies, 108/3613, 3617.

boune, *adj.* ready, 53/1698, 72/2344 ; boun, 81/2686 ; bown, 52/1678. O.N. *búinn.*

bountevouse, *adj.* bounteous, 120/ 4011.

bour, *sb.* chamber, 15/448 ; facetiously, for a dog's kennel, 22/668.

boystly, *adv.* rudely, boisterously, 5/104, 6/163.

bracyd, *pret. s.* embraced, 2/25, 46/ 1485, 52/1659.

braunce, *sb.* branch, 84/2785.

brede, *sb.* breadth, 17/528.

brennyng, *adj.* burning, 72/2351.

brent, *pp.* burnt, 72/2354.

breyde, *vb.* struggle, 56/1826 ; breyde a-wey, start away, 113/ 3775 ; *pret. s.* breyd vp, started up, 11/316 ; *pp.* i-brayid, out, drawn out, 118/3935. *See* Coleridge *s. v.* 'Braid,' and Stratmann *s. v.* 'Breiden.'

bribour, *sb.* thief, 17/524. *See* Prompt. Parv., *s. v.* 'Brybowre,' and note.

bridd, *sb.* bird, 27/814.

brigg, *sb.* bridge, 87/2897, 88/2923.

brithern, *sb.* brethren, 25/759; bretheryn, 26/765.

brode, *sb.* breeding, 6/160. See note, p. 179.

broke, *imp. s.* use, enjoy, 3/66. A.S. *brucan.* See Gloss. Index to *Havelok* (E. E. T. S.), *s. v.* 'Brouke.'

bronde, *sb.* brand from the fire, 19/585. 'Bronde of fire. *Facula, fax, ticio, torris,* C. F.'—*Prompt. Parv.*

Brooches and rings offered by the Canterbury pilgrims, 5/134.

brouȝt, 97/3212, got (with child).

brussh, *sb.* ? fluff, 46/1482. But Halliwell gives 'Brush (1) Stubble. *Staff.*'

bryng hym in, decoy him, 54/1750.

Burgess No. 2 of Falsetown, engages Beryn in talk, p. 53.

burgyn, *vb.* bud, 23/692.

burh, *sb.* borough, town, 25/744.

burrith, *pres. pl.* stick like burrs, 79/2601.

bussh, *vb.* push, 6/156.

but, *prep.* save, except, 3/44, *et passim;* but yf, 7/186, *et passim.*

but, *sb.* a drive, butt, thrust, push, 41/1287. Cf. *Havelok* (E.E.T.S.), l. 1040.

butte, but the, 14/410, 29/885, 49/1590, 98/3250.

by, *prep.* = in, 25/745, 65/2131; on, 64/2064; with, 75/2444, 100/3328; of, *de,* 1/10, 96/3185; be, 108/3598. *See* be.

by & by, one after the other, one by one, separately, 10/293. 'By and by. *Sigillatim*' (Prompt. Parv.). '*Sigillatim,* fro seel to seel.' (Medulla. Harl. MS. 2257).— Way. 'Two yonge knightes liggyng *by and by.*'—Chaucer, Knight's Tale, l. 153.

bye = ? but, 16/478. See note, p. 182.

bydë, *vb.* wait, 118/3956. Scanned as a dissyllable here.

by-nym. See be-nym.

bysely, *adv.* busily, diligently, 70/2279.

bythynch, *vb.* devise, bethink, provide, 36/1141; *pret. s.* be-þouȝt, 43/1375; *pp.* be-þouȝt, 108/3612.

byword, *sb.* proverb, 69/2243, 96/3183. *Cf.* comyn seying.

Caldey, Chaldee, 81/2662.

Canterbury brooches, 7/175. *See* signes.

Canterbury pilgrims, the, arrive at Canterbury, p. 1; their visit to the cathedral described, pp. 5-7; they dine, pp. 7-8; go out sight-seeing, pp. 9-10; sup, pp. 13-14; the steady pilgrims go to bed after supper, the rakes sit up drinking and singing, p. 14; they leave Canterbury, p. 22.

capes, *pres. s.* 1/8, ? feathers over at the top; cf. 'caping, caping-stone,' 'coping - stone.—F. capes = gapes.—W. W. S.

cardiakill, *sb.* heart-burn, 16/493. καρδιαλγία.

carnel ende, *sb.* death, end of life in the flesh, 81/2688.

case, *sb.* chance, fortune, 56/1805.

case, in case, if, 100/3316.

cast, *vb.* plot, 36/1141; *pp.* i-cast, 61/1964.

catell, *sb.* chattels, personal property, 61/1993, 66/2163, 116/3874.

cause to [*i. e.* to do so], 86/2860.

cautele, *sb.* artifice, 31/959; *pl.* cawtelis, 51/1658.

Centenarian, Geffrey a, 74/2439.

centence, *sb.* meaning, sentence, 1/3, 24/731.

chaffare, *sb.* merchandise, 73/2408.

char vp, *adv.* ajar, 12/355. 'Char. (3) Ajar. *North.*'—Halliwell.

charge, *sb.* care, thought, 5/125, 63/2034.

charge, *vb.* care for, 44/1387.

charge, *sb.* cargo, 59/1917.

charge, *vb.* load, 47/1512, 95/3146, 109/3637; *pp.* chargit, 70/2276.

chasid, *pret. s.* followed up, 91/3020. See note, p. 198.

chast, *vb.* chasten, 34/1058, 44/1396, 103/3440.

CHAUCER'S daisies, 22/683.

chaunce, *sb.* good fortune, 24/728. See note, p. 184.

chek, *sb.* trick, mischief, 16/471, 30/914.

Cheker-of-the-Hope, an inn at Canterbury, 1/14. See note, p. 176.

chekkir, *sb.* chess-board, 54/1735.

cher, have, *imp.* look cheerfully, kindly, 32/986.

chere, *sb.* entertainment, semblance, aspect, 2/25, *et passim.*

chere, *sb.* = chare, work, 18/538. See note, p. 183.

cherely, *adv.* dearly, 29/892.

chese, *vb.* choose, 37/1166, 58/1865, 1874; *pret. s.* 31/952; *imp. s.* 58/1869, 59/1925, 60/1947.

chese, *sb.* the chess-board and men, 54/1732; ches, /1733.

Chess-board, a, and its pieces described, 54/1733-34.

chircheward, churchward, 28/858. *See* -ward.

child, *sb.* page, 53/1709, 67/2189.

chokelyng, *pres. p.* gurgling, 14/413.

chongit, *pp.* changed, 27/812.

chynys, *sb.* chinks, corners, 72/2353.

Civil Law, rules of, 64/2068-70; 79/2596, 2602-7; 87/2866-70; 106/3531-33; twenty-four jurors learned in the law in a trial at, 115/3857.

clapp, *vb.* talk fast, prate, 74/2423; *pret. s.* clappid, 90/3005.

cleen, *adv.* completely, 88/2909. 'Men i-armyd cleen,' *i. e.* in full armour.

CLEKAM, Sir, a name given to Geffrey, 75/2450. ? from the clacking on the ground of his crutch, and the 'stilt under his knee,' 73/2380, or the beggar's clappers which he probably carried, or his tongue: 'Geffrey evir clappid, as doith a watir myll,' 90/3005. 'Claquette: f. A Lazers Clicket, or Clapper.' Cotgrave—F. See note, p. 195.

clepeist, 2 *pres. s.* callest, namest, 91/3024; *pret. s.* cleped, 3/65; clepid, 14/415, *et passim; pret. pl.* 92/3048; *imp. pl.* clepeth, 75/

2460; *pp.* i-clepid, 26/791, *et passim;* clepid, 27/805, *et passim.*

clepid ? *crepid,* crepitate, break wind, 27/810. See note, p. 186.

clerge, *sb.* learning, 9/252, 265; clergy, 83/2749.

Clerk, the, of Oxenford, defends the Friar's tale of a Summoner, p. 9.

cloith, *sb.* cloth, 117/3930.

cloute, *vb.* clout, patch, 97/3240.

clyȝte, *pret. s.* closed, clenched, 77/2515. From a *vb.* 'clicchen'— Strat. conj.

cold sot, cold sweat, 16/493.

colyn swerd, Cologne sword, 20/621. *See* footnote, p. 20.

comand, 'som comand,' some one coming, 74/2426.

comannd, *pres. p.* coming, 75/2451; comyng, 103/3418.

combirment, *sb.* embarrassment, 79/2604.

compers, *sb. pl.* fellows, 6/145; comperis, 51/1644, 107/3581. 'Compere, falawe (compyre, P.). *Compar, coequalis.'* — *Prompt. Parv.*

comyn seying, *sb.* proverb, 63/2037. *Cf.* byword.

comyng, to, *gerund. inf.* to come, 12/347. See Morris's *Historical Outlines of English Accidence,* 1877, p. 177 (4).

con, *vb.* acknowledge, give, 39/1227. In all other instances the *pres.* of this *vb.* = can *or* know; the *pret.* = could *or* knew.—1 *pres. s.* can, 3/60, *et passim;* 2 *pres. s.* canst, 6/155; *pres. s.* can, 7/183, *et passim;* conne, 118/3956; 1 *pres. pl.* con, 102/3408: 2 *pres. pl.* con, 12/343, 80/2636; *pres. pl.* can, 31/958; 1 *pret. s.* coud, 4/80, 11/326; coude, 51/1652; couthe, 70/2279; 2 *pret. s.* cowdist, 100/3336: *pret. s.* coude, 21/628, *et passim;* coud, 17/527, 51/1634, 69/2250, 81/2674; couth, 16/482, 65/2109; couthe, 37/1166; 2 *pl.* couth, 4/100; coude, 98/3274; *pret. pl.* coude, 22/667, 49/1581, 51/1628, 102/3381; coud, 62/2004: cowd, 77/2547; couth, 6/165, 60/1943; couthe, 27/817.

cond, *vb.* con luct, 119/3995.

congir, *vb.* conjure, 12/339 ; *pp.* i-congerid, 16/489.

connyng, *sb.* knowledge, wisdom, 11/308, 28/841, 38/1206, 49/1576, 83/2755, 100/3328, 103/3414.

consequent, *adv.* consequently, 88/2230.

CONSTANTINE III., emperor of Rome, 26/783.

contre, men of, men of [his own] country, 7/172 ; of contre, from [his own] country, 70/2294.

Cook, the, sits up drinking with the Miller, p. 14.

corage, *sb.* courage, daring, 16/470 ; heart, disposition, 30/914.

corouse, *adj.* curious, elaborate, 117/3924.

cors, *sb.* body, 52/1686 ; corps, 98/3246.

cosshon, *sb.* cushion, 52/1660.

cote, *sb.* bodice, 4/88.

cotelere, *sb.* 70/2297 ; cutler, 99/3296, 3303 ; 113/3792.

couchid, *pp.* set, 114/3794. *See* i-couchid.

coude no chere, knew no pleasure, 120/4005.

counselles, *adj.* without counsel, 71/2313 ; counsaillis, 55/1791 ; counsallis, 27/808

countid more with, accounted of, 28/842.

countirplede, *sb.* counterplead, 79/2602.

Court, the, at Falsetown opens at 9 a.m. 87/2878.

court ward, to the court, 92/3054. *See* -ward.

couthe, *adj.* known, 97/3231. A.S. *cuð.*

couʒid, *pp.* coughed, 11/323.

covenab.ll, *adj.* accordant, 9/246.

coverture, *sb.* cover, 37/1147.

crafft, *sb.* ? [sailors'] craft, business, skild trade, 49/1575. *Cp.* 'crafft of tanery,' tanner's trade, 97/2327. Or ' crafft' = *ship.*

crakid, *pp.* boasted, 23/706.

crane lyne, *sb.* the rope or line that ran over the pulley in the crane on board the ship, 90/2999.—F.

CRASSUS ASULUS, 27/805.

criour, *sb.* crier, 93/3084.

cripill, *sb.* cripple, 74/2439 ; crepill, 73/2379, &c.

cristyanite, *sb.* Christendom, 114/3794.

crope, *pp.* crept, 97/3232.

cros-saill, make, to haul the yards square across, 90/2995. *Cf.* 'wend þe saill a-cross,' 86/2837, *and* ' the saylis stonden al a-cros,' 87/2899. See note, p. 197.

crouch, *sb.* crutch, 73/2381, 76/2509 ; cruch, 86/2856.

cry, *sb.* proclamation, 109/3628.

cry, have the, obtain public notice and approval, 93/3080. Cp. ' *Cry, out of.* Out of all estimation . . . " I should have these maps *out o' cry now,* if we could see men peep out of door in 'em." — *Puritan,* iii. 5 ; Suppl. Sh. ii. 588.'—Nares.—F.

curtesy, *sb.* etiquette, 6/135 ; politeness, 11/323.

cury fauel, *sb.* flattery, currying favour, 12/362.

cusky, drouʒe to, ? went to sleep, 14/423. Urry, in his Gl., says (*s. v.*): ' the words (*to slepe*) which follow it seem to have been at first a Gloss in the margin for explaining the CB (Cambro-Briton or Welsh) *Cusky* or *Cysgu,* to sleep.'—F. J. Vipan.

cut, *sb.* horse, 41/1288.

cut, *sb.* ? lot, 41/1309. *See* Proverbs and Phrases, *s. v.* cut, and note on p. 189.

Cutler, a, of Falsetown, gives evidence for Macaign, p. 99.

daunser, *sb.* ? danger, liability to punishment, 79/2616. 'Quidquid jure stricto, atque adeo confiscationi obnoxium est sive ratione feudi, sive ex conductione : ita ut res dicatur esse in *dangerio domini* feudalis, quæ, nisi quod de ea statutum est adimpleatur, confiscari . possit.'—D'Arnis, *s. v.* ' Dangerium.'

daw, *sb.* day, 79/2585 ; *pl.* dawis, 25/733.

daw, do out of, kill, 79/2585.

dawnyng, *sb.* day dawn, 90/2991.

Decay of nature nowadays, 77/2518-20.

dede, maken al thing, make things quiet, pleasant, 37/1167.

dele, euery, every whit, 60/1934; euerydele, 59/1899; nevir a —, never a whit, 62/1996; no —, no whit, 11/307; som —, somewhat, 14/403. A.S. *dœl.*

dele, sorrow, 38/1183. *See* dole.

deme, *vb.* judge, 9/248, *et passim; pret. s.* demed, 119/3991; *pret. pl.* demed, 116/3872; demyd, 116/3865; *subj. pres.* 1 *pl.* deme, 116/3869; 2 *pl.* 103/3437; *pp.* i-demed, 4/96.

Denmark, Isope born in, 81/2673. See note, p. 195.

dentour, *sb.* indenture, 84/2791.

deol, sorrow. *See* dole.

depart, *vb.* part, divide, 44/1416, 101/3374, 102/3401, 106/3530; *pp.* departid, 69/2266.

dere. *vb.* harm, 59/1926, 84/2787. A.S. *derian.*

desperate, (?) *sb.* desperation, 105/3493.

dessautly, *adv.* constantly, 26/790, 49/1563. 'Dessable. Constantly. *North.'*—Halliwell. See note, p. 185.

desseyvabill, *adj.* deceitful, 50/1621, 51/1658.

deth-day, 40/1262.

devise, *sb.* skill, device, 80/2644, 83/2749.

devise, *vb.* contrive, describe, 83/2755; *pres.* 1 *s.* devise, 84/2767; *pres. p.* devising, 9/239.

devoir, *sb.* duty, 47/1487.

devyne, *vb.* describe, understand, 117/3924; 2 *pres. pl.* 90/2989.

deyse, *sb.* dais, 117/3931.

diete, *sb.* ? way of living, 45/1431.

dietes, *sb. pl.* days, 25/749.

diffence, *sb.* resistance, 61/1981.

dischauce yewe, *imp. pl.* ? take off your shoes, 16/471. F. *Déchausser.* See note, p. 181.

discryve, *vb.* describe, set forth, 35/1100, 81/2658.

disë, *sb. pl.* dice, 89/2953.

disese, *sb.* grief, vexation, 3/51, 27/817, 72/2371, 106/3552.

disfetirly, *adv.* misshapenly, 77/2515.

disfigure, *vb.* 76/2504.

disgisenes, *sb.* disguisedness, disguise, 77/2523.

diskennyng, (?) ignoring, 2/20. See note, p. 176.

diskeuerith, *imp. pl.* discover, 68/2231; *pres. p.* diskyueryng, 6/151.

dispiracioune, *sb.* desperation, 110/3680.

dissimilyng, *pres. p.* dissembling, 31/956.

distance, *sb.* discord, 87/2891.

disteynyd, *pp.* distained, defiled, 12/341.

distract, *pp.* distraught, 78/2555; distrakt, 102/3379.

disware, *adj.* unawares, doubtful, 83/2726, 92/3046, 98/3266. (In 83/2726, of = out of. See note, p. 196.)

docers, *sb. pl.* tapestry, 27/833. F. *dossier.* Lat. *dosserium.* See *Prompt. Parv.* s. vv. 'Docere' and 'Dorcere.'

doctryne, *sb.* wisdom, 39/1245, 81/2663.

Dog, the Welsh, at the Cheker-of-the-Hope, 21/631—51.

dole, *sb.* sorrow, 42/1331, *et passim;* dele, 38/1183; deol, 72/2363.

dome, *sb.* judgment, 65/2102, 77/2535; doom, 101/3376; *pl.* domus, 26/766; domes, 780.

doon, *vb.* do, cause, make, 5/118; do, 52/1684, 86/2859; *pres. s.* doith, 37/1151, 43/1371; *pres. pl.* doith, 23/692; doth, 37/1154; doon, 75/2462; *imp. pl.* doith, 6/158, 37/1151, 44/1384; *pp.* i-doon, 26/781, 62/2024; i-do, 52/1683, 88/2921; do, 18/471, 60/1951, 78/2573, 119/3984. *auxil. vb.* doith, 26/768, 83/2744. *See* to done *and* daw, do out of.

dore up = ? open. See note, p. 182.

dorward, towards the door, 16/477. *See* -ward.

Doseperis, Douzepairs, the Twelve Peers, 26/776; dosiperis, 783.

dotaunce, *sb.* fear, awe, 25/738. O.F. *doutance.*

dout, *vb.* fear, 9/240, 50/1599; 1 *pres. s.* dout, 72/2367; *imp. pl.* doutith, 69/2236.

doute, *or* dout, *sb.* doubt, fear, 10/279, 88/2915, *et passim;* dowte, 106/3530.

drad, feared, 67/2194. *See* drede.

drauʒte, *sb.* a move at chess, 55/1779, 56/1812.

Dreams go by contraries, 5/108.

drede, *vb.* fear, 12/337; 1 *pret. s.* dred, 3/55; *pret. s.* drad, 67/2194. *See* a-dred.

dres, *vb.* go, 51/1645, 93/3086; *pret. s.* dressid. made ready, 52/1660; *imp. s.* dres the, turn thee, 91/3032.

Drinking from the same cup, a sign of friendship, 93/3076.

dromodarijs, *sb. pl.* dromonds, swift vessels, 70/2275. See note, p. 193.

drouʒe, *pret. s.* made a move at chess, 56/1822; *imp.* draw, 56/1809.

dure, *vb.* endure, 55/1783; remain, 76/2503; *pres. p.* duryng, lasting, 105/3486.

dures, *sb.* hardship, 60/1934.

dwell, *vb.* remain, or listen. A.S. *dwellan.* See *Sir Tristrem,* Fytte III., stanza 72.

dyner while, dinner-time, 87/2881. *See* while.

dynerward, to dinner, 7/170. *See* -ward.

Dyonyse, a stone of a very cold nature, in Isope's hell, 83/2731. *See* Stone, a.

Ebrewe, Hebrew, 81/2661.

echone, each one, 2/38, *et passim;* echon, 21/655, 49/1569; echoon, 87/2883; echeon, 118/3937.

efft, *adv.* again, 80/2643; efft ageyn, again, 8/221, 44/1396, 55/1777, 78/2549; efft sone, soon after, 5/117; efft-sone, 11/326; efft-sonys, 116/3888.

egall, *adj.* equal, 35/1104.

egallich, *adv.* equally, justly, 26/781.

egge, *sb.* edge, margin, 19/587, 22/

679. 'egge of þe firmament,' horizon, 22/679.

egir, *adj.* eager, angry, 5/105. F. *aigre.*

elder more, older, 97/3240.

ellis, *adj.* else, other, 36/1122, 80/2624. See note, p. 195.

elyng, *adj.* wretched, 31/967. 'Dan. *elendig.* O.N. *eligr.*'—Coleridge, *s. v.* 'Eling.' 'þere þe catte is a kitoun. þe courte is ful *elyng.*'— Piers Plowman (E. E. T. S.), Text B. prol. l. 190.

encheson, *sb.* occasion, reason, 79/2590, 97/3218.

encombirment, *sb.* embarrassment, 113/3785.

ende *or* end, courteous, 47/1491, 52/1671. *See* hende.

endenting, *pres. p.* ? snapping, biting, 57/1851; *pp.* endendit, set, 99/3301. Fr. '*Endenter.* To indent, snip, notch, iag on the edges; also, to set or make teeth in.'— Cotgrave.

enditen, *vb.* speak, rehearse, 25/760; endite, 95/3162.

endlong, *adv.* along, 51/1634.

endreyte, *sb.* ? place (F. *endroit*), 14/404. endreyte ? = entreat = treatment.—F. J. Vipan.

endyng day, life's end, 32/974, 986. 'vourtene ʒer he[Edred] was kyng, and at ys *ende day,*' &c.—Robert of Gloucester, ed. 1810, p. 279, l. 3.

Engelond, England, 26/772.

England conquered by Julius Cæsar, 26/772.

engyne, *sb.* contrivance, 84/2758; gynne, 19/570; gyn, 82/2708.

engyne, *vb.* beguile, 47/1501, 68/2214, 76/2508; *pp.* engyned, 104/3479.

enpeche, *pres. pl.* impeach, 79/2590.

enpechement, *sb.* impeachment, 82/2703, 85/2795.

enpledit, *pp.* impleaded, 74/2415.

enselid, *pp.* sealed, 119/3980.

ensensid, *pp.* instructed, taught, 68/2213, 73/2406.

ensurid, *pret. s.* plighted troth, promised, bound, 69/2260; ensurid, *pp.* 63/2051, 80/2638; ensuryd, 36/1122, 85/2805.

entende, *vb.* understand, 26/777. F. *entendre.*

ententiflich, *adv.* attentively, 9/239; entyntyflich, 104/3483.

entere, *vb.* bury, 34/1047 ; *pp.* enterid, 35/1089.

enteryng, *sb.* burial, 34/1046.

er, *adv.* ere, 116/3888. *See* or.

ere, *sb.* ear, 8/205, 33/1022 ; *pl.* eris, 22/660, 56/1800, 100/3324. 'Leyd to his ere,' listened intently, 8/205.

ere, *sb.* hair, 42/1350.

ertly, *adj.* earthly, 37/1175.

estate, *sb.* condition in life, rank, 44/1387, 80/2651, ; *pl.* estatis, 15/442 ; statis, 2/19 ; states, 6/140.

estris, *sb. pl.* inner parts of a house, chambers, 18/556, 28/837.

ethir-is, either's, 5/126. *Cf.* ffifft-is, *s. v.* ffifft ; *and* his.

EVANDIR, Steward of Falsetown, hears Syrophanes's charge against Beryn, pp. 57-8 ; and the blind man's charge, pp. 63-4 ; and the deserted wife's, pp. 65-6 ; and Macaign's accusation, pp. 69-71 ; presides at Beryn's trial, pp. 93—115 ; gives judgment against Syrophanes, p. 107 ; goes to see Hanybald's merchandise, p. 107 ; advises him to restore Beryn's goods, p. 109 ; consults burgesses learned in the law, and gives judgment for the defendant, p 116.

eve a-fore, on the evening before, 82/2701.

euen long, *adv.* straight along, 62/2007.

evenaunte *adj.*, F. *avenant*, seemly, 28/837.

everich, *adj.* each one, every, 5/132, 6/140, 39/1212, 40/1256, 117/3922.

everichone, each one, every one, 23/689, 61/1986 ; everichon, 102/3382, 109/3641 ; everychon, 92/3068 ; evirichon, 94/3130 ; euery-choon, 26/792 ; everichoon, 60/1948 ; every-choon, 94/3112.

euery dele, everydele, every whit, 59/1899, 60/1934. *See* dele.

evese, *sb.* eaves, 72/2354.

evil, *adv.* evilly, ill, 33/1012.

evil, ? read 'well', Urry's correction, 73/2398.

evill-thewid, *adj.* ill given, of evil habits, 67/2177. A.S. *yfel* and *þeáw.*

evir more a-mong, at intervals, 110/3686. *See* a-amongis.

excellent, *pres. p.* excelling, 36/1110 ; *adj.* 36/1114.

ey, *sb.* eye, 56/1800 : *pl.* eyen, 2/34, *et passim ;* eye, 111/3724 ; yen, 63/2047.

eye. *sb.* awe, restraint, 34/1053. A.S. *ege. See* hey.

factur, *sb.* capability, 9/247. '*Facture :* f. The facture, workmanship, framing, making of a thing;' . . .—Cotgrave. See note, p. 179.

fale, many, 39/1224. *See* fele.

fallace, *sb.* deceit, 60/1944. Lat. *fallacia.*

Falsetown men, the, their device for beguiling strangers, 50-1/1623-28 ; back one another in swearing falsely, 79/2589-2601 ; for fear of Isope, 2610-16 ; Geffrey and Beryn tame them, 120/4017-20.

fare, *sb.* demeanour, 31/967.

fare, *vb.* go, 82/2699 ; *imp. pl.* farith feir, go on fairly, go softly, 57/1831.

fast, *adv.* diligently, earnestly, 87/2881, 119/3985. *Cf.* Barbour's *Bruce,* i. 42.

FAUNUS, senator of Rome, marries Agea, p. 28 ; spoils his son Beryn, pp. 29-30 ; receives Agea's dying injunctions, p. 32 ; is grieved at Beryn's disreputable life, p. 35 ; marries Rame, p. 36 ; lectures Beryn and threatens to disinherit him, pp. 39-40 ; is reconciled to Beryn, and agrees to set him up as a merchant, pp. 45-6, carries out the agreement, p. 48.

faute, *sb.* fault, 57/1838.

fawe, fain, 62/2022, 120/4017. *See* feyn.

fay, *sb.* faith, 24/720, 63/2032, 90/3003, 96/3193, 100/3338 ; fey, 58/1886, 109/3648.

feir, *sb.* fire, 38/1187 ; feire, 18/551 ; feer, 72/2355.

fele, *adj.* many, 96/3177, 3205, 97/

3221, 110/3667 ; fale, 39/1224
('I sey no fale,' I say not many
[words].) A.S. *feala.* 'Fale.'—
Robert of Gloucester, ed. 1810,
p. 146, l. 4.

fele, *vb.* meditate, 61/1988.

fell (*for* fill), full, 90/3006.

fellich, *adv.* felly, cruelly, 11/311.

fenaunce. *See* fynaunce.

fences, *sb. pl.* ? defences, prohibitions, 27/824. See note, p. 186.

fentyse, *sb.* deceit, 47/1487. O.F. *faintise.*

fere, *sb.* companion, 13/389, 31/966, 37/1174, 46/1476, 52/1683 ; *pl.* feris, 96/3201.

ferforth, *adv.* fully, far, 24/731, 76/2503, 85/2807, 94/3134, 114/3799, 116/3875.

ferm. *pres. pl.* affirm, 79/2615.

ferth, fourth, 27/809, 49/1570, 113/3764, 117/3929.

fese a-wey, *vb.* drive away, 12/351. A.S. *fêsian.*

fet, *pret. s.* fetched, 3/61 ; *pl.* 86/2849 ; *pp.* i-fett, 29/890 ; i-fet, 44/1395.

fetously, *adv.* skilfully, 6/141. O.F. *adj.* faictis.

feyn, *adj.* fain, 86/2864, 100/3334, 108/3607, 116/3896 ; fawe, 62/2022, 120/4017.

feyn, *vb.* ornament, trill, 3/70. (E.E. feȝen.)—F. See note, p. 177.

feyner, *adj.* fainer, readier, 65/2124.

feynyd, *pret. s.* (?) for *feyndyd,* attempted, 6/141. See note, p. 178.

ffeer, *vb.* terrify, 33/1013.

ffifft, fifth, 95/3158 ; ffifft-is, fifth's, 27/815. Cf. ethir-is, *and* his.

ffrauk, *sb.* 39/1228. '*Franc:* A peece of money worth, in old time, but one Sol Tournois ['the tenth part of our shilling.' — *Cotg.*]; now it goes for twentie ; which amount vnto ij s. sterl.'— Cotgrave.

ffrountis, *sb. pl.* fronts, 50/1609. 'Frownt, or frunt of a churche or oþer howsys. *Frontispicium,* C. F. Cath.'—*Prompt. Parv.*

fikil, *adj.* deceitful, 41/1283.

fill, *adj.* full, 94/3117 ; fell, 90/3006.

fisnamy, *sb.* physiognomy, 96/3196.

fit, *sb.* turn, tustle, 41/1309. 'So mery a fytt [of swiving] ne had sche nat ful yore.' — Chaucer, *Reeves Tale,* l. 310.—F.

flaptaill, *sb.* whore, 41/1283 : cf. Fr. '*Culeter.* To wag or stirre the buttockes vp and downe ; to moue the taile in a wanton time, or with the taile keep time vnto a wanton musicke.'—Cotgrave.—F.

flood, *sb.* sea, 53/1718 ; salt flood, 92/3058.

floure, *sb.* flower, 111/3694 ; *pl.* flouris, 23/692. O.F. *flour.*

flowe, *pp.* flown, 108/3616.

fnese, *vb.* sneeze, 2/42. 'fneosen, *sternuere.*' — Stratmann (quoting 'fnese' in *Beryn,* 2/42). See note, p. 176.

fole of kynde, a natural fool, 89/2967 ; see l. 2937-8.

fonde, *vb.* seek, 82/2698 ; *pret. s.* fond, 17/529. A.S. *fandian.*

Fools have shorn heads, 102/3407, 103/3426, 113/3779.

foon, *sb. pl.* foes, 26/771 ; ffoon, 80/2630.

for, *prep.* = on account of, 2/34, 3/51, 15/440, 21/644, 72/2358, 97/3241 ; ffor, 32/973 ; ffor = ? from, 28/854 ; = in spite of, 112/3759 : *conj.* = because, 43/1370, 63/2052 ; ffor = in order that, 7/172.

forby, *adv.* near, 83/2728.

fore stage, *sb.* forecastle, fore part of the ship, 88/2934.

for-in, *adj.* ? foreign, 90/2989.

formally, *adv.* in good form, 104/3457.

fors, no, no matter, 13/396, 61/1984 ; no force, 72/2375.

for-skramyd, *pp.* shrunk, distorted, 73/2381. *Scram,* distorted (Westmoreland) ; *scrambled,* deprived of the use of some limb by a nervous contraction of the muscles.—F.

Fortifications of Canterbury inspected by the Knight and his companions, 9/237-44.

FORTUNE, 31/943.

fourm, *sb.* form, making, 9/247 ; fourm of kynde, natural disposition, *ib.*

fourm, *sb.* form, bench, 93/3079.

fray, *vb.* frighten, 33/1013; be afraid, 42/1335.

frelich, *adj.* freely, unconcernedly, 33/1024.

frendshipp, *sb.* friends, 106/3526.

Friar, the, tries to take the holy water sprinkler at the church door, p. 6; has his eye on the Summoner, p. 7; reminds the Host of his promised supper, p. 8; visits an acquaintance of the Monk, p. 10.

Friars, knavery of, alluded to, 12/362; compared to the Falsetown men, 51/1643-4.

ful riȝte, *adv.* straight, 48/1546.

fynall, *adj.* last, 80/2624.

fynaunce, *sb.* fine, penalty, 64/2079, 79/2610; fenaunce, 77/2534.

fynd, *vb.* provide for, 65/2120, 97/3219.

fyne, *vb.* pay a fine, 64/2078, 92/3062.

fyne, *or* ffynys, to make, pay a fine, 115/3851, 116/3872.

fyne force, of, of necessity, 65/2110.

gagid, *pret. s.* gave security to abide judgment, 113/3778.

gall, *sb.* gall, ill humour, 14/402, 43/1382, 48/1552. A.S. *gealla.*

galle, *sb.* gall, sore place, 37/1150; gall, 107/3564. 'galle, *O. Icel.* galli, *gall, vitium, vulnus.*' — Stratmann.

game, *sb.* jest, 57/1843, 89/2941, 98/3263.

game, set a [of chess], set the chessmen in their places, 54/1744.

gamyd, *pret. pl.* jested, 95/3160.

Garden of the 'Cheker of the Hope' described, 10/289-294.

gascoyn, *sb.* Gascon wine, 10/280.

GEFFREY, the sham cripple of Falsetown, pursues Beryn, and offers to help him, pp. 73-6; his surprising activity, pp. 76-7; promises his help if Beryn will take him back to Rome, pp. 77-8; his account of the Falsetown men, and their duke Isope, pp. 79-82; and of Isope's house, pp. 82-5; sets off on a visit to Isope, p. 85; returns and blames Beryn for his

faint-heartedness, p. 87; plays the fool before the Falsetown men, pp. 88-9; bandys words with Hanybald, p. 90; chaffs Hanybald and Beryn, pp. 91-2; Evander, p. 93; the plaintiffs generally, p. 94; Hanybald, p. 95; the blind man, p. 96; and Beryn, about his wife and son, pp. 97-8; encourages Beryn, pp. 98-9; says he'll make the plaintiffs smart, p. 100; comforts Beryn and the Romans, p. 102; answers Syrophanes, pp. 103-6; outwits Hanybald, pp. 107-9; answers the blind man, pp. 110-12; poses Beryn's sham wife, p. 113; turns the tables on Macaign, pp. 113-15; tells Beryn what answer to send to Isope, p. 118.

ges, *vb.* guess, 65/2121, *pres.* 1 *s.* 66/2153.

gesolreut, 57/1837,? G, *sol* (G), *re* (D), *ut* (C).

'Qwan ilke note til other lepes ·
　and makes hem a-sawt,
That we calles a *moyson* · in
　gesolreutȝ en hawt.'
　　Reliquiæ Antiquæ, i. 292.—F.
See note, p. 191.

gist, *sb.* guest, 15/461; *pl.* gistis, 18/550.

gladder, *adj.* more glad, 93/3078. *See* long the gladder.

glose, *vb.* deceive, speak falsely, 31/958, 54/1741.

glow, *vb.* ? read *clow* = *claw*, 41/1308. See note, p. 188.

glyde, *vb.* pass by, 20/608; downe glyde, slip down, 74/2427.

goglyng, *pres. p.* ? shaking, wagging, 6/163.

gonde, going, 19/574. *See* goon.

gonne, *sb.* gun, 9/241.

good, *sb.* property, wealth, 64/2075, 81/2677, 116/3876.

Good old days, 77/2518-20.

goodshipp, *sb.* goodness, 40/1247.

goon, *vb.* go, 5/104, 89/2958, 113/3788; 1 *pres. s.* goon, 26/791; *pres. s.* gone, 13/374; 1 *pres. pl.* goon, 115/3855; *pres. p.* gonde, 19/574; gond, 31/944; *pp.* ago, 20/599, 114/3799; a-go, 40/1265,

70/2277; a-goo, 91/3033; i-goo, 84/2782; go, 76/2505, 85/2812.

governaunce, *sb.* behaviour, conduct, 9/248, 102/3399, 119/3990; ? self-control, 71/2337; good management, 82/2694; control, discipline, 87/2892.

grace, *sb.* aid, succour, 64/2066.

graine, *sb.* grief, 22/673, 29/896. A.S. *grama*.

gre, *sb.* pleasure, 63/2060.

Greece, Isope brought up in, 81/2674-75.

gren, *sb.* gin, snare, 116/3394. *See* Halliwell, *s. v.* 'Green.' Dame Julocke said of the trap in which Tibert was caught, 'in the deucles name was the *grynne* there sette / &c.'—Caxton's *Reynard the Fox*, Cap. x., Arber's ed., p. 22.

grenyth, *pres. pl.* grow green, 23/687.

grete clerge, much learning, 9/252. *See* clerge.

Grew, Greek, 81/2661.

greynyd, *adj.* dyed in grain, *i. e.* scarlet, 92/3065.

grise, *vb.* be horror-struck, 66/2140, 85/2801. A.S. *agrisan*.

groundit, *pp.* established, 25/757.

groundly, *adv.* deeply, seriously, 120/4001.

guerdon, *sb.* reward, 76/2486.

guy, *vb.* guide, 46/1458.

GYLHOCHET, a name Geffrey gives himself, 92/3048, 103/3421; Gylhoget, 100/3315; Gylochet, 3336.

gyn, gynne, contrivance, 19/570; 82/2708. *See* engyne.

hale, *vb.* haul, pull, 49/1581, 57/1831, 90/2997, 2999, 91/3016; *pret. s.* halid, 2/27; *pp.* hale, 89/2948; halyd, 114/3817.

halffyndele. *sb.* half-part, 35/1084. A.S. *healf*, half, and *dael*, part.

halk, *sb.* corner, 44/1407.

halowid, *pp.* halloo'd, shouted for, 2/21.

halsow, *vb.* predict, interpret, 5/107. 'hálsien, *A.Sax.* hálsian, hélsien (*augurari, obsecrare*), &c.' — Stratmann. 'Halson. To promise or bid fair, good, or bad; to predict. *Devon.*'—Halliwell.

halue, *sb.* half, side, 64/2064; helve, 67/2178.

HANYBALD, Provost of Falsetown, cheats Beryn, pp. 58-61; sees Beryn preparing to sail, and stops him, pp. 87-8; his word-fence with Geffroy, p. 90; asks Geffrey his name, p. 92; states his case against Beryn, pp. 94-5; claims the whole of Beryn's goods, p. 101; is outwitted by Geffrey and gives Beryn sureties for damages, pp. 108-10; says he shall never recover his losses, p. 116.

hap, *sb.* chance, ill-fortune, 11/302, 38/1185, 61/1990, 67/2198; *pl.* happis, 73/2400; happous, 67/2178.

hap, *vb.* happen, 54/1739.

harmys, held hym to his, 22/674, ? kept his injuries to himself. See note, p. 184.

harowe, out &, 62/2010. 'Harowe now, out and well away! he cryde, &c.'—*Faerie Queene*, II. vi. 43.

HARPOUR, the late Mr. Jenkyn, tribute paid to his memory by his wife, Kit the Tapster, p. 16.

hauntid, 1 *pret. s.* frequented, 71/2319. F. *hanter*.

haut, *adj.* high, 57/1837. F. *haut.*

havith, *subj. pres.* 2 *pl.* have, 69/2243; *pp.* i-had, 30/903, 63/2050.

hazard, *sb.* dice-play, 30/924, 38/1211.

hazardours, *sb. pl.* dicers, 44/1408.

hazardry, *sb.* dice-playing, 40/1250.

he, *pron.* ? she, 23/690. A.S. *heo*.

he, *pron.* they, 85/2826, 94/3111. A.S. *hi*.

hegg, *sb.* hedge, 1/8.

hele, *sb.* health, welfare, 3/46, 15/466.

hele, *vb.* conceal, 70/2293, 96/3195. A.S. *helan*.

helve, side, 67/2178. *See* halue.

hem, *pron.* them, 1/4, *et passim*; ham, 7/178.

hem, ? for *adv.* here, 9/264.

hen, *adv.* hence, 60/1930.

hend, *adj.* courteous, gentle, 10/287; ende, 47/1491; end, 52/1671.

hent, *pret. s.* caught, 74/2424, 2429; *pp.* i-hent, 2431.

her, their, 49/1569. *See* hir.

herbegage, *sb.* inn, lodging, 13/379, 21/627. O.F. *herberjage.* L. Lat. herbergagium. — Roquefort, *s. v.* 'Heberge.'

herbery, *sb.* herb-garden, 10/289. O.F. *herbier, herberie.*—Roquefort.

hert fill, heart's fill, 90/3006, 94/3117.

hertiest, *adj.* most courageous, 84/2777.

hertis rote, heart's root, 3/59.

hertis swete, *sb.* sweetheart, 48/1536.

hertly, *adj.* hearty, 8/201, 37/1173, 118/3949.

hest, *sb.* promise, command, 88/2901, 101/3362, 105/3514, 119/3971.

hey, *sb.* (A.S. *ege*) awe, restraint, 30/903. *See* eye.

hir, hire, *pron.* her, 2/25, 39, *et passim.*

hir, *pron.* their, 1/13, *et passim;* her, 49/1569.

hire, *adv.* here, 17/517.

his, the genitive in *es*, 62/2003, 112/3732. *Cf.* ethir-is; *and* ffifft-is, *s. v.* ffifft.

hit, *pron.* it, 29/892. *Cf.* hown.

hiȝe noon, i. e. *midday*, or the tip-top point of the wheel of fortune, 31/945.—W. W. S.

hiȝte, *pret. s.* named, 27/799.

hiȝte, 2 *pret. s.* promised, 102/3397; hiȝte, *pp.* 106/3540. *See* behote.

ho, *pron.* who = whoever, 106/3520.

holich, *adv.* wholly, 1/6; hoolich, 116/3873.

Holy Roman Empire, 25/733-42.

Holy Sepulchre, pilgrimages to the, 105/3489.

hond, *vb.* lay hands on, handle, 62/2020; *pres. s.* hondis, 118/3946.

honde, *sb.* hand, 48/1532, 58/1880; hond, 57/1838; *pl.* hondis, 2/37.

hongit. *See* be-hongit.

honoure, *sb.* fief, domain, 28/849, 40/1261, 46/1469; honour, 48/1524, 72/2358. 'Honor, * * * *fief, domaine.*'—Roquefort.

hoost, *sb.* inn, 10/294. O.F. *ost* or *host,* inn, hostel.

hoot, *adj.* hot, 41/1317.

Horse, a gentle heart's feeling towards his, 52/1686-88.

Host, the, orders the pilgrim's dinner, p. 2 ; reproves the irreverence of the Pardoner and his friends, p. 6 ; promises the pilgrims a supper at Southwark, p. 8 ; sends the noisy pilgrims to bed, p. 14 ; his rhapsody on the fine morning, pp. 22-3 ; wants some one to tell the first tale, p. 23.

hown, *adj.* own, 38/1179. *Cf.* hit.

howsing, *sb. pl.* housen, houses, 27/831. Here out-buildings are most likely meant.

huch, *pron.* which, 7/176, 17/517.

huche, *sb.* chest, 76/2510. F. '*Huche,* a Hutch or Binne.'—Cotgrave.—F. 'That Arke or *Hucche* * * * Tytus ledde with hym to Rome,' &c. *Maundevile,* ed. Halliwell, 1866, p. 85.

hul by hul, side by side, 15/455.

hullid, *pret. s.* covered, embraced, 46/1477. O.H. Germ. *hullen;* pret. *hulda.* — Stratmann, *s. v.* 'hulien.' See note, p. 190.

husst, *pp.* husht, 92/3067.

hy, *vb.* hie, haste, 109/3631 ; hiȝe, 39/1236; *imp.* hyen, 95/3170.

hyust, *interj.* hist! 18/536.

[*Some past participles are here collected.*]

i-answerd, *pp.* answered, 94/3111.

i-armyd, *pp.* armed, 88/2909.

i-blowe, *pp.* blown, in blossom, 41/1315.

i-bore, *pp.* managed, 116/3875.

i-bound, *pp.* bound, 99/3294.

i-brayid, drawn, 118/3935. *See* breyde.

i-cappid, *pp.* wearing caps or hoods, 55/1772.

i-cast, plotted, 61/1964. *See* casten.

i-closid, *pp.* closed, 82/2721.

i-colerid, *pp.* coloured, disguised, 51/1658.

i-congerid, conjured, 16/489. *See* congir.

i-couchid, *pp.* set, 99/3300; couchid, 114/3794.

i-demed, judged, 4/96. *See* deme.

i-di3te, *pp.* put to rights, set in order, equipped, made ready, 22/657, 37/1172, 45/1437, 52/1687; in-dight, 88/2927. A.S. *dihtan.*

i-dyned, *pp.* dined, 87/2883.

i-entrid, *pp.* entered, 112/3760.

i-esid, *pp.* eased, 80/2628.

i-ete, *pp.* eaten, 84/2782.

i-fett, fetched, 29/890. *See* fet.

i-fourmyd, *pp.* formed, 84/2761.

i-frethid, *pp.* protected, 10/292. A.S. , *freoðian,* to set apart, protect.

i-fretid, *pp.* fretted, 117/3926.

i-goo, gone, 84/2782. *See* goon.

i-hent, caught, 74/2431. *See* hent.

i-herd. *See* i-here (below).

i-here, *vb.* hear, 91/3021 ; *pp.* i-herd, 115/3863. A.S. *gehéran.*

i-hold, *pp.* held, thought, 93/3082; bound, obliged, 108/3595.

i-hurid, *pp.* wearing headgear, 55/1772. 'HOWE, or hure. heed hyllynge.'—*Prompt. Parv.* See the note thereon, and also *Halliwell,* s. v. HURE.

i-iapid, mocked, 104/3459. *See* iapid.

i-ioyned, *pp.* joined, 82/2721.

i-knet. *See* i-knyt.

i-knowe, known, 91/3037. *See* knawe.

i-knyt, *pp.* knit, *i. e.* married, 40/1280; i-knet, knotted, 89/2947.

i-lassid, *pp.* lessened, 25/754; lassid, 3/44.

i-led, *pp.* laden, 48/1526.

i-lerid, *pp.* learned, 101/3364, 115/3857. *See* lere.

i-leve, ? *pp.* lived, 65/2121.

i-loggit, lodged, 5/131, 11/304, 13/374. *See* loggit.

i-loke, *pp.* locked, embraced, 96/3207.

i-lore, lost, 39/1216. *See* lese.

i-lost, *pp.* lost, 113/3784.

i-makid, *pp.* made, 10/291.

i-massid, *pp.* when it was al, when mass was over, 5/102.

i-matid, *pp.* mated at chess, 54/1749, 55/1767, 93/3093, 105/3512.

i-merkid, *pp.* stamped, as a coin is, 15/434.

i-met, *pp.* met, 92/3056.

i-mevid, spoken, 8/199, 82/2704, 112/3758. *See* meve.

i-mynt, *pp.* minted, 15/434.

i-myryd, *pp.* ? bemired, stuck in the bog, 102/3388.

i-myssid, *pp.* misst, misstated, 104/3449.

i-nayid, *pp.* denied, 86/2829.

i-paid, *pp.* paid, 71/2320.

i-parid, *pp.* adorned. 10/291. F. *parer.*

i-peynyd, distressed, 63/2046. *See* peyne.

i-pikid, *pp.* cleansed, brushed up, 54/1734. 'PYKYD, or purgyd fro fylthe, or oper thynge grevows. *Purgatus.'*—*Prompt. Parv.*

i-pilt, *pp.* struck, 18/559. *See* Stratmann, *s. v.* 'bulten.'

i-pleynyd, complained, 63/2045. *See* pleyne.

i-previd, *pp.* proved, 112/3738.

i-pulsshid, *pp.* polished, 54/1734.

i-rasid, *pp.* shaved, 88/2936, 91/3032. F. *raser.*

i-rau3t, caught, 73/2389. *See* rau3te.

i-rayd, *pp.* arrayed, 88/2927.

i-raylid, *pp.* railed, 10/291.

i-seelid, *pp.* ? settled (Urry reads *ysetlid*), 78/2583. 'i-secled,' became sick. *Laȝamon,* 30549.—F.

i-sesid, *pp.* possessed, 58/1880; sesid, 48/1549, 63/2061.

i-set, seated, 92/3055. *See* sat.

i-set, fixed, 26/798; set, 54/1746. *See* setten.

i-shethid, *pp.* sheathed, in a scabbard, 117/3925.

i-sod, ? buried, 39/1217. A.S. *seoðan.* See note, p. 188.

i-sotyd, *pp.* besotted, 36/1138.

i-spilt, *pp.* ruined, 75/2452. A.S. *spillan.*

i-spronge, spread, 68/2213. *See* sprang.

i-steryd, *pp.* steered, 107/3564.

i-swept, *pp.* swept, 108/3590.

i-take, taken, 63/2042, 98/3248. *See* take.

i-thankid, *pp.* thankt, 117/3903.

i-told, *pp.* told, said, 69/2258.

i-went, brought about, 40/1264; contrived, 48/1522. *See* wenden.

i-wrou3t, *pp.* done, 91/3009, 102/3385.

ilche, *adj.* same, 1/11, *et passim;* ilke, 46/1467, *et passim;* ilk, 5/119, 116/3889.

i-lich, *adj.* like, 25/736; lich, 114/3796; liche, 117/3930; lych, 28/836.

i-lich, *adv.* alike, 14/402.

i-lome, *adv.* frequently, 41/1312; lome, 53/1701, 65/2101, 67/2191, 70/2275; lom, 11/330. A.S. *gelome.*

imaginacioun, *sb.* image, simile, 34/1061.

in, *prep.* upon, 65/2109, 67/2197.

in fere, together, 10/268, 277, 50/1603, 60/1940, 91/3025; in feer, 15/433; i-fere, 74/2421.

in hast, in haste, quickly, 82/2718.

in parcell. *See* parcell.

in town, at hand, 2/18. See note, p. 176.

in-dight, equipped, 88/2927. *See* i-diȝte.

influence, *sb.* inflow, quantity, 77/2527.

inlich, *adv.* inly, deeply, 28/867; inly, 47/1515, 80/2643.

inner, more within, further inside, 84/2790.

innocent, *sb.* innocence, 68/2207.

i-nowe, *adv.* enough, 8/220; i-nowȝe, 17/529.

insoluble, *adj.* unanswerable, unsolvable, 80/2622.

intelleccioune, *sb.* mind, will, 75/2473.

into, *prep* unto, 48/1533, 98/3268, 119/3976; in-to, 40/1272, 50/1592, 92/3054, 110/3687.

isope, *sb.* hyssop, 10/292.

ISOPE, Duke, Geffrey's account of him and his house, pp. 80-5; sends an embassy to Beryn with presents, pp. 117-18; and a safe conduct, p. 119; weds his daughter to Beryn, p. 120.

it *for* he, used in speaking of a child, 97/3237.

iangill, *vb.* prate, 99/3280; *pres. p.* iangelyng, 57/1851; ianglyng, 92/3054. 'Jangler, * * * blâmer, jaser, caqueter, bavarder, * * * railler, plaisanter, se moquer; joculari.'—Roquefort.

iape, *sb.* jest, 62/2012; *pl.* iapis, 1/7, 103/3428.

iapid, *pret. s.* jested, mocked, 89/2969; *pp.* i-iapid, 104/3459.

iogelour, *sb.* juggler, 111/3693.

Judges should be like Marcus Stoycus, 27/804.

iugg, *sb.* judge, 107/3561.

JULIANE, S., besoⁿght by the Pardoner to send the Tapster to the devil, 21/626.

IULIUS CEZAR, 26/766; Cezare, 773.

iuly, *adj.* gay, lively, 74/2441. O.F. *jolif.* 'So iuly [marginal collation ynly] fayre she was of her fygure.' — Hardyng's *Chronicle,* ed. Ellis, 1812, 124/15.

karff a too. *pret. s.* carved or cut in two, 19/588. A.S. *ceorfan.*

karse, *sb.* cross, 31/971. A.S. *cerse.*

keke, *vb.* look hard at, 29/900.

kelen, *vb.* cool, 16/470. A.S. *célan.*

kenebowe, in, akimbo. 57/1838.

kepe, *sb.* care, 72/2356.

kepe, *pres.* 1 *s.* care, 15/465.

keueryng, *sb.* covering, ceiling, 83/2723.

kiss : men kiss each other to settle an agreement, 78/2572. Cf. *tuk le meyn.*

kissid, *pret. pl.* kissed, licked, as flames do, 72/2354.

kist, *pret.* 1 *s.* cast, 89/2955; 3 *s.* 70/2283.

Kitt, ? a name for an amorous damsel, 3/66. Cf. 15/443, 33/1011.

kitt, *pret. s.* cut, 13/393.

knave child, male child, 96/3207.

knawe, ? *vb.* acknowledge, display, 84/2758. (See note, p. 196.) *pp.* i-knowe, 91/3037.

Knight, the, settles the precedence of the pilgrims at the church door, p. 6; changes his clothes and goes into the town, p. 8; criticises the fortifications, p. 9; ironically commends the Clerk's defence of the Friar, p. 9; acts as Marshall at supper, p. 13.

knor, *sb.* swelling in the flesh, 76/2514. 'cnarre, L. Germ. knarre, knar (gnar), tuber, vertex;' &c.—Stratmann.

knot, *sb.* ' knotte yn the fleshe, vndyr th skynne. *Glandula.*'—*Prompt. Parv.* 76/2514.

knowlechid, *pp.* acknowledged, 115/3833.

kynd, *adj.* natural, 72/2345.

kynde, *sb.* nature, natural disposition, 9/247, *et passim ;* kynd, 6/160, 96/3196.

laid their heads together, consulted, 118/3960.

lakk, ? fault, 52/1682. See note, p. 191.

lap, *sb.* skirt, 70/2286.

las & more, less and greater, 49/1578, 53/1696, 68/2212. *Cf.* les or more.

lassh, *pret. s.* let, shed, 2/34. O.Fr. *lascher,* laxare. *See* Stratmann, s. v. ' lasken.'

lassid, lessened, 25/754. *See* i-lassid.

last, *sb.* ballast, 90/2996. ' *Lest et Lestage,* Gallis præterea dicitur pro sabulo navibus injecto ut stabiliores navigent, the ballace, vel rectius, ballance of the ship: eodemq; sensu occurit vox in Stat. de *Caleis,* 22. Ric. 2. ca[p.] 18.'— Spelman. 'fech more last' = bear a heavier burden, draw more water.

launch out a bote, 86/2845.

lauȝe, *vb.* laugh, 90/3006 ; lawȝe, 94/3117, 100/3335 ; *pret. s.* louȝe, 89/2964 ; lowȝe, 92/3252 ; *pl.* lauȝhid, 93/3084 ; lawuȝid, 95/3161 ; lawȝid, 96/3202 ; lowȝe, 103/3420 ; lauȝid, 104/3461.

leche, *sb.* leech, physician, 39/1242, 109/3628.

leem, *sb.* flame, 72/2352, 83/2729. A.S. *leoma.* See note in *Prompt. Parv.* s. v. LEEM.

leffe, *sb.* leaf, 107/3582 ; *pl.* levis, 1/9.

leffe, *adj.* lief, willing, 107/3566.

legeman, *sb.* liege man, 77/2530.

legg, *vb.* lay, wager, 55/1765 ; *pret. pl.* leyde, 57/1860 ; *subj. pres.* 1 *s.* ley, 54/1761.

lele, *adj.* true, upright, 107/3561. O.F. *léal.*

Leopards, Isope's, hate man's breath, 83/2745.

lere, *adj.* empty, 60/1953.

lere, *vb.* learn, teach, 26/790, 115/3830, 120/4008 ; *pres.* 1 *s.* lere, 87/2870; *pret. s.* leryd, 118/3962 ; *pp.* i-lerid, 101/3364, 115/3857.

leris, *sb. pl.* faces, 96/3202. A.S. *hleor.*

les or more, 70/2278.

lese, *sb. pl.* lies, 66/2141.

lese, *vb.* lose, 2/41, *et passim ;* *pres.* 2 *s.* 100/3318 ; *pp.* i-lore, 39/1216; lore, 60/1955, 112/3731.

lesing, *sb.* loss, 15/440, 96/3177.

lesing, *pres. p.* speaking falsely, 79/2611. A.S. *leasian.*

let, *vb.* hinder, 33/1015, 47/1516, 61/1965, 71/2319.

lete, *pret. s.* let, permitted, 40/1253, 97/3212 ; *imp.* let, leave, 6/157 (' let stond,' leave alone, let be) ; let, cause, 44/1396, 46/1466, *et passim ;* lete, 54/1744, 88/2917 ; *pp.* lete, let [fall], shed, 96/3176.

lett, *sb.* hindrance, 58/1892 ; let, 92/3069, 111/3718.

leue, *vb.* ? better, ' lene,' 18/562. ' Leue ' is the A.S. *lýfan* = allow, permit: ' lene,' the A.S. *lænan* = lend, give. Consult index to *Havelok,* ed. Skeat (E. E. T. S.), s. v. Leue, on this point.

leute, *sb.* good faith, 101/3368. O.F. *léauté.*

leve, *vb.* believe, 37/1161 ; *pres.* 1 *s.* leve, 29/876, 47/1514, 78/2558 ; 2 *pl.* levith, 41/1286 ; 3 *pl.* 102/3401 ; *pret.* 1 *s.* leuyd, 63/2049 ; 3 *pl.* levid, 102/3380 ; *imp. s.* leve, 40/1252, 57/1848 ; *pl.* levith, 46/1454 ; *pp.* levid, 64/2087.

levir, rather, 26/796, *et passim ;* wel levir, much rather, 92/3038. In 71/2336, 118/3934, levir = *more pleasant,* or *grateful.*

levith, *imp. pl.* leave, 68/2222 ; *pp.* levid, 43/1368.

lewde, *or* lewd, *adj.* ignorant, stupid, 51/1627, 72/2366, *et passim ;* leude, 99/3276. In 84/2766, it means *ill-mannered ;* in 88/2919, *unfit, clumsy ;* and in 93/3081, perhaps, *grotesque.*

lewder, *adj.* more stupid, 77/2538.

libardis, *sb. pl.* leopards, 83/2741.

maletalent, *sb.* malice, 112/3759. O.F. *maltalent*.

man, *sb.* chess-man, 56/1821.

Manciple, the, goes into the town, p. 10; sings after supper, p. 14.

marchantfare, *sb.* merchant's voyage, 109/3625. A.S. *fær*, journey.

marchis, *sb. pl.* marches, country, 53/1702, 55/1775, 76/2491, 110/3677, 119/3982.

MARCUS STOYCUS, ? Cato of Utica, 27/799.

Marshall, a, his office at supper, 13/387.

mase, *sb. pl.*maces, 56/1806.

masid, *adj.* crazy, 96/3190, 3203, 98/3253.

mastris, *gen. s.* master's, 53/1710, 67/2189, 112/3741; mastris, *sb. pl.* masters, 111/3726. *Cf.* raftris.

mastry, *sb.* mastery, cunning, skill, 11/320. Fr. *maistrie*.

may, *vb.* be troubled, 62/2018. Fr. '*s'esmayer*. To be sad, pensive, astonyed, carefull; to take thought.' (Cotgrave.)—F.

maystowe, mayst thou, 91/3021.

mede, *sb.* meed, reward, 7/186.

meene honde, third party, 48/1532.

MELAN, Macaign's father, Beryn accused of murdering, p. 70; evidence in the case, pp. 99-100; Geffrey's answer, pp. 113-15.

mell, *vb.* meddle, 116/3890; *pres. s.* mel, 80/2648. O.F. *meller.*—Roquefort.

men, *sb.* used like the F. *on*, 34/1066.

mende, *sb.* mind, 95/3152. The *Prompt. Parv.* has: 'Mende. *Memoria, mencio, mens.*'

mendit, amended, 34/1045. *See* a-mend.

Merchant, the, helps the Host in making up the accounts, p. 14; praises the Host's tact in ruling the pilgrims, and offers to tell the first tale, pp. 23-4.

Merchants, terms of partnership between, 110/3675-76.

mercylese, *adj.* merciless, 71/2314.

merellis, *sb.* nine men's morris, 40/1250. See note, p. 187.

mere y, *adv.* merrily, 22/676, 678.

mery, ? *sb.* merriment, 70/2289. See note, p. 194.

mes, *sb.* mess, dish, 55/1773, 85/2818, 110/3688. Fr. '*Més:* m. A messe, or seruice of meat; a course of dishes at table.' *Cotgrave.*—F.

message, *sb.* messenger, 44/1401. O.F. *message.* L.Lat. *messagerius.* —See *Roquefort,* s. v. ' Messadge.'

messe, *sb.* mass, 34/1046; mas, 111/3710.

mete, *sb.* meal, 117/3919.

mete, *vb.* dream, 4/101. A.S. *mætan.*

meve, *vb.* move, touch upon, 5/128, 79/2593; *pp.* i-mevid, spoken, uttered, 8/199, 82/2704, 112/3758; administered, 112/3737; mevid, spoken, 115/3852.

meyne, *sb.* company, ship's crew, household, 9/237, 59/1923, 114/3819; meyny, 102/3379. Applied to chess-men, 54/1733.

meynten, *vb.* assist, 100/3327; meyntenyth, *pres. s.* maintain in law, back up in a suit, 100/3323.

Miller, the, sets the Pardoner right on a question of blazonry, p. 6; steals Canterbury brooches, p. 7; sits up drinking with the Cook, p. 14.

Ml = Mille = 1000, 52/1677.—W. W. S.

mo, *adj.* more, 17/516, *et passim.*

moblis, *sb. pl.* goods, movables, 47/1511. F. *meuble.*

mocioune, *sb.* proposition, motion, 9/264,79/2593; mocioun,60/1932.

mode, *sb.* temper, spirit, 5/105, 45/1421, 53/1725, 65/2129, 101/3373; anger, 72/2363; mood, 17/502.

mode, ? *adj.* moody, 38/1196. See note, p. 187.

Modern times bad, 77/2518.

moilled, *pret. s.* wetted, 6/139, slobbered; mollid, 46/1477. F. *mouiller.*

mold, man of, earth-born, mortal man, 63/2043. *Cf. Henry V.* III. ii. 23.

Monk, the, characterized by the Summoner, p. 7; invites the Parson and the Friar to go with him to see an acquaintance, p. 10.

monstrefulle, *adj.* monstrous, 84/2767.

moon, *sb.* moan, complaint, 96/3190.

more, *sb.* root, 34/1056. '* * * on o More þei growed.'—*Piers Plowman*, Text B, pass. xvi. l. 58 (E. E. T. S.). Still common in Dorset.

more, þe, & eke the lase, the greater and the less also, 107/3558. *See* las & more.

most greatest, 110/3681.

motehall, *sb.* town-hall, 88/2922. A.S. *mót-heal.*

mourned, *pret. pl.* were deep in thought, 6/151. See note, p. 178.

mowe = may, 25/755, *et passim;* mow, 25/749.

mut, *adj.* mute, 35/1096 ; muet, 64/2065 ; mewet, 2081 ; mwet, 66/2147.

mut = mayest, *or* may, with *opt.* sense, 3/57, 5/116, 33/1012 ; = must, 29/891, *et passim.*

mydmorowe, *sb.* mid-morning, *i. e.* 9 a.m. 1/13.

myere, *sb.* mere, lake, 11/304.

myrthis, *sb. pl.* pleasantry, amusement, 1/4, 8/203, 103/3428, 119/4000. Applied to the performance of a conjuror, 111/3693, 3697.

my3tfull, *adj.* mighty, 71/2339, 102/3383.

mys-do, *pp.* done amiss, 107/3568.

mys-wrou3t, *pp.* done amiss, 43/1360.

mytens, *sb. pl.* gloves, 97/3239. O.F. *mitaine.* See *Halliwell*, s. v. 'Mitaine'; and *Prompt. Parv. s. v.* 'Myteyne,' with the note thereon.

nad (ne had), *pret. s.* had not, 117/3902.

napron, *sb.* apron, 2/33. O.F. *naperon.*

nas (ne was) was not, 30/907, 49/1581, 111/3695.

nat, *adv.* not, 2/31, *et passim;* nowt, 4/71 ; nou3te, 45/1426. *See* nat.

ne, now, 104/3478. *See* noweth.

ne, *conj.* nor, 1/5, *et passim.*

Negative, in Civil Law, rule relating to a, 64/2067-8, 79/2602-6.

nempt, *pret.* 1 s. mentioned, called, 114/3811 ; *pret. s.* nempnid, 17/516.

ner (ne were), *pres.* 2 *s. subj.* were not, 33/1019 ; *pres. s.* nere, 39/1220 ; ner, 83/2730.

ner þe latter, nevertheless, 5/120 ; — lattir, 94/3119.

nere, *vb.* draw near, approach, 21/642.

nere, *adv.* ne'er, 59/1918.

nere & nere, nearer and nearer, 29/879, 74/2424.

nere end. *See* nere hond.

nere hond, nearly, 16/474, 73/2389; nere end, 5/123. *See* ny hond.

nere 3it, nearer yet, 95/3168.

nethirles, *adv.* nevertheless, 53/1722.

nevir a dele, never a whit, 62/1996. *See* dele.

next, *adv.* nearest, 60/1943.

ney, *vb.* neigh, 98/3245.

no dele, no whit, 11/307. *See* dele.

nobley, *sb.* pomp, nobleness, 118/3957, 119/3969. O.F. *noblois.* Roquefort, *s. v.* 'Nobilite.'

nol (ne wol), *pres.* 1 s. will not, 7/190 ; nyl (ne wil), 47/1517 ; nolt (ne wolt), 2 s. wilt not, 61/1973; nyl, 1 *pl.* 94/3110.

nold (ne wold), *pret.* 1 s. would not, 4/89 ; *pret. s.* 6/142, 30/910, 66/2160.

noll, *sb.* head, 98/3259. A.S. *hnoll.*

non-obstant, *prep.* notwithstanding, 75/2467. F. *nonobstant.*

nonys, for þe, for the occasion, 18/544, 79/2613, 94/3126; the nonys, 111/3726. See note in *Prompt. Parv. s. v.* 'For the nonys.'

note, I, I know not, 3/62, *et passim ;* not, 53/1699.

nou3t, nothing, 41/1291 ; nau3t, 71/2333.

nou3te, not, 45/1426. *See* nat.

noweth, *adv.* now, 115/3831 ; nowe3, 97/3213 ; ne, 104/3478.

nowt, not, 4/71. *See* nat.

Nun, the, a monk at Canterbury Cathedral wants to see her face, p. 6.

nyce, *adj.* foolish, 1/7, 75/2445, 88/2933, 103/3416, 3420. In 9/262 it seems to mean *wicked.* 'Nice:

Oaths and Adjurations.

God, have, my trowith, 17/510, 97/3226.

——, hem ȝeld, God reward them, 52/1680.

——, hym graunte wynnyng, riȝte as he hath a-servid, 95/3163.

——, so, me help, 44/1402.

——, wold to, 4/100.

—— woot, God knows, 12/339.

Goddis blessing have þow, 3/66.

good will be my chaunce, 24/728.

graunt mercy, 3/56, 47/1489, 59/1907, 68/2232 ; graunte mercy, 45/1443, 115/3840 ; gromercy, 39/1223.

heven quene, þat bare Criste in hir barme (*i. e.* bosom), by, 75/2457. Cf. 4/79.

Jame, by, 33/1016. *See* God, be.

Iohn, be seynt, 39/1220. *See* 68/2226.

Iudas sold, for (*i. e.* by) hym þat, 63/2044.

lady, our, gyve hym sorowe, 7/183, 16/489.

lady Mary, þat bare Ihesu on hir arm, by our, 4/79. *Cf.* 75/2457.

lord, 12/346, 16/492, 56/1803.

Lord God, 52/1661.

mas, by him þat first made, 111/3710.

Petir, by, 33/1016. *See* God, be.

rood, by the, 53/1726. *Cf.* 23/717.

sorowe com on thy hede, 99/3277.

Thomas shryne, by seynt, 8/221.

trowith, be my, 5/116, 20/602, 78/2558, 93/3105, 94/3110, 98/3253.

——, be, of my body, 70/2288.

——, have God my, 17/510, 97/3226.

Trynyte, by the, 98/3257.

---

oeptas, *sb.* oetas = utas, *i. e.* octave, 8 days ; *i. e.* a week after (W. W. S.), 19/590. See foot-note, p. 19.

of, *prep.* = by, 93/3082 ; = for, by reason of, 36/1109, 52/1682, 57/1856, 72/2367, 89/2964, 92/3052, 103/3420, 118/3966 ; = for, for the sake of, 106/3527 ; = in, at, 55/1788 ; = from, away from, 33/1015, 49/1584, 70/2294, 72/2368, 102/3393, 103/3428 ; = with, 48/1526.

of = off, 115/3836.

of-bove, *adv.* above, 83/2723.

of lyve, *for* on lyve, in life, *i. e.* alive, 71/2311. *See* i-leve *and* on lyve.

of newe, recently, 79/2592.

of wele, ? our weal, 80/2624.

offter, *adv.* oftner, 4/98.

Ointment, the cure all, 109/3628-30.

Old times, the good, 25/745, 28/842.

on, *prep.* in, 36/1137, 113/3771, 117/3920.

on, *adv.* off, 51/1645.

on lyve, in life, *i. e.* alive, 36/1137, 37/1174, 70/2289, 117/3920. *See* i-leve *and* of lyve.

on-do, undone, quashed, 93/3074. *See* vndo.

on-know, *adj.* unknown, 110/3671 ; vnknowe, 114/3802.

onys, *adv.* once, 14/406, *et passim.*

opyn, *adj.* open, plain, 107/3559, 114/3797. ' In opyn & no roun,' 48/1529, means : *openly and not in secret.*

or, *adv.* ere, 2/17, *et passim.*

orden, *vb.* order, appoint, 12/365 ; *pret.* 1 *s.* ordeyned, 16/487 ; *pret. pl.* 2/17, 68/2234 ; *pp.* 92/3066.

orient, *adj.* ? shining, 117/3926.

othir whils a-mongis, sometimes, 30/933. *See* amongis.

ouȝwher, *adv.* anywhere, 37/1166.

outid, *pp.* sold, 73/2408. See note, p. 194.

out-stert, *vb.* spring forth, 114/3826 ; *pret. s.* escaped [his lips], 46/1467. *See* a-stert.

ouer al about, all over, in every part, 76/2513.

ouyr eve, over night, 23/706.

ovir þe bord, overboard, over the side of the ship, 87/2886.

ovir-do, *pp.* over done, too much, 4/91.

ovir grove, *vb.* overgrow, 34/1065.

ovir-pleid, *pp.* over played, *i. e.* beaten, 104/3472.

ovirtwart. *adj.* perverse, 46/1459.

ovir-musid, *pp.* outplotted, out-witted, 104/3481. ' *Muser.* To muse, dreame, studie, bethinke himselfe of.' &c.—Cotgrave.

owt, *pret. s.* owed, 37/1161 ; ouȝt,

plener, *adj.* full, 26/787. O.F. *plenier.* See *Planier* in Roquefort.

plentivouse, *adj.* fertile, 47/1496. O.F. *plentivous.* See *Plantieux* in *Roquefort.*

plete, *vb.* plead, 115/3838; *pres. s.* pletith, 64/2064.

pley, *sb.* conjuring, 111/3719, 112/3728; *pl.* pleyis, 111/3699, 3712.

pleyer, *sb.* conjuror, 110/3690, 111/3698.

pleying, *pres. p.* playing, moving, 22/679.

pleyn, *adj.* full, 37/1151, 107/3559, 108/3600, 112/3733. F. *plein.*

pleyne *or* pleyn, *vb.* complain, 30/919, 68/2209, 70/2274, 79/2597, 112/3757; *pres. s.* pleynyth, 66/2145, 101/3350, 113/3765; *pres. pl.* pleyn, 94/3110, 116/3888; *pp.* i-pleynyd, 63/2045; pleynyd, 66/2143.

pleynlich, *adv.* fully, 119/3989.

pleyntyff, *sb.* plaintiff, 87/2870.

Ploughman, the, precedence granted him at the church door, p. 6. The Ploughman is the Parson's 'brothur' (Prol. *Cant. Tales,* l. 529); here the Ploughman (?) is the Parson's 'fere' (6/137). But see note, p. 178.

plukking, *sb.* pulling, 72/2368.

Poets feign words to make ryme, 75/2462.

poll, *sb.* head, 98/3260.

pompery, *sb.* ? pumping, 81/2668.

popis se, the Pope's see, *i. e.* Rome, 25/741.

port, *sb.* bearing, demeanour, 81/2686, 90/2974, 120/3999.

port, *sb.* porthole, hole near the waterline, 90/3001.

port-colyse, *sb.* portcullis, 82/2719.

pose, *sb.* rheum, 19/578.

possessioune, *sb.* property, 10/271. 'POSSESSIONATUS.—Habens bona solo (W. Thorn). Interdum nude pro eo qui in rei possessione est. Sic *sacerdotes possessionati* dicuntur qui aliquod beneficium possident. *Possessionati monachi,* Gal. *moines rentés,* dotati, quibus attributæ sunt possessiones. (*Act. ad Conc. Basil).'*—D'Arnis.

pour, *vb.* look intently, pore, 22/667; *pret. s.* pourid, 11/311; *pret. pl.* 6/149.

poynt, in, immediately, forthwith, 88/2907, 90/2981, 102/3400. Under *Point,* Roquefort gives: 'quant *point* est, quand il est temps, à propos.'

poyse, *sb.* poesy, 81/2664.

practik, *sb.* treachery, 38/1188.

praunce, *vb.* dance about, quarrel, make a disturbance, 102/3400; *pres. s.* 80/2648. 'Penader. To bound, *praunce,* brag, vaunt, braue it.'—Cotgrave.

preche, *vb.*? *for* prece = press, 73/2388. See note, p. 194.

prechement, *sb.* sermon, 40/1263.

preff, *sb.* proof, trial, 17/511.

preff, *vb.* prove, 66/2144.

prelatis, *sb. pl.* clergymen, 6/137, 13/386. 'Prelati Ecclesiæ vocantur nedum superiores, ut Episcopi, sed etiam inferiores, ut Archidiaconi, Presbyteri, Plebani, & Rectores Ecclesiarum.'—*Spelman,* s. v. Prelatus. Sir John the Parson of Wrotham is called: 'An honest country *Prelate,* who laments

  To see such foul disorder in the Church.'—*The History of Sir John Oldcastle,* Shakspere Fol. 3, p. 34, col. 2.

present, *sb.* presence, 82/2796.

prest, *adj.* ready, 56/1822, 95/3153. O.F. *prest.*

preve, *sb.* proof, trial, question, existence, 58/1903.

prikke, *vb.* spur, 62/2012.

Prioress, the, goes with the Wife of Bath to see the inn-garden, p. 10.

pro, contra, things for and against, 78/2577.

probacy, *sb.* proof of assertions, 79/2595.

Probate Law, 64/2066-70. See *Civil Law.*

profir, *sb.* offer, 117/3911.

prudenciall, *adv.* prudently, 13/381.

pry, *pres. 2 pl.* enquire (taking *sotil* to be an *adv.*), 107/3554. Or for *pry* read *be.* See note, p. 199.

Proverbs and Phrases.

al hole !, all's well ! 2/43. See note, p. 176.

asse, lewder (more stupid) þen an, 77/2538.

bagg of trechery, vndid þe, 38/1182. *Cf.* 23/701.

bale, aftir, comyth bote, 118/3956. 'Bale,' woe, A.S. *bealu.* 'Bot,' amends, A.S. *bót.*

ball, They shull be behynd, & wee shul have þe, 78/2580. This may be a metaphor taken from the game called Hurling, thus described by Strutt : 'The contending parties endeavoured to force the ball one from the other, and they who could retain it long enough to cast it beyond an appointed boundary were the conquerors.' See *Sports and Pastimes*, bk. II. ch. iii. p. 98, ed. Hone, 1845.

begynnyng, Who take heed of þe, what fal shal of þe ende, He leyith a bussh to-fore the gap, þer fortune wold in ryde, 55/1788-89.

berd, I can wipen al this ple cleene from your, 110/3658.

berd, make his, 15/436, 16/485, 20/622.

Beyard, a man to seruesabill, ledith offte b. from his owne stabill, 96/3183-84. Bayard was a common name for a horse ; *see* Halliwell, *s. v.* 'Bayard.' Rinaldo's destrier was called Baiardo.—*Orl. Fur.* I. xxxii.

brennyd cat dredith feir, 4/78. 'Brend child fire drediþ.'—*Prov. of Hending*, st. 24. 'Puer noviter combustus timet ignem.'—*Cronica Jocelini de Brakelonda*, ed. Rokewode (Camden Soc.), p. 3.

brond, stappid oppon a, stepped upon a hot brand, 19/585. *Cf.* the A.S. ordeal of redhot ploughshares.—W. W. S.

button, set of himself the store of a, 111/3696. *Cf.* 'fly, it is nat worth a,' and 'karse, vaylith nat a.'

cat, fese (*i. e.* drive) a-wey þe, 12/351.

cloudis, aftir mysty, þere comyth a cler sonne, 118/3955. 'After sharpe shoures · moste shene is þe sonne.'—*Piers Plowman* (E. E. T. S.), Text B, xviii. 409.—W. W. S.

clowdis, Lo ! how the, worchyn, eche man to mete his mach, 4/83.

company, who doith after, may lyve the bet in rest, 6/162.

covenante, yee woll hold me, & I woll ȝew also, 78/2569. See note, p. 195.

cupp, þe, he drank with-out, 11/306. *Cf.* 15/460.

'cut,' as who seyd, 41/1288. Like one who says '*cut*.' This is an abbreviation for 'draw cut', or 'kepe cut' (41/1309). *I. e.* put up with the lot you have drawn : = as you've made your bed, so you must lie on it.—W. W. S.

cut, kepe thy, 41/1309, 56/1805. See note, p. 189.

day, the, is short, the work is long, 109/3631.

deol (sorrow), evil avengit he *h*is, þat for a litill mode (passion), and angir to his neyȝbour, sellith a-wey his good, &c., 72/2363-64.

doggis lyden, *i. e.* Latin, language, 16/482.

doith as othir doith, 37/1151.

dub him knyȝt, 15/456.

fals, as, a thing, as God hym-selff is trewe, 79/2591.

fete, thow shalt . . . stond on thyn owne, 40/1254.

fethirles bolt, to shete a, 55/1764.

flower, bear the, *i.e.* be the first, 111/3694.

fly, it is nat worth a, 99/3278. *Cf.* 'button, set of himself,' &c., and 'karse, vaylith,' &c.

galle, touch no man the, 37/1150. Galle = gall, sore place.

garlik, pull, 5/123. Make a man pull garlic, sell him, and disgust him.—F. See note, p. 177.

Goddis cope, he shall be as sikir as of, *i. e.* he may be as sure of having God's head (A.S. *copp*) or cope, cloak (Lat. *capa*), 15/453.

goldfynch, glad as eny, 16/476.

gren, cauȝt even by the shyn . . . in our owne, 116/3893-94. 'Gren' = gin, snare.

had-I-wist, 72/2348. A common proverb. To several instances cited in a note to *Tell Troth* (New Sh. Soc.), p. 193, may be added: 'The Adulterous Falmouth Squire,' l. 35, in *Political, Religious, and Love Poems* (E. E. T. S), p. 94.

half a myle, in las then, 54/1737. Cf. 15/468.

hipp, i-cauȝte somewhat oppon the, 55/1780-81.

hors, as, þat evir trottid, trewlich I ȝew tell, it were hard to make hym, aftir to ambill well, 39/939-40.

Hurlewaynes meyne, familiæ Harlequini, 1/8. See note, p. 175.

i-mynt, offt is more better i-merkid then there is, 15/434. This proverb contains an allusion to the practice of issuing base money. Coin is often stamped (i-merkid) so as to pass for more than it is worth; folk often seem better than they are. 'Merkyd, . . . *Signatus.*'—*Prompt. Parv.* A.S. *mynetian*, to coin money.

Judas, as fals as, 99/3282.

karse, vaylith nat a, is not worth a cress (A.S. *cerse*), 31/971. Halliwell quotes from Gower under 'kerse': 'Men witen welle whiche hath the werse, And so to me *nis* ('tis not) *worth a kerse.*'

kite, went lowe for the, 46/1478, bowed herself as if to avoid Faunus's pounce; pretending that he was a kite.

kynd, þe, of brode (natural disposition), 6/160.

kynde woll have his cours, Nature will have her way, 4/86.

lawe, the, goith by no lanys, but holdith forth the streyt way, even as doith a lyne, 101/3358-59. Cf. 103/3441.

lyne, even as a, 34/1070, 101/3359.

male, vnlace his, 23/701. Cf. 38/1182. Cf. 'Unbokeled is the male.' Ch., *Mill. Prol.* l. 7.—W. W. S.

moon, in crokeing of þe, in the crook of the moon, 13/398. See note, p. 181.

murdir, ther may no man hele (*i. e.* conceal), þat it woll out atte last, 70/2293. Cf. Ch. *Nonne Preste's Tale*, l. 237.—W. W. S.

myle, within this, 15/468. Cf. 54/1737, and see note, p. 191.

nayll, to dryv in bet þe, 104/3464.

part as it comyth, of rouȝe & eke of smoth, take yeur, 37/1152.

pecok, I make a-vowe to þe, 15/462. This seems to be a burlesque allusion to the mediæval fashion of making vows. Jacques le Clercq relates how Philip the Good, duke of Burgundy, banqueting at Lille in 1453, was presented by his herald, Toison d'Or, with a roasted pheasant, 'que on nomme autrement colimoge, moult joliment joli;' and the duke then took an oath to lead an army against the Turks. The pheasant was also presented to the princes and nobles assembled, who 'feirent plusieurs grands vœux, desquels je n'en parlerai pour tant qu'ils ne feurent pas accomplis ne faits, et si seroit la chose trop longue à racompter.'—*Memoires*, ed. Buchon, tom. xiii. p. 168 (*Chroniques de Monstrelet*).

peny, wele settith he his, þat þe pound therby savith, 69/2244.

pot, to, who comyth last, 101/3366.

'quek,' the, *i. e.* quick, alive, 89/2945. A make-believe game of Geffrey's.

right as wolde rammys hornyd, 6/152.

rynge, shoke (shook) a, 55/1762.

Sir John (applied to a layman), 90/2984. See note, p. 198.

sour, aftir, when swete is com, it is a plesant mes, 110/3688. Cf. 29/898.

spone, & wee hewe a-mys eny maner, 103/3430. Spone = chip, splinter of wood. (A.S. *spón*.)

styll as ony stone, 21/653.

swete, aftir, þe soure comyth, ful

offt, in many a place, 29/898. *Cf.* 110/3688.

taberd, touch his, 7/190. A tabard was a short coat or mantle. The term has been latterly confined to a herald's coat.—See *Halliwell*, s. v. 'Tabard.' 'In a *tabbard* he [the Ploughman] rood upon a mere.'—Prol. *Cant. Tales*, l. 541.

tole, tyme is nowe to worchen with som othir, 100/3342.

touȝte, make it nevir so, 57/1830. Touȝte = tough, difficult.

trowith, the, evir atte ende, woll be previd, how so men evir trend, 63/2037-38.

twinkling of an eye, in the, 94/3107.

wedir at will, 49/1560. See note, p. 190.

whele, the [of Fortune], was i-chaungit in-to a-nothir cours, 39/1234.

——, wronge went my, 38/1184.

wherof, wold to God I had, 51/1652. See note, p. 191.

wyvis tayll, setten al his wisdom on his, 40/1278.

ȝolke, telle ȝewe þe, & put þe white a-way, 24/732.

———

prowes, *sb.* integrity, 81/2686. 'Prueste: Honneur, probité; *probitas.*' —Roquefort.

pryme, *sb.* prime (9 a.m.), 87/2878.

pryme-rosis, *sb. pl.* primroses, 23/693.

pryvvy, *sb.* proof, 113/3791 ; pryue, 114/3797.

pryvvy, *adj.* intimate, 120/4002.

pryuyte, *sb.* mystery, 82/2710. 'of riȝte pryuyte,' in great privacy, 11/324. '*Pryuyte.* Misterium, secretum, archanum.'—*Prompt. Parv.* :
'Wher thou schalt knowen of our *privete*
More than a maister of divinité.'— Chaucer's *Freres Tale*, ll. 339, 340.

Ptolemy the astronomer, his skill in astronomy, 83/2754 ; designs Isope's garden, 83/2755.

pulcritude, *sb.* beauty, 36/1109. Lat. *pulchritudo.*

pull, *sb.* spell, short space of time, 108/3616.

purchase, *vb.* procure, 38/1188. See *Pourchacer* in Roquefort.

purpensid, *pp.* premeditated, 68/2214. O.F. *porpenser.*

purposid, *pp.* designed, 82/2722.

purs, *vb.* purse, pocket, 109/3634.

pursuith, *pres. s.* sues, accuses, 87/2867 ; *pres. pl.* pursu, 68/2208.

purveaunce, *sb.* foresight, precaution, 48/1540. O.F. *pourveance.*

putaigne, *sb.* 40/1275. 'Putain: f. a whore, queane, punke, drab, flurt, strumpet, harlot, cockatrice, naughty pack, light huswife, common hackney.'—Cotgrave.

putto, put to, 81/2675. *Cf.* 'went to,' 16/478, in MS. 'wentto.'

pyne, *sb.* pain, 35/1088. A.S. *pín.*

pyrid, *pret. pl.* peered, 6/149. *See* pire.

pyry, *sb.* pear-tree, 41/1315. Lat. *pirum.* '*Piries* and plom-trees · were puffed to þe erthe.'—*Piers Plowman*, Text B. pass. V. l. 16 (E. E. T. S.).

quarter nyȝt, 9 p.m. 16/474.

quek, *adj.* alive, 81/2655. *See* quyk. The 'quek'; a make-believe game of Geffrey, 89/2945.

querelouse, *adj.* querulous, litigious, 64/2071.

queynt, *adj.* subtle, ingenious, 12/349, 82/2708.

queynt, *pp.* quencht, settled, 106/3534.

queyntlich, *adv.* adroitly, slily, 94/3129, 97/3210.

quod, *pret. s.* quoth, 2/23, *et passim.*

quyete, put hem in, hushed them up, 30/934.

quyk, *adj.* quick, alive, 84/2758 ; quek, 81/2655.

quyt, *adj.* quit, free, 74/2410 ; quyte, 106/3534, 3537 ; 108/3601.

quyte, *vb.* requite, acquit, 76/2488, 80/2653, 106/3519; quyt, 69/2254; *pres.* 1 *s.* quyte, 7/186.

rage, *sb.* rashness, 13/380.

rage, *vb.* sport, 72/2346. O.F. *ragier.* —Roquefort.

rakith, *pres. s.* rushes, 83/2743;
pret. s. rakid, 55/1791, 114/3815.

RAME, second wife of Faunus, sets
him against his son Beryn, pp.
37-9; fears she's gone too far,
pp. 43-4; is pleased with Beryn's
proposal and Faunus's assent, pp.
46-7; and rejoiced to get rid of
Beryn, p. 48.

ransakid, *pp.* ransacked, conveyed
away, 109/3652.

rathir, *adj.* earlier, long past, 2/26.

raumpith, *pres. s.* runs, 84/2780.
'*Ramper.* To creepe, runne,
crawle, or traile itselfe along on
the ground, &c.'—Cotgrave.

rauȝte, *pret. pl.* reached, came, 6/
168; *pp.* i-rauȝt, caught, 73/2389.

ravid, *pp.* taken away, 105/3503.

rayd, *pret. s.* arrayed, dressed, 114/
3812; rayid, 117/3916; *pp.* rayid,
89/2970; = furnished, 48/1545.
See aray.

rebawdy, *sb.* dissipation, 40/1249;
rebawdry, 40/1257.

rechen, *vb.* reckon, enumerate, 17/
517.

red (? A.S. *ræd*), a ful even, ? a
very true opinion, 4/99. See
note, p. 177.

rede, *sb.* counsel, 20/615. *et passim.*

rede, *pres. 1 s.* counsel, 73/2404, 83/
2735, 2740. A.S. *rǽdan.*

reedynes, *sb. pl.* ? tidings, 99/3291.
? Du. 'Rede, or ofte Speake.
Reason, Speech, or Oration.'—
Hexham. I suppose it's from
rede, advise. 'Advise me of the
arrival of So-and-So.'—F. J. F.

Reeve, the, goes into the town, p.
10; sings after supper, p. 14.

refourmyd, *pp.* reformed, set right,
103/3438.

refreit, *sb.* burden of a song, 38/
1200. '*Refreyt*, of a respowne.
Antistropha.'—*Prompt. Parv.*

refreyn, *imp. s* restrain, 83/2745.

refute, *sb.* refuge, 86/2840. O.F.
refuy. See note on *Refuge* in
Prompt. Parv. '*Refuite*: f. a
flight or course, a running or
flying backe; an euasion or
auoidance.'—Cotgrave.

rekelagis, *sb. pl.* diversions, 40/

1267. '*Rigolage*, ... Ris, risée,
raillerie, plaisanterie, moquerie;
suite d'une affaire, libertinage.'—
Roquefort. See note, p. 188.

rekenydist, *pret* 2 *s.* reckoned, stated
an account, 63/2035.

releff, *vb.* relieve, 118/3954. *See*
releve.

relevacioun, *sb.* relief, 110/3687.
Lat. *relevatio.*

releve, *vb.* get up, arise, 77/2548,
118/3966. F. *se relever.*

releve, *vb.* relieve, 110/3682; releff,
118/3954; *pp.* relevid, 117/3899.

Relics kissed by pilgrims at St.
Thomas's shrine, Canterbury, 6/
166-67.

remedy, *vb.* help, 102/3402.

renne, *vb.* run, 73/2390, 2393; 83/
2725.

rennyng, *sb.* running, 73/2402.

repase, *vb.* return, 77/2537.

repeir, *vb.* return, 85/2828; *imp. s.*
repeir, 82/2706; *pres. p.* repeyryng, 119/3984. O.F. *repairer,*
repeirer.—Roquefort.

repenyng, 14/411, ? stillness. Dutch
Repen, to be still or quiet.—
Hexham, A.D. 1660.—F. J. F.

repeyryng, *verb. sb.* return, 85/2814.
See repeir.

repreff, *sb.* reproach, 9/253, 107/
3565.

repreve, *vb.* accuse, 79/2594; *pp.*
reprevid, 64/2088.

reprouabill, *adj.* blameable, 9/256.

rere soper, late supper, 12/365.
'*Regoubillonner.* To make a reare
supper, steale an after supper,
banquet late anights.'—Cotgrave.
See note on *Rere sopere* in *Prompt.
Parv.*

rerid vp, *pret. s.* roused up, 88/2905.

rese, *sb.* a rush of emotion; here of
anger, 16/498, 18/548. A.S. *rǽs.*

rese, *vb.* rush, 30/910. A.S. *rǽsan.*

reservid, *pp.* kept back, 72/2372.

respite, *vb.* delay, 106/3538.

responsaill; ? surety, 80/2623. L.
responsalis, qui pro aliis spondet;
répondant, caution (Vet. Gl.).—
D'Arnis.—F. J. F.

retourn, *imp. s.* send back, 91/3007.

reve, *sb.* servant, 90/3003. '*Reve,*

lordys serwawnte. *Prepositus.'*
—*Prompt. Parv.*

reve, *vb.* take away, 31/942 ; *pp.* ravid, 105/3503.

reward, *sb.* regard ; 'take reward,' care, 71/2326.

rewe, *vb.* have ruth, pity, 32/982 ; *imp. s.* rew, 39/1242.

riall, *adj.* royal, noble, 72/2343, 79/2612,82/2707, 107/3561,118/3939, 119/3977.

riallich, *adv.* royally, lavishly, 46/1453.

rid, *pret. s.* rode, 46/1471 ; *pret. pl.* rood, rode (at anchor), 87/2897.

rigg, *sb.* back, 20/594, 41/1298. A.S. *hrycg.*

Rod, the, its educational value, 34/1060-1.

rodylese, *adj.* rudless, pale, 31/951.

Rome, 25/752 ; Room, 25/735. The former spelling occurs seven times, the latter twelve. *Cf.* 1 *Henry VI.* III. i. 51, with *John,* III. i. 180.

ROMULUS, 25/758, 26/765.

ROMUS, Remus, 25/758, 26/765.

romyd, *pret. pl.* roamed, wandered, 92/3054.

rood, *pret. pl.* rode, 87/2897. *See* rid.

rote, *sb.* root, spring, 120/4015.

root, *vb.* rot, 34/1057.

rothir, *sb.* rudder, 8/212, 92/3060. A.S. *roðer. See* strothir.

roun, *sb.* whisper, 48/1529. Roune = rune = mystery.—W. W. S.

roune, *vb.* whisper, 35/1076, 62/2002, 86/2852 ; roun, 20/606 ; rown, 77/2522 ; *pres. p.* rownyng, 7/179.

rouse, *sb.* talk, noise, 52/1669, 108/3610.

rout, *sb.* company, 14/405 ; route, 20/613, 22/670, 26/763, 88/2923.

route, *vb.* snore, 84/2766. ' *Rowtyn,* yn slepe, *Sterto.'*—*Prompt. Parv.* A.S. *hrutan.*

routhe, *sb.* ruth, 74/2417 ; rowith, 66/2135.

rowe, *adj.* rough, harsh, 17/520, 40/1272.

rowe, *vb.* rest, 10/284. O.H. Germ. *ruowan (quiescere)?* So Stratmann, s. v. *rowen.*

ruddok, *sb.* redbreast, 22/685.

rudines, *sb.* rudeness, lack of art, 24/729.

ruyne, *sb.* Rhenish wine, 10/280.

ryding best, horse, 52/1687.

ryding knot, slip knot, 89/2947.

Rye, Sussex, impaired of late years, 25/756. *See* Winchelsea.

ryff,*adj.* rife, 44/1392 ; ryve, abounding, 67/2174.

rynge, *sb.* bell, 55/1762.

rype, *vb.* ripen, encrease, 22/677 ; ripe, 41/1316.

ryve, *adj.* abounding, 67/2174. *See* ryff.

saal, *sb.* soul, 81/2682.

sad, *adj.* grave, 14/408, 68/2232, 81/2678.

saff, *adj.* safe, 50/1594, 84/2786, 119/3995.

saff, *adv.* save, except, 22/660, *et passim ;* saffe, 77/2520 ; save, 7/178, 79/2588.

Sailors shrive each other in a tempest, 49/1578-79 ; and make vows, 105/3487-91.

Sails across the mast, a sign of starting, 87/2899. *See* cros saill.

Salamonys sawis. the *Proverbs of Solomon,* 81/2666.

sale, set at, offer for sale, 7/188 ; *pret. s.* sette, &c., 99/3282 ; *pp.* i-set, &c., 14/429. *See* setten.

salidone, *sb.* ? a precious stone, chalcedony, 99/3302. See note, p. 196.

sapience, *sb.* wisdom, 75/2467.

sat, *pret. s.* lay, was situate, 2/36, 19/590 ; sete, 19/591 ; *pret. pl.* souȝt, sat, 6/148 ; sett, sat, 13/389 ; set, 54/1729 ; *pp.* i-set, 92/3055.

sat, *impers.* became, befitted, 118/3966.

sauge, *sb.* sage, 10/292. F. *sauge.*

saunce, *adv.* without, 66/2150. F. *sans.*

save condit. safe conduct, 119/3972 ; saff condit, 119/3980.

saverid, *pret. s.* understood, 118/3964. O.F. *saver.*

saw, *sb.* speech, saying, 58/1882 ; sawe, 64/2070 ; *pl.* sawis, 81/2666.

scapidist, *pret.* 2 *s.* escapest, 70/
2288 ; scapiddist, 89/2951.

Sciences, the seven, 81/2667. Gram-
mar, logic, and rhetoric formed
the *trivium ;* arithmetic, geom-
etry, music, and astronomy, the
quadrivium.

sclawe. *See* sclee.

sclee, *vb.* slay, 27/816, 71/2327 ; *pp.*
sclawe, 26/796.

scliper, *adj.* slippery, deceitful, 51/
1641. A.S. *slipur,* slippy. *Lye.*
—F. J. F.

sclope, *vb.* sleep, 15/454.

sclynk, *vb.* slink, 100/3334.

sclytt, *adj.* slit, 96/3204.

sclyue, *sb.* sleeve, 43/1356 ; sclyve,
99/3292.

scole, *sb.* schooling, teaching, 73/
2403.

se at eye, (?) see with eye, 25/755.
Cf. tell with mouth, 70/2280.

seche, *vb.* seek, 32/1004, 52/1665 ;
sech, 19/563, 99/3298 ; sechen
(visit), 105/3490 ; siche, 114/
3795 ; seke, 81/2680 ; *pret. s.*
souȝt, 21/632, 33/1034 ; *pres. p.*
seching, 112/3730 ; sheching, 44/
1407 ; *pp.* souȝte (visit), 7/172,
45/1425.

see bord, *sb.* the plank to cover up
the port-hole, 90/3001.—F. J. F.

seen, *vb.* see, 23/693 ; se *or* see, 6/
144, 48/1548, *et passim ; pres.* 1 *s.*
sigh, 50/1595 ; *pres.* 2 *s.* seist,
7/180 ; *pres. s.* seeth, 42/1332 ;
pres. 2 *pl.* seth, 61/1986 ; *pret.*
1 *s.* sawe, 17/515, *et passim ;*
pret. s. sawe, 11/311, *et passim ;*
seid, 7/178 ; seyd, 113/3771 ;
imp. s. se, 88/2926 ; *imp. pl.*
seith, 23/696, 95/3159 ; seth, 41/
1300 ; *subj. pres.* 2 *s.* se, 83/2738 ;
3 *s.* 84/2780 ; *pp.* i-sey, 53/1705 ;
seyn, 56/1804, 59/1905, 95/3142,
107/3574, 110/3691 ; sey, 52/1673,
93/3079, 111/3697 ; seen, 52/1673.

selde, *adv.* seldom, 35/1093 ; seld,
56/1804.

selondyn, *sb.* 83/2723. ? a silk, or
Fr. '*Selenite.* A light, white, and
transparent stone, easily cleft into
thin flakes, whereof the Arabians,
among whom it growes, make

their glasse, and glasen win-
dowes.'—Cotgrave.—F. J. F. See
note, p. 196.

selve, *sb.* salve, 108/3588.

sely, *adj.* innocent, 56/1803. A.S.
sélig.

semblant, *sb.* seeming, 75/2471.

semen, make, cause to appear, 84/
2775. *Cf.* soth, make seme, 15/
446.

semybousy, *adj.* half tipsy, 23/706.

semyvif,*adj.* half alive, *i. e.* half dead,
68/2202. '*Semiuyf* he semed.'—
Piers Plowman, B. Text, pass.
xvii, l. 55 (E. E. T. S.).

SENECA, 81/2666.

sent, *vb.* assent, 50/1614.

sentyn, *pres. pl.* diffuse fragrance,
84/2765.

serkill celestyne, *primum mobile,*
35/1087. See note, p. 187.

sesid, *pp.* scised, 48/1549, 63/2061.
See i-sesid.

sesours, *sb.* scissors, 88/2918 ; sisours, 88/2916.

setten, *vb.* guide, 8/213 ; = place,
40/1278 ; *pres. s.* settith, 69/2244 ;
pret. 1 *s.* set, valued, cared, 71/
2333 ; *pret. s.* 41/1291, 44/1386,
111/3696 ; = hit, 19/577 ; = set
out, 62/1999 ; = laid, put, 62/
2013. 70/2290 ; disposed, arranged,
113/3781 ; *pret. pl.* set of, cared
for, 86/2838 ; *imp. s.* set = put,
ordain, 43/1363 : *pp.* i-set, fixed,
26/798 ; = set, 54/1746 ; set =
put, 40/1272 ; = appointed, 93/
3089, 97/3217. *See* 'game, set
a,' *and* 'sale, set at.'

sett, set = sat, 13/389, 54/1729.
See sat.

Seven Sages, the, of Rome, their
names and characters, pp. 26-7 ;
advise the emperor how to con-
sole Faunus, p. 35 ; are not so
wise as Isope, 81/2659-60.

sevile law, civil law, 81/2665.

sew, *sb.* soup, 10/290.

seyne, say, 50/1608 ; seyn, 87/2890 ;
sey, 8/215, *et passim ;* say, 44/
1414, 82/2696 ; *pres.* 1 *s.* sey, 2/
32, *et passim.* In 4/76, 52/1666
= tell. *pres.* 2 *s.* seyist, 15/458 ;
seyst, 20/616, 91/3015, 102/3411 ;

pres. s. seith, 50/1593, *et passim;* seyith, 113/3765 ; sayith, 41/1286; *pres.* 2 *pl.* sey, 4/75, *et passim; pres. pl.* seyn, 40/1276 ; *pret.* 1 *s.* seyd, 45/1427, 57/1846, 57/1849 ; *pret. s.* seyd, 3/48, *et passim;* seid, 16/489, *et passim;* seit, 87/2877 ; *pret.* 2 *pl.* seyde, 63/2056 ; *pret. pl.* seyde, 30/916, 92/3059 ; seyd, 35/1101, *et passim;* seyden with = found for, 116/3871 ; seid, 8/226, 109/3646 ; *imp. s.* sey, 58/1866, 91/3020 ; *imp. pl.* seith, 13/382 ; *subj. pres. s.* sey, 79/2614; *pp.* i-seyde, 39/1237 ; i-seyd, 20/616, 59/1912, 100/3323 ; = told, 57/1845 (*cf.* 4/76, 52/1666); i-sayd = said, 8/223, 54/1738 ; seyde, 56/1825 ; seyd, 108/3589.

seyntis, sechen, *i. e.* visit saints' shrines, 105/3490.

seynture, *sb.* belt, 117/3925. F. *ceinture.*

shakill, *sb.* twisted band, 34/1064.

shape, *vb.* dispose, make, 87/2875, 88/2913 ; *pret. s.* shope, 87/2879.

sheching, *pres. p.* seeking, 44/1407. See seche.

sherith my berd, cut off my beard, 88/2916.

shete, *vb.* shoot, 55/1764.

shippis ward, toward ships, 62/1999, 91/3032, 116/3878. *See* ——ward.

shoke, *pret. s.* shook, 55/1762.

shoon, *sb. pl.* shoes, 97/3240.

shoon, *pret. s.* shone, 41/1317.

shope, *pret. s.* made, 87/2879. *See* shape.

shor, *pp.* shorn, 102/3407, 113/3779 ; shore, 103/3426.

shorting, *verb. sb.* shortening, 8/209, 23/700 ; shortyng, 46/1461.

shrewdnes, *sb.* malice, 7/189.

shrewid, *adj.* wicked, perverted, 15/464, 79/2613 ; shrewde, 51/1628 ; shrewd, 35/1079. '*Schrewyd.* Pravatus, depravatus.' — *Prompt. Parv.*

shrewis, *sb. pl.* bad folk, 41/1282.

shryne, *sb.* shrine, object of veneration, 36/1114.

shryve, *vb.* shrive, 105/3487 ; *pret. s.* shroff, 49/1579.

siche, *vb.* seek, 114/3795. *See* seche.

signes, *sb. pl.* pilgrims' tokens, 7/171, 191 ; signys, 7/175. Lat. *signum.*

sikir, *adj.* sure, 15/453, *et passim.*

sikirlich, *adv.* surely, certainly, 13/372, *et passim;* sikirliche, 46/1454 ; sikirly, 48/1542.

sikirnes, *sb.* security, 85/2814, *et passim.*

sikirnes, in, certainly, in good faith, 92/3038, 109/3648.

sisours, a peir, a pair of scissors, 88/2916.

SITHERO, Cicero, 822.

sithis, *sb. pl.* times, 11/328, &c. ; sith, 57/1845.

sitting, *adj.* befitting, due, 34/1041. *Cf.* sat, 118/3966.

skape, *vb.* escape, 62/2011.

skaunce. *See* a-scaunce.

skill, *sb.* knowledge, artifice, 51/1628.

smale, *adv.* small, 23/686.

smaught, *pp.* tasted, 94/3122. A.S. *smeccan.* See *smecchen* in Stratmann.

smote in, struck, seized, 42/1340, 72/2355.

snache, *vb.* snap at one as a dog does, 21/651, 46/1460.

snell, *adv.* quickly, 36/1120 ; snelle, 53/1694 ; snel, 54/1750 ; snele, 82/2706.

sofft, *adj.* soft, foolish, 97/3233.

sokeyng, *verb sb.* suckling, 65/2128.

solas, *sb.* recreation, 110/3678, 119/3996.

solase, ? *adj.* cosy, recreative, 45/1432.

solue, *vb.* solfa, 13/396.

som, *adj.* some, 41/1282. Used here ironically for 'almost all.' *Cf.* these lines in B. Sawin Esq.'s 3rd letter, *Biglow Papers,* p. 120, ed. 1859.

'he come an' grinned,
    He showed his ivory some, I
        guess,' &c.

som dele, somewhat, 14/403. *See* dele.

some, *adj.* peaceable, 97/3233. A.S. *gesóm.*

sommon, ? some men, 9/264.

sondys, *sb. pl.* things sent, gifts,

118/3945. 'Sond, or 3yfte sent. Eccennium.' — Prompt. Parv. Often, 'messages'; also 'men sent,' 'messengers.' See sande in Stratmann.

Songs.

'now, loue, þou do me ri3·e,' 3/70. 'Doubil me this bourdon,' = 'Chorus, gentlemen'! 14/413.

sonner, adv. sooner, 4/97.

sope, sb. sup, 105/3497.

sorys, sb. pl. sores, wounds, 22/662; soris, 10·/3589.

sot, sb. sweat, 16/493.

sote, adj. sweet. 22/682.

sotes, sb. pl. fools, 6/147. F. sot.

soth, make seme, appear true, 15/445. Cf. semen, make, 84/2775.

SOTHER LEGIFEER, 26/794.

soule, adj. sole, 32/989, 35/1095.

soune, vb. sound, utter, 74/2412.

sou3t, pret. pl. sat, 6/148. See sat.

sou3t, sou3te, soughr. See seche.

soverens, my = my Lords, 112/3746. Cf. 'Soveren sirs,' 104/3465.

spech, imp.? patch, 39/1229. 'Spetch. To patch. Yorksh.'—Halliwell.

speche-tyme, sb. time of converse, 75/2461.

spedful, adj. helpful, 114/3800.

spene, vb. spend, 47/1520. 'Nede y mot spene that y spared 3ore.'— Political Songs (Camd. Soc.), p. 151.

spetouse, adj. savage, 21/635.

spetously, adv. savagely, 21/641, 30/910; spitouslich, 17/520.

spone, sb. spoon, 103/3430. Here used in its original sense of chip (A.S. spón).—W. W. S.

sportis, sb. pl.? portis, gates, 28/837.

sprang, pret. s. spread, 33/1031; pp. i-spronge, 68/2213. A.S. springan = (1) to spring; (2) to sprinkle. Cf. note to Havelok, ed. Skeat, l. 959.—W. W. S.

spryng, vb. sprinkle, 6/142. A.S. sprengan.

spryngill, sb. holy water brush, 6/138; spryngil, 6/141.

spurn, vb. wince, shrink, or spin off, 86/2862. 'Spurnyn (or wyncyn) calcitro.' Prompt. Parv.—F. J. F.

Squire, the, thinks of his lady love while his father is discussing the fortifications, p. 9.

stabill, vb. make sure, 61/1976.

stage, sb. deck, tier, 46/1464.

stall, sb. place, seat, 68/2201. A.S. steal.

stallid. pp. fixed, ordained, 79/2610. A.S. steallian.

stan dede, adj. stone-dead, 42/1341; standede, 114/3816, 3828.

stappe, vb. walk, step, 7/192, 74/2433; stap, 62/2010; stapp, 70/2285, 98/3243; pret. s. stappid, 11/309, 19/585.

statis, sb. pl. rank, 6/140. See estate.

Stepmothers unkind, 41/1282, 72/2360.

stere, vb. stir. bustle, 7/198, 28/859; pres. s. sterith, 18/548.

sterris, sb. pl. stars, 81/2657. A.S. steorra.

stert, vb. spring, hasten, 2/35, et passim; pret. s. stert, 3/61, et passim.

stervid, pret. s. died, 71/2332; pp. 3/55.

Stichomythia between Geffrey and Hanybald, 90/2996-3004.

stillith, imp. pl. still, calm, 78/2565.

stilt, sb. wooden leg, 73/2380, 75/2451, 76/2509.

stodied, pret. pl. pondered, 104/3461. See studied.

stond, vb. stand, 12/355, et passim; stoude, 20/617; pres. 1 s. stond, 80/2636, 92/3051; stonde, 95/3155, 98/3271; pres. s. stondith, 38/1207, et passim; stont, 55/1785, 67/2169. 95/3173; stant, 84/2759; pres. 2 pl. stonden, 69/2253; pres. pl. stondein, 1/10; stont, 79/2595, 88/2911; stond, 102/3400; pret. s. stode, 42/1322, et passim; stood, 64/2065, 77/2543; pret. pl. stoden, 14/417; stode, 44/1410, 55/1772, 64/2076, 90/2972; stooden, 95/3164; imp. s. stond, 95/3168; pp. stonden, 76/2500.

stond, let, imp. let be, 6/157. See let.

Stone, a, of a very fiery nature in Isope's hall, 83/2727-29. See Dyonyse.

stont an hond, presses on me, concerns me, 95/3173.

stonyd, *pp.* astonished, 64/2088. *See* a-stonyd.

store, hold no, make no account, 1/4. Straw lain on by Beryn's father during Passion-week. *See* Passion-week.

stre, *sb.* straw, 72/2350.

strengthis, *sb. pl.* fortifications, 9/239.

streyte, *adj.* strict, 14/403, 109/3643; streyt, 79/2609; = narrow, 84/2790.

streytly, *adv.* accurately, 4/95.

strodir, *sb.* ? rudder, 58/1884. *See* strothir.

stronde, *sb.* strand, shore, 67/2199, &c.; strond, 58/1879, 88/2909.

strondward, toward the shore, 94/3138. *See* -ward.

strothir, *sb.* ? = rothir, rudder, 49/1580; strodir, 58/1884. *See* rothir, and note, p. 191.

stroute, *pres.* 2 *s.* assertest, boastest, 57/1840.

stroye, *vb.* destroy, 68/2206.

studied, *pret. s.* pondered, 55/1793; *pret. pl.* stodied, 104/3461.

stuffid, *adj.* well-provided, stored, wealthy, 54/1730. 'Stuffyd wythe stoore. *Instauratus.*' — *Prompt. Parv. Cf.* Chaucer's 'A bettre envyned (= supplied with wine) man was nowhere noon.' 'The Frankeleyn,' in Prol. l. 342.— F. J. F.

styed, *pret. s.* climbed, 50/1592; *imp. s.* sty, 49/1588. A.S. *stigan.*

STYPIO, Scipio, 27/822.

Summoner, the, wants to share the Miller's plunder, p. 7; vows vengeance on the Friar, p. 7; joins the Pardoner in singing after supper, p. 14.

surmysid, *pp.* charged, 64/2092, 74/2411, 80/2631, 110/3665.

suyd, *pp.* sued, 64/2075.

suyr, *pres.* 1 *s.* pledge, promise, 47/1486, 58/1886, 74/2418.

swat, *pret. s.* sweated, 56/1813, 70/2299; swet, 62/2007.

swele, *vb.* burn, 72/2349. A.S. *swelan.*

swerd, *sb.* sword, 118/3946.

swere, *sb.* neck, 2/40, 12/361. A.S. *sweora.*

swetyng, *sb.* term of endearment, 2/36; sweting, 11/327. *Cf.* 'hertis rote' *and* 'hertis swete.'

sweven, *sb.* dream, 4/100, 5/115; swevyn, 5/106; *pl.* swevenys, 5/108. A.S. *swefen.*

swith, *adv.* quickly, 19/583.

swowe, *sb.* swoon, 42/1341.

swynke, *vb.* labour, 65/2124. A.S. *swincan.*

syde bonde, *sb.* the Bond to secure quiet enjoyment of land sold, given in old time to a purchaser when the Release or Conveyance of the land was handed to him, 48/1531.—F. J. F.

SYDRAK, ? Sirach, the father of Jesus, author of *Ecclesiasticus*, 81/2666.

syn, *sb.* sinew, 19/588.

syn, *prep.* since, 2/29.

SYROPHANES, Burgess No. 1 of Falsetown, welcomes Beryn, pp. 51-2; pumps Beryn's man, p. 53; plays chess with Beryn and beats him, pp. 54-56; brings him before Evandir, Steward of Falsetown, pp. 57-8; his charge against Beryn, p. 93; asserts his prior claim to Beryn's goods, p. 101; can't answer Geffrey, and is sentenced to pay damages to Beryn, pp. 106-7.

taberd, *sb.* mantle, 7/190.

tablis, *sb.* tables, *i. e.* backgammon, 40/1250.

tach, *sb.* disposition, habit, 4/84, 46/1459; *pl.* tacchis, 35/1079. Under 'Teche, tece,' &c., Roquefort says: 'Ces mots se prenoient en mauvaise part lorsqu'ils étoient précédés du mot *male*, et ils signifioient, défaut, mauvaise habitude, vice, crime; mais ils étoient employés en bonne part pour, qualité, perfection, vertu, preuve, signe, marque, disposition.' The *Prompt. Parv.* has: 'Tetch'e, or maner of condycyone, *Mos, condicio.*' 'Tache' is thus glossed by Cotgrave: 'A spot, staine, blemish;

mole, natural mark ; also, a reproach, disgrace, disreputation,
blot vnto a mans good name.'

take, vb. give, hand over, entrust,
107/3567, 108/3608, 112/3744,
115/3842 ; 1 pret. s. toke, 63/
2049, 95/3170, 96/3179 : pret. s.
toke, 12/364, 67/2184, 70/2300 ;
imp. s. take, 67/2185, 95/3171 ;
pp. i-take, taken, 63/2042, 98/
3248 ; take = given, 72/2369. In
63/2049, 67/2184, 2185, 95/3170,
and 96/3179 the word = 'entrust.'
'Takyn̄', or delyncryn̄ a thynge
to a-nother. Trado.' 'Takyn̄',
or betakyn' a thynge to a-nother.
Committo.'—Prompt. Parv.

takelyng, sb. tackle, 86/2837.

talent, sb. inclination, liking, 13/
367, 108/3620. O.F. talent. 'Tal-
ant' in Roquefort. See maletalent.

talowe, vb. grease, 90/2996.

talyng, pres. p. narrating, 8/202.

Tapster, the, flirts with the Pardoner,
pp. 2-5 ; makes an assignation
with him, p. 12 ; her faithless
conduct, pp. 14-17 ; and unconcern, 19/580.

'He [the Frere] knew wel the
tavernes in every toun,
And every ostiller or gay
tapstere,' &c.
Prol. Cant. Tales, ll. 240, 241.

Tapsters not to be trusted, 21/655.

tapstry, sb. tap-room, 10/299, 11/309.

tauc, pres. 2 pl. ? deal, 63/2061.
Halliwell glosses this word thus :
'To kick ; to fidget about, es-
pecially with the feet ; to rage.
Var. dial.' 'Taving, irregular
motion ; picking the bed-clothes
in febrile delirium.' Willan.
Archæol., vol. xvi. in Brockett.—
F. J. F. See note, p. 192.

tell with mouth, 70/2280. Cf. 'se
at eye.'

telle, vb. talk, 89/2966 ; tell, 118/
3960.

tend, imp. 1 s. attend, 80/2641.

tent, sb. intent, 5/126.

terrene, adj. earthly, 25/751.

that or þat, with optative force, 20/
601, 33/1012, 40/1265, 95/3163,
99/3277 ;—pron. = who, 39/1229,

et passim :— adv. = [ere] that,
33/1008 ;—how, 71/2315 :—conj.
= but, 3/56, 70/2293 ;—that =
imprecative as, 78/2560.

þat þat, that [man] that, 66/2160.

thé, pron. they, 61/1962, 81/2660,
85/2813 ; þé, 113/3782.

thè, pron. thee, 61/1978, 79/2599.

the, vb. thrive, 33/1012. A.S. þeón.

then, adv. thence, 61/1962.

ther a-geyn, prep. there-against, on
the other hand, 9/243 ; þere ageyns,
67/2176.

ther a-mong, there amidst, mingled,
105/3485. See a-mongis.

þer & þer, here and there, 62/2002.

þere, adv. where, 2/27, et passim ;
ther, 61/1990.

therforth, there forwards, 84/2782.

þey, adv. though, 79/2602.

tho, pron. those, 77/2518, 81/2681,
95/3149, 110/3677, 111/3694 ; þo,
68/2234 ; tho = those that, 26/
769, 109/3629 ; = that, 29/885.

tho, adv. then, 3/46, et passim.

þo, pron. those, 68/2234. See tho.

THOLOMEUS, Ptolemy the astronomer, 83/2753.

þowe, pron. thou, 33/1012.

thrallis, sb. pl. slaves, 85/2820.
A.S. þrœl.

throff, pret. s. throve, 29/889.

thrustelis, sb. pl. throstles (a kind of
thrush), 22/684 : 'Thrustylle, bryd
(thrusshill or thrustyll, P.). Me-
rula, Diu.' (Prompt. Parv.)—
F. J. F.

till, prep. to, 60/1945, 88/2905, 119/
3972 ; til, 104/3456, 105/3487.

tire, 2 pres. pl. strain, exact, 78/
2565. F. tirer.

tite, the, it betides thee, it will happen to thee, 61/1978. Tite = tit
= tideth.—W. W. S. See note,
p. 192.

to, prep. at, 32/999.

to-brast, pret. s. burst, 31/964, 49/
1577.

to comyng, gerund. inf. to come,
12/347. See 'comyng, to.'

to done, to do, 2/37.

to-rent, pret. s. was torn to tatters,
74/2432.

to smyte, vb. smite hard, 46/1456.

to-tere, *vb.* tear to pieces, 33/1014;
pret. s. to-tare, 42/1350; *pp.* to-
tore, ragged, 39/1215, 1229, 97/
3239, 103/3416; = ? torn (with
sorrow), 45/1443.

todir, other, 45/1424.

todirs, other's, 93/3094.

to-fore, *adv.* before, 1/2, *et passim;*
to-forn, 110/3684.

toke, *pret.* 1 *s.* gave, 63/2049, &c.
See take.

Tokens (*See* signes) bought by the
Canterbury pilgrims, 7/171-73;
they stick them in their caps,
7/191.

tole. *See* tool.

tool, *sb.* tool, 89/2938; tole, 100/3342.

toon, the one, 6/153, 58/1865.

top, *vb.* clip, 88/2917.

topcastell, *sb.* 50/1592. 'Corbis,
galea, *Erasmo.* Cage. The top of
yᵉ mast, which is made like a
basket, whereunto they clime to
descry the land.'—Higins's *No-
menclator*, 1585, p. 223, col. 1.

touȝte, *adj.* tough, difficult, 57/1830.

traunce, *sb.* quandary, condition of
amazement and fear, 77/2533.

travaill, *sb.* toil, 9/246.

travers, *vb.* cross, oppose, 102/3411.
F. *traverser.*

trayde, *pp.* betrayed, 102/3380.

tre, *sb.* wood, 60/1950, 86/2856.

Tree, a, in Isope's garden described,
84/2784-85; its virtue, 84/2786.

tregetours, *sb. pl.* magicians, con-
jurors, 84/2771; tregitouris, 96/
3180. O.F. *tresgetteres.*—Roquefort. *See* Tyrwhitt's long note on
this word, in his ed. of Chaucer's
Cant. Tales.—F. J. F.

tregetrie, *sb.* magic, 84/2774.

trend, *pres. pl.* turn about, 63/2038.

trest, *sb.* ? beam (or projection),
14/424. O.Fr. *traste;* It. *trasto,* a
transom or crossbeam; W. *transt,*
a rafter; Bret. *treust,* beam, rafter.
Wedgwood, under *trestle;* Littré,
under *treteau.*—F.J.F. See note,
p. 181.

tretid, *pp.* discoursed, 73/2399. F.
traiter.

trist, *sb.* trust, 66/2161, 88/2912.

tristen, *vb.* trust, 48/1544; *pret. s.*

trist, 98/3267; *imp. s.* trest, 59/
1910; *imp. pl.* tristith, 115/3848.

trobilnes, *sb.* sorrow, 45/1417.

trompis, *sb. pl.* trumps, 88/2906,
117/3918. From *Prompt. Parv.*,
s. v. 'Trumpet,' it appears that
'trumpet' was the diminutive of
'trump.'

trotting, *sb.* 73/2402.

trowith, *sb.* troth, trust, 5/116, *et
passim;* trowes, 2/38.

trown, *vb.* (?) troll, sing, 3/70.—
F. J. F. See note, p. 177.

trus, *vb.* truss, 22/660; *imp. s.* trus,
56/1828, 91/3033. 'Trousser. To
trusse, tuck, packe, bind or gird in,
plucke or twitch vp.'—Cotgrave.

tuk le meyn, ? *touche la main,* be
friends, or strike a bargain, 59/
1922. '*Toucher en la main de.*
To shake hands with, or take by
the hand, in signe of friendship.
Il toucha la main entre leurs mains.
He layed his hands betweene
theirs, or gave them his hand that
he would be theirs.' Cotgrave:
u. *main.*—F. J. F.

turment, *sb.* torment, suffering, 22/
664, 68/2203, 105/3493, 117/3898.

turmentid, *pp.* persecuted, 68/2212,
76/2493, 79/2586.

twist, *sb.* door-fastening, 16/478.

twynt, *sb.* jot, 15/433.

Thus lafte they the leder that hem
wrong ladde,
And tymed no *twynte,* but tolled
her cornes, &c.
Deposition of Richard II. (Camden Soc.), 17/18.

twynyth, *pres. s.* separates, 23/686;
1 *pres. pl.* twyn, 73/2403.

tyle-stonys, *sb. pl.* tiles, 60/1950, 107/
3583. *Prompt. Parv.* glosses,
'Tylestone:' '*Tegula. later.*' It
might thus mean either a roofing
tile, or a brick.

vnaservid, *pp.* unserved, not attend-
ed to, 3/56. See note, p. 176.

vnbore, *pp.* unborn, 92/3040.

vndaungerid, *pp.* unindangered, secure, 74/2410.

vndirmyned, *pp.* undermined, 104/
3480.

vndo, *vb.* interpret, 4/100 ; *pp.* vndo, broken, 101/3355 ; on-do, undone, quashed, 93/3074.

vn-knowe, *adj.* unknown, 114/3802. *See* on-know.

vnlacyd, *pret. s.* unlaced, 74/2426 ; vnlasid, opened, 3/67.

vnneth, *adv.* scarcely, 38/1197, 42/ 1322, 74/2412, 112/3734 ; vnncthis, 34/1066.

vnquert, *sb.* discheer, discomfort, trouble, 63/2057. 'Quert, *sb.* = joy. Ps. lxiii. 11 ; lxxxviii. 27.' F. *cœur, queor.*—Coleridge. And see 'Quert' in Wedgwood.

vnryȝte, *sb.* injustice, wrong, 18/ 557. A.S. *unriht.*

vntrowith, *sb.* faithlessness, 97/3209, 101/3349.

vnyd, *pp.* united, combined, 111/ 3724.

vp riȝt a-fore, straight before, 83/ 2736.

vse, 1 *pres. s.* fo'low, practise, make use of, 4/84 ; *pres. s.* vsith, 80/ 2650 ; *pres. pl.* vsyn, 69/2239 ; vsen, 79/2596 ; *subj. pres. s.* vse, 39/1230.

vttir, *adj.* outer, 117/3928.

vttirlich, *adv.* utterly, fully, 28/848, 48/1537, 63/2051, 86/2830 ; vt-tirly, to extremity, 115/3844.

vaillith, *pres. s.* avails, 65/2098. *See* a-vaile.

valowe, *sb.* value, 76/2501.

variaunce, *sb.* changeableness, 38/ 1135.

vaunce, *vb.* advance, 12/340.

vaylith, *pres. s.* avails, 116/3883, 118/ 3958. *See* a-vaile.

vel, *adv.* well, very, 41/1283. *See* wel.

vend, *vb.* go, 17/523. *See* wenden.

verry, *adj.* true, sheer, 9/256, 17/ 500, *et passim.* O.F. *verai.*

vexacioun, *sb.* vexation, 115/3842. *See* wexacioun.

visenage, *sb.* term of abuse, 33/1012 : ? from *visage,* or '*Voisine:* f. A she neighbour. *Voisinage:* m. Neigh-bourhood, nighnesse, necrenesse.' Cotgrave.—F. J. F. See note, p. 186.

vlyes, *sb. pl.* flies, 72/2349.

void, *vb.* depart, flee, 62/2104, 70/

2287, 75/2456, 90/2981 ; *pret. s.* voidit, 45/1424 : *imp. s.* (reflexive sense) void, 45/1426 ; *imp. pl.* voidith, 65/2098 ; *pp.* voidit, 70/ 2285.

voise, in his, in his natural uncon-cernd tones, 59/1918.—F. J. F. See note, p. 192.

vombe (*v* = *w*), *sb.* womb, belly, 28/ 859, 41/1298.

vomman (*v* = *w*), *sb.* woman, 10/ 287, *et passim:*—voman, 65/2121 ; —womman, 15/436 ; *gen. s.* vom-mans. 29/872 ; *pl.* vymmen, 28/ 863, *et passim ;* vommen, 11/325, 15/440, 96/3205, 117/3919, 118/ 3945.

waite, *vb.* keep watch, observe, 54/ 1744 ; *pret. s.* waytid, 14/424, 19/ 576, 51/1637 ; *imp. s.* weyte, 49/ 1589 ; *subj. pres.* 2 *s.* weyte, 20/ 614. O.F. *waiter.*

wan, *pret. s.* won, gained, 51/1642, &c. *See* wone.

wanlase, *sb.* 87/2874, 'Wanlass, a Term in Hunting, as *Driving the Wanlass,* i. e. the driving of Deer to a stand, which in some Latin Records is termed *Fugatio Wan-lassi ad Stabulum,* and in Domes-day Book, *Stabilitio Venationis.*' Kersey's Phillips, 1706. I believe the word is. as explaind by Mr. Hensleigh Wedgwood, *windlass,* a winding course, ' and thus doe we of wisedome and of reach, with *windlesses,* and with assaies of bias, By indirections finde direc-tions out.'—*Hamlet,* II. i., Fol. p. 259, col. 2 (Booth, p. 749). See Wedgwood in *Philol. Soc. Trans.,* 1873, p. 68.—F. J. F. See note, p. 197.

ward. *sb.* award, 107/3568.

-ward, *versus,* chircheward, fro, 28/ 858, —— unto the, 42/1333, —— to, 42/1320 ; court ward, in-to þe, 92/3054 ; dorward, to kittis, 16/ 477 ; dynerward, to, 7/170, —— to the, 7/192 ; shippis ward, to his, 62/1999, —— 116/3878, —— to þe, 91/3032, shipward, to, 6 / 2185 ; strondward, to the, 94/3138.

with þis (this), provided that, 24/729, 119/3972.

withdrawe, *vb.* draw from, shun, 40/1257.

withseyith, 2 *pres. pl.* deny, 104/3467 ; *pp.* withseyd, 104/3471.

witith, *imp. pl.* know, 60/1955. *See* witt.

witt, *vb.* know, 63/2036 ; wyt, 36/1140 ; wete, 106/3544 ; 1 *pres. s.* woot, 32/975, *et passim;* wote, 72/2372 ; 2 *pres. s.* wotist, 3/45 ; wost, 17/509, 106/3531 ; *pres. s.* woot, 12/339, 38/1201, 94/3116 ; 1 *pres. pl.* wetith, 106/3539 ; 2 *pres. pl.* woot, 13/385, 15/438, 54/1751 ; wotith, 90/2990 ; *pret. s.* and *pret. pl.* wist *or* wiste, 7/177, *et passim;* *imp. pl.* wetith, 29/880, 31/960 ; witith, 60/1955 ; wotith, 111/3723 ; woot, 10/276 ; *subj.* 2 *pret. s.* wiste, 41/1311.

wold nat, would not do, avail, 35/1082.

wonde, *vb.* ? fear, 82/2697. A.S. *wandian.* See note, p. 196.

wondir, *adj.* wonderful, 82/2710, 85/2802.

wondir, *adv.* wonderfully, 5/116, *et passim.*

wone, *sb.* habit, 39/1244. A.S. *wune.*

wone, *vb.* won, 9/242 ; *pret. s.* wan, 51/1642, 54/1747 : wan oppon hym londe, gained ground upon him, 73/2384.

woo, *sb.* woe, 38/1176.

wood, *adj.* mad, 16/498, *et passim.* A.S. *wód.*

woodman, *sb.* madman, 43/1351, 60/1957.

woodnes, *sb.* madness, 41/1289.

wook, *sb.* week, 18/547, 19/578 ; passion-woke, 114/3804 ; *pl.* wookis, 34/1047.

Woollen robes of grained colour (scarlet) worn by Beryn and his men, 92/3065.

woot, 1 *pres. s., pres. s.,* 2 *pres. pl., imp. pl.* know, 32/975 ; 38/1201 ; 13/385 ; 10/276. *See* witt.

worch, *vb.* work, do, 37/1154, 50/1618, 100/3342 ; wirchen, 105/3499 ; *pres. pl.* worchyn, 4/83 ;

imp. s. worch, 59/1897 ; *imp. pl.* worchith, 6/160.

wordit, *pret. s.* worded, spoke, 98/3261.

wordlich, *adj.* worldly, 66/2161.

wormys, *sb. pl.* serpents, 84/2776.

wose, *sb.* ooze, mud, 54/1742. A.S. *wós.*

wosshid, *pret. s.* wished, 67/2192.

wost, 2 *pres. s.* knowest, 17/509. *See* witt.

wote, wotist, wotith, 1 *pres. s.,* 2 *pres. s., pres. pl.* and *imp. pl.* know, knowest, 72/2372 ; 3/45, 90/2990 ; 111/3723. *See* witt.

wowe, *sb.* wall, 108/3614.

wrake, *sb.* mischief, 60/1932. A.S. *wræc.*

wrench, *sb.* trick, 36/1142. A.S. *wrence.*

wry, *vb.* twist, turn, 77/2516 ; *pres. s.* wriythe, 84/2791 ; *imp. pl.* wrijth, 103/3436.

wyled, *pret. pl.* beguiled, deceitfully turned, 82/2691.—F. J. F.

wyt, *vb.* know, 36/1140. *See* witt.

y, *pron.* I, 14/407, 74/2430.

yen, *sb. pl.* eyes, 63/2047. *See* ey.

ymmemorat, *adj.* ? unmentioned, 80/2626. Lat. *immemoratus.*

ynmagytyff, *adj.* inventive, 106/3529. See note, p. 198.

yelp, *vb.* boast, 69/2266. *See* ȝelpe.

Yeoman, the, sings after supper, p. 14.

ȝede, *pret. s.* went, 33/1034, 97/3210.

ȝeer, *sb.* year, 27/811 ; *pl.* ȝeris, 34/1065.

ȝeld, *vb.* yield, requite, 52/1680.

ȝelpe, *vb.* boast, 98/3268 ; yelp, 69/2266. A.S. *gelpan.*

ȝemen, *sb. pl.* yeomen, 90/2997.

ȝerd, *sb.* rod, 34/1060, 41/1314, 71/2324, 103/3417.

ȝit, *pron.* it, 65/2098.

ȝore, *adv.* long ago, formerly, 3/54, 70/2273. A.S. *geare.*

ȝowith, *sb.* youth, 34/1039, 1052, 1055 ; ȝouthe, 34/1058 ; yowith, 55/1790.

&, *for* and, if, 3/45, *et passim.*

www.ingramcontent.com/pod-product-compliance
Lightning Source LLC
Chambersburg PA
CBHW021138020726
47500CB00003B/1138